THE GIRL AT THE BAR

Fireflies Publishing, LLC

THE GIRL AT THE BAR
Copyright © 2016 by Fireflies Publishing, LLC
LCCN Number: 2016961547

ISBN-10: 0-9984358-1-3
ISBN-13: 978-0-9984358-1-7

Nicholas Nash
Facebook: @AuthorNicholasNash
Instagram: @NicholasNashAuthor
Email: thegirlatthebar@gmail.com

Book Cover Design by Panagiotis Lampridis
Book Design by István Szabó, Ifj.

THE GIRL AT THE BAR

BY
NICHOLAS NASH

TABLE OF CONTENTS

CHAPTER 1

DAY 1, THURSDAY
THE KING & DUKE BAR, NEW YORK CITY

She was wearing a gorgeous black dress.

The first things he noticed about her were her slender legs and her delicate wrists. She wore a thin diamond bracelet that sparkled in the low light of the hotel bar as she drank her martini, seemingly unaware of her surroundings. She was a gorgeous golden blonde with features that were tough to look away from, or ever forget.

She pulled out her purse and started going through it when something fell out. She bent over to pick the fallen object, half sitting on the bar stool when he walked over to help her pick it up.

He didn't know what got over him but he had to help her. He had to get noticed by her, to be an infinitesimally small part of her life, even if it was for just a few moments. He reached out for the object, just a few moments quicker than her, their hands almost colliding mid-air when, to his horror, he noticed the object was a tampon. Rather than recoil, he swallowed his fear and embarrassment, cupped the tampon and handed it gently and discretely back to her. She skillfully grabbed it from his hand and before he knew it, the tampon was back in her purse. She looked up and gave him a wide smile.

"Hi, I'm Rebecca. It's nice to meet you."

"I'm uh, I'm uh… I'm so sorry. I just didn't know it was a, a, you know, a…"

She burst out laughing and he took the bar stool next to her, still red in the face but feeling better knowing she found the whole episode amusing, probably even more so given his reaction. He introduced himself trying not to think about the tampon incident.

"I'm Ragnar, Ragnar Johnson."

"Scandinavian?"

"Yes and no. I'm American but the name is Scandinavian. Norwegian actually. Believe it or not, my parents named me after a character from an Ayn Rand novel."

"Atlas Shrugged, I know. The capitalist pirate." She was suppressing a chuckle and smiling.

"Well, here's the whole story. My parents adored Ayn Rand, her ideas and her books. They decided to name their children after key characters from that book."

"So you have a sibling named John Galt?"

"Close enough. Two brothers, John Johnson and Francisco Johnson. Thankfully, we all got to keep our family last name. Can you imagine me as a Ragnar Danneskjöld?"

They chatted about what had brought her to New York City. She told him that she was a medical executive and was traveling to the city for a major cancer conference that was well-attended every year by executives of large pharmaceutical and biotech companies, academic researchers, oncologists, as well as sales and marketing executives from across the spectrum of companies. Her company was presenting results for and launching their latest cancer drug, a highly publicized next-generation miracle drug.

Before Rebecca joined her company, she was an assistant cancer researcher in the laboratory of Dr. Steven Gupta. Dr. Gupta was the country's leading cancer researcher, whose groundbreaking discoveries in the field of cancer had fueled the laboratories of several large and small pharmaceutical and biotech companies.

"So Dr. Gupta is probably one of the richest doctors on the planet, I presume?" he asked.

"On the contrary, he's been so immersed in his quest to cure cancer, academic glory and possibly a Nobel Prize in medicine that he never really benefited financially from his discoveries. In an effort to continue to push his research through the labs of the giant pharmaceutical companies at the fastest possible pace, he licensed out all his research without any real thought about himself." Ragnar sensed a tinge of sadness in her face, and in a fleeting moment it was replaced by the same warm smile as before and she turned to sip her martini.

He thought that not only was Rebecca beautiful but she was also a smart, intelligent and a compassionate person who cared about the work she did for the broader good of humanity.

"And what brings you here today, Mr. Knight in Shining Armor, besides rescuing ladies who've dropped their tampons?"

No lie he could've made up would match up to what she was in reality. After all, he did get more than he bargained for since he first set eyes on her sitting alone at the bar. No lies, just the truth. The plain and simple truth. It did not matter to him anymore what she would think of him.

"I'm an unemployed trader. Nothing is more cliché than a jobless, failed trader in New York, I guess."

Rebecca put her hand on his indicating, without any spoken words, that she was sorry and sympathetic.

"I lost my job at one of the large investment banks in the city a few months ago. I worked on a trading desk, tracking complicated securities and setting up even more complicated trades. I was always good at numbers growing up. I thrived as a quantitative analyst at the bank. A quantitative analyst analyses reams and reams of trading information to identify trends and signals in the data that could help in predicting the direction of securities prices, and hopefully makes money in the process. I worked on setting up trades in arcane securities and made money day in and day out, for the first few years till one day the house of cards came tumbling down."

He glanced at her to see her reaction. "Following a quick turn of events those trades lost hundreds of millions of dollars for the bank within days and I was thrown out of there, before I could catch my breath or even understand what happened. It turns out we were picking up pennies in front of a steamroller. We lost multiples of what we made in the last few years. I had a lot of my personal money invested in the same trades too. Not sure if I'm ever going to find another job again after that disaster."

She was probably stunned by the admission but did not show it.

"Anyways, I was at the Bowery Ballroom earlier tonight to watch my favorite indie rock band. They're from New Zealand and they're in the city for a couple of shows. Thought I'd stop for a drink after the show before calling it a night. My place is close by from here."

She smiled. "You know this happened to my father too when I was young. He lost his job in security at the local Wal-Mart after an employee was caught for theft. She was skimming cash and shoplifting with the help of some other employees before they finally caught her. My father lost his job in the cleanup that followed. It took him over a couple of years before he found his next job. He was a changed person after that but he always said that those two years were the happiest days of his life."

"I kind of miss the excitement and the thrill of the trading desk. I trade on and off with my own money but it's not much to begin with. New York's an expensive place." He pensively stared at the beer he had ordered but not sipped yet.

"You know, I was a huge fan of 80s hair bands." she said steering the conversation in a different direction.

"Why am I not surprised? So what's your favorite 80s band?"

"Guns N' Roses. You?"

"Def Leppard. Favorite GN'R song?" he asked, trying to imagine her head banging to Welcome to the Jungle.

"Rocket Queen. What about your favorite Leppard song?" She was clearly waiting for his reaction to her answer.

"Uh, Rocket Queen, huh. Mine's uhh, it's probably Bringin' On the Heartbreak. You know the moaning in Rocket Queen is really Axl Rose getting nasty with..."

She nodded. "Umm hmm, that's what I like about the song." She said with an evil grin on her face, like she just got caught with a guilty secret. "Never would've counted you as a mushy type, though."

They spent the next few hours talking about the 80s bands, must-go places in New York City, curing cancer, his former job, her days as a researcher and her father. The chemistry was undeniable and he was intoxicated by her beauty and intelligence and yet down-to-earth manner. He knew she felt their chemistry too.

"This is going to sound a bit strange but do you mind if I crash at your place tonight? There's construction that starts at night just outside my hotel window. Kept me up most of the night yesterday. I know it sounds strange but..."

"No, no, no problem. You're welcome to spend the night. It's a small place but I'm happy to spend the night on the sofa tonight. It's quite cozy, honestly. You can take my bed." Ragnar tried to be the nice guy and not too direct.

He sensed a hint of disappointment in her voice for a moment and then she was herself again. "Let me pick up a few things from my room and I'll be right back. I'll see you in the lobby in a few. Thanks Ragnar, I really appreciate it"

"Don't mention it. I'll wait for you downstairs."

CHAPTER 2

DAY 2, EARLY HOURS OF FRIDAY MORNING EAST VILLAGE, NEW YORK CITY

Rebecca stepped out of the bathroom wearing just her black bra and matching panties. She looked immaculately sexy in her underwear. Her beauty had a sort of fragility to it. Ragnar felt as though touching her may somehow damage the very thing that made her beautiful.

"Are you just going to sit there on the couch and make a lady feel naked? Drop your clothes fast, mister, so I don't feel under-dressed and change my mind." Her tone almost had a commanding quality to it and she crossed her hands as a gesture for him to hurry up.

He quickly got out of his clothes down to his underwear and walked up to her. He went down on his knees and started kissing her bare stomach. She put her hands in his hair and held his head as he continued to kiss her, gently at first and then more aggressively.

He pulled down her panties and started kissing her below. He held her hand and led her to the couch. He laid her down, gently pulled her legs apart and started licking her. Her moaning got louder and louder as she started to lose control and enjoy his warm tongue.

Her eyes were closed and she was whispering, "Give it to me. Please. Come up and put it in me. I need it, Ragnar."

He pulled himself on top of her, pulled her bra above her breasts, put one of her nipples into his mouth and started guiding himself between her legs with one hand. She shuddered and groaned when he put her nipple in his mouth but did not pull herself away. Her hand helped guide him as he entered her and started to thrust himself in her.

After a few minutes of love making, he got up, picked her up in his arms and walked over to his bedroom. He gently put her on the bed. She enjoyed being handled by him. He turned her over on her stomach and guided himself back into her. He lay down on her and held her face in his arms and kissed her on her face again and again while thrusting himself even harder. She responded by kissing him back and pushing her hips back against his body. Their bodies moved in rhythm together faster and faster. She broke off the kissing as she neared her orgasm, arched her back and screamed and shuddered as she came. He continued to thrust inside her and seeing her orgasm pushed him over the edge as he moaned and reached his own. His body went limp and he stayed on top of her for several minutes.

She moved from under him but he continued to embrace her from the side. He knew this was one of the best nights of his life, being here with this beautiful and intelligent woman he hardly knew. He knew he was going to ache for her if he never saw her again.

Before he fell asleep, he made a mental note to get her number and tell her that he would like to see her again. They fell off to sleep as he continued to embrace her from behind.

CHAPTER 3

3 MONTHS EARLIER
NEW YORK TIMES

Lincoln Myers Pegs Losses related
to Bond Desk at over $2 Billion

BY JAMES GOLD

Lincoln Myers & Company, one of the top five investment banks, said yesterday that it suffered losses of over $2 billion this week stemming from wagers on a basket of securities tied to interest rates as well as domestic and international stock indices.

Executives at other bond trading desks could not recall an occasion when a securities firm lost so much within such a short period of time – apparently in no more than three days.

While Lincoln Myers executives attributed the losses largely to unauthorized trading by one of its senior officials, executives at Lincoln Myers and other Wall Street firms said most of the trades had been approved and suggested that the losses point to errors in judgment.

Warren Lewis, the Chief Executive Officer of Lincoln Myers, in a hastily arranged conference call, cited a "seriously flawed, poorly conceived, overly complex and poorly executed trades" as the primary cause of the losses.

Further, on the same call he emphasized that the bank was "taking appropriate steps to identify the individuals responsible for the outsized losses, increasing oversight and determining the right team structures to make sure such lapses do not occur in the future."

CHAPTER 4

DAY 2, FRIDAY
EAST VILLAGE, NEW YORK CITY

The first thing that Ragnar noticed when he woke up was that Rebecca was gone. The sun was streaming through the windows and the whole room was lit up. Ragnar looked at his iPhone. It read 8:54 am. He had not set a morning alarm. It was Friday morning and it was not like he had a job to show up for or even a job interview. It had been several weeks since he had his last interview. He opened his laptop, while still in bed, to check for any emails from prospective employers. It seemed like no one was really jumping up and down to meet a down and out-of-his-luck trader who had lost a boatload of money.

He remembered his last interview where the CEO met with him and showed him around the "trading" floor. While the CEO raved on about how Maximus Global Trading was an up and coming top notch trading outfit, Ragnar knew it was just another bucket shop staffed with sleazy, smooth talking salesmen who sold questionable penny stocks to unsuspecting buyers across the country, with promises of quick profits. The salesmen at these bucket shops had perfected their script and would almost never let a working stiff get away with their money. But even they balked at hiring Ragnar. A burning dumpster was more likely to get a job there than him.

Ragnar jumped out of bed and ran through his routine in his head. A quick shower, a run, a simple breakfast, push-ups and pull-ups, shower again and then back to the classified sections. Maybe it was time to broaden out his search and look for job opportunities outside New York City. The city that had sheltered, clothed and fed him seemed to have turned its back on him now. Maybe it was time for a change, he thought.

As he was thinking about his life, he caught a scent of Rebecca lingering in his bedroom and his heart ached at the thought of never seeing her again. Other than her scent, which he knew would not last forever, there was no trace of her. It was almost as if the encounter last night was a happy dream that felt all too real.

Ragnar walked into the bathroom, which was bare other than a few crumpled unwashed clothes when he noticed Rebecca's bra hanging over the mirror. She had clearly left it there for him as a memento of their night together. There was no note, no number and no goodbye message, just the bra.

Maybe he could find the conference she was attending in midtown and track her down. But then again, if she wanted to stay in touch, she would've left her number. Why go through the trouble of hanging the bra as a souvenir and not leave a number or email if she wanted to stay in touch?

He pulled the bra down, put it close to his face, took a deep breath to smell the lingering fragrance of her body, waited for a few minutes for the longing feeling to pass and then threw the bra into the open laundry bag.

CHAPTER 5

DAY 4, SUNDAY
BEVERLY HILLS, CALIFORNIA

Julia Fitzpatrick paced back and forth in the living room of her Mediterranean-style mansion on her cellphone. The estate, a nine thousand square foot mansion, once belonged to the head of one of the Hollywood studios and had remained with that family for over three decades. The home, built in the 1930s, had nine bedrooms, twelve bathrooms, a four car garage and a driveway that sported a black Porsche 718 Boxster, a bright red Ferrari 458 Italia, a white Maserati GranTurismo and a silver Tesla Roadster. The mansion also had an open swimming pool surrounded by buildings on three sides.

Julia's short hair was tied back and she looked visibly irritated. Julia, at slightly over fifty-five years of age, had manly features and a prominent Adam's apple. Julia had been born a boy, James Charles Fitzpatrick, to Irish immigrants in Brooklyn. Her father, Joseph Fitzpatrick, was a small shoe storeowner, and mother, Nicole O'Sullivan, was a garment worker at a factory in the Red Hook neighborhood of Brooklyn.

Julia's father died of a stroke when she was only seven years old. She barely remembered what he looked like. She had seen pictures of her father but did not know if the memories of him were real or false images that her mind created based on the knowledge and pictures of the father she once had.

The loss of a father figure at such a young age had a profound impact on Julia, a child with photographic memory and a sharp intellect, yet socially inept and unable to communicate at a basic level with those around her. Julia suffered from borderline Asperger syndrome. Despite the inability to connect socially, young James Fitzpatrick was forged in steel with an iron will and a burning desire to succeed.

Young James always knew he was wired very differently from those around him. In addition to being distinctly different, James suffered from gender identity issues as well, though without having any true appreciation of this, which James attributed to his social awkwardness.

Nicole attributed young James's mannerisms to being a shy and reserved child, so she was always more protective of him. Correspondingly, his mother was the only person James felt he could be close to and who understood him, or at least somewhat understood him and the full extent of his problems.

At school, James immediately stood out as one of the most brilliant students, as he blazed through the materials. James was a standout student at school and topped every science and math class that he was in. At the same time, he was probably the loneliest kid at school.

He barely interacted with any other students and was awkward in all his interactions with his teachers.

When a teacher called him out in class, congratulating him for his academic performance or commending him for a complex math problem that he solved in class or an outstanding piece of literature that he submitted as part of his assignments, James would stand up and just stare without as much as a smile. No "thank you" or any other words of acknowledgement came to his mind. If the teachers knew him any less, they would've thought he was arrogant but they all recognized that this child was special and a true genius. A child with an intellect far superior to one they would ever see in their lifetime.

James skipped three grades at school by the time he was done. Having always felt that something was wrong about him and his biology, James decided to pursue medicine and was admitted to the Yale School of Medicine. Leaving Brooklyn for school felt like he was moving an ocean away.

While at Yale, James was admitted as a research fellow for a prestigious yet demanding cancer research program. As part of the program, he worked in the research laboratory for a leading cancer researcher, Dr. Kevin Fischer. He immersed himself in the research to understand the effects of cancer on the human body at the cellular level. His work involved discovering medicines to slow the progression of and cure cancer.

In his studies, he found that cancer is the name given to a group of related diseases. Unlike several other diseases, which are caused by external organisms such as viruses or bacteria, cancer is caused when the body's cells divide uncontrollably and multiply rapidly without check.

Cell division is a process that the human body uses for normal growth. Each parent cell divides into two daughter cells, which help build normal tissues, or replace cells that have died due to ageing or damage. Healthy cells in the body stop dividing when there is no longer a need to produce daughter cells. Cancer cells, on the other hand, continue to produce copies relentlessly, overwhelming the body either through the formation of solid tumors or disrupting the functioning of blood cells.

For the first time, James felt truly at home. He felt like he was built for the isolation of the research laboratory. He was a bundle of energy with a raw intellect, suited for research, coupled with a near absence of human feelings and emotions, the need to connect with others or even the need to unwind and blow off steam.

It wasn't long before Dr. Fischer recognized his talent as a standout researcher whose imagination was only exceeded by the brilliance of his work. James was identifying cause and effect connections for cancer that had never been identified before. He was able to identify interactions of the dreaded disease and its progression at the molecular level that were previously unknown.

Dr. Fischer took James under his wing to mentor and guide him, knowing fully well that he would have the privilege of James working for him for a brief period of time. Talent and brilliance like his was a rarity that one would encounter maybe once in a lifetime, if you were incredibly lucky. Dr. Fischer felt a fatherly affection towards James, while James, unable to reciprocate his feelings, responded the only way he knew how, by working harder and with even more intensity.

While at the laboratory, James grew close to Nancy Mulligan, a fellow researcher. Nancy was in some respects the polar opposite of James. Nancy was a lean blonde with a bubbly personality. She looked like someone who belonged on a beach in California, surfing and sunbathing all day instead of toiling in an academic lab.

A team celebration after a breakthrough in the lab at a local pub, involving several rounds of tequila shots, led to a chance encounter between James and Nancy ending up at Nancy's place. Despite the opposite personalities, James and Nancy instantly connected physically. But that was also the first time that James felt his inner woman and the need to be treated like one in bed. Nancy knew he was different and special. Why would he not be different in bed too? She accepted his being different, tender and passionate in bed, though she did not suspect his gender identity issues then. While the physical relationship between them did not last long, Nancy and James (and later Julia) became lifelong friends and close colleagues.

Julia looked at herself in the mirror as she continued to talk on her cellphone. "What do you mean she has disappeared? Did you try to trace her cell phone? Look at the GPS history from her iPhone, her credit card transactions, hotel security cameras and her internet browsing history. Just find her somehow, will you?"

Julia listened to the voice on the other end. "I'm doing everything I can. You think I'd leave any stone unturned? I know how important she is and what she means to you. We're going to find her. Really soon, I promise, Julia."

"Don't make promises you can't keep, Raoul. Let me know as soon as you learn anything, anything at all. Just call me when you do." Julia sighed and then hung up. Rebecca was one of the most promising cancer researchers she had ever met. Julia recruited her to Atticus Biopharma after watching her progress in Dr. Steven Gupta's academic cancer research lab. Julia had grown close to Rebecca since she joined Atticus Biopharma. For her, Rebecca was the child that Julia never had. Rebecca was the closest thing to family for her.

Julia, the CEO of Atticus Biopharma, the company she founded, had made it her life's mission to find cures for diseases that had plagued mankind for time immemorial. In addition to tackling cancer, the number one priority for the company, Atticus Biopharma was a leader in therapies for several rare diseases. Diseases that affected a very small percentage of the total population, defined as any disease that affects 1 in about every 1,500 to 200,000 people.

The labs at Atticus Biopharma were brimming with promising developing treatments for rare diseases ranging from Duchenne muscular dystrophy, a degenerative disease that affects mostly boys who do not survive beyond their teen years to spinal muscular atrophy, a disease that affects nerve cells in the spinal cord and is the number one genetic cause of death in infants.

Julia named the company after a lead character from a highly popular literary masterpiece that she enjoyed reading as a child. The name of the company was meant to signify justice – her way to trying to right the wrongs done to those robbed of a normal, fulfilling life due to a deadly disease that they either inherited or that struck them later in life, cutting short their journey.

Julia dialed Nancy's number. "Nance, they still haven't found her. I'm heading to New York. Meet me at the airport." Julia hung up and dialed another number. "Get my plane ready at Van Nuys. I want to leave for New York City right away."

CHAPTER 6

DAY 5, MONDAY
EAST VILLAGE, NEW YORK CITY

Ragnar heard a loud knock on the door. It was a Monday morning and he wasn't expecting anyone today. He had stopped the deliveries from *FreshDirect*, a popular online food delivery service in New York City, last month. As he started to cut back on his expenses, those grocery bills were on the chopping block. Ragnar would now walk several blocks to a neighborhood grocery store that stocked cheaper unbranded versions of the basic stuff, cornflakes, bread and the like.

"Mr. Johnson?"

"Yes, that's me."

"I am detective Timothy Burns and this is detective Roberta Lopez. We'd like to ask you a few questions about Rebecca Chase. She was last seen with you on Thursday night leaving the King & Duke bar. The bartender gave us your address. Said you were a regular there and left with her. Can we come in and ask you a few questions?"

Timothy Burns was a tough and built middle-aged man with red hair and a faint Irish accent. Roberta, on the other hand, was a delicate looking woman with a petite frame but a very determined face. Her hair was tied back in a no nonsense style and she looked ready to engage in hand-to-hand combat at a moment's notice.

"Sure, come on in. Did you say last seen? Is she, like, uhh, uh, go… missing?"

The two detectives walked into the small living room area. "That's correct, Mr. Johnson. She's been reported missing by her fiancé. She was last seen leaving the bar with you on Thursday night and hasn't been seen since. She was due to present the findings of her latest cancer research as the lead researcher for the experimental cancer vaccine, ATCS-1010, at an oncology conference on Friday morning in midtown, but did not show up for that."

Ragnar's head was spinning taking in all of this information within a short period of time. Rebecca did not sport a ring that night and there was no mention of a fiancé or boyfriend of any sort. She also said she was a medical professional, a pretty generic description of her job, and not the lead cancer researcher for an experimental cancer vaccine.

"Mr. Johnson," Roberta started before Ragnar interrupted her.

"You can call me Ragnar."

"Ragnar, can you run us through the events of Thursday night without leaving out any details? Also, have you heard from her since then?"

"Yeah, sure. Happy to. But I last saw her that night. I haven't heard from her since then."

Ragnar started running the two detectives through the events of Thursday night, how he met Rebecca, how he could not get his eyes off her and how they ended up at his apartment as a result of a rather direct suggestion from Rebecca.

Ragnar could sense uneasiness in Roberta's face when he stated the fact that he spent the night with her but did not know when she left his apartment. He could sense that she was making scathing judgments about him in her head.

"Are you going to find her? I didn't feel like she was running away from anyone or anything the night I met her. You think someone had something to do with this? Someone who didn't like her or maybe her, uh, fiancé?"

"Of course you didn't feel anything was wrong. You were busy getting your knob..." Timothy gave Roberta a quick hand motion to stop her mid-sentence.

"Well, Ragnar, if you remember anything about that night, please give Roberta or me a call. We appreciate your time today. We may reach out to you again for additional questions."

"Of course, of course. Anything I can do to help, err, help find her, uhh, find Rebecca."

Ragnar showed the detectives out. He just knew it in his bones that this was not going to be the last of this Rebecca mess. He had an uneasy feeling in the pit of his stomach that something was seriously wrong. It just didn't add up. Call it a quantitative analyst's instinct. Something about the whole series of events of that night and Rebecca's sudden disappearance in the middle of an important conference, one that probably meant a lot to Rebecca, pointed to deeper undercurrents. He just could not place a finger on what that could be.

Rebecca, relatively carefree, talks to a stranger at the bar, goes home with him, ends up in bed with him and then wakes up, likely in the middle of the night, takes her things (just her purse and the clothes she wore, in this case) and disappears into the ether. And all she leaves behind is her... dammit, he just realized that she left her bra behind and he did not mention that to the detectives a few minutes ago. Not that it mattered much, he thought.

CHAPTER 7

FOUR YEARS EARLIER
CAMBRIDGE, MASSACHUSETTS

Dr. Steven Gupta peered at the sample one last time through the microscope and glanced again at his large computer screen to review all the readings one last time. Dr. Gupta had spent virtually his entire academic career at the university in Cambridge understanding how various forms of cancer evaded the body's immune system.

Dr. Gupta's research was geared towards answering some fundamental questions about cancer. What if the body's immune system could be taught to identify cancer cells and not get fooled by the cancer's evasion techniques? What if the body's immune cells could be taught to attack cancer cells? What if one could modify immune cells, known as T cells, to provide them with "receptors" or artificial detectors, to track and summon a concerted attack on cancer cells?

Behind Dr. Gupta stood his team of three bright lab researchers, Rebecca Chase, an athletic blonde, Gustav Henriksen, a brilliant mathematician-turned-cancer researcher whose parents had moved to the United States when he was just two-years old from a rural farm in Denmark, and Christy Cassidy a tall leggy girl with short blonde hair. Dr. Gupta looked up at his three protégés. "This is it. This better work."

Dr. Gupta had met with the parents of five-year old Joshua Nelson a little over two months ago. Joshua was suffering from leukemia, a common form of cancer in children. Joshua had failed several treatments including chemotherapy and several conventional cancer drugs. The cancer kept progressing and Joshua was getting sicker by the day.

In a last ditch effort, Joshua's doctor in suburban Chicago referred him to an old classmate of his, Dr. Gupta, who was working on an experimental treatment for cancer that seemed to work exceedingly well in lab rats but was as yet untested in humans. He had seen Dr. Gupta present his findings at a cancer conference in San Francisco the year before.

Dr. Gupta had successfully attached receptors, or a detection system, on immune cells that could identify cancer cells, attach modified immune cells to the cancer cells and kill them. The attaching of the cancer detecting receptors to immune cells was his big breakthrough.

In order to move this experimental treatment forward, Dr. Gupta was, at that time, gearing up for a clinical trial on humans.

A clinical trial for a drug is a study to compare the effectiveness and safety of the drug to treat a specific disease. A clinical trial involves enrolling volunteers, who are often patients suffering from the disease for which the drug is being developed. The volunteers are administered the drug and the effects are studied against patients who are not on that drug.

There are several ethical dilemmas related to trials on patients. The drug may not work, patients may experience severe side effects and in some extreme cases, patients may even die in a clinical trial. Only a small percentage of drugs tested in clinical trials become an approved drug.

The subjects of Dr. Gupta's clinical trial would be late-stage cancer patients, those who really had nothing to lose, patients that had failed every other therapy and were willing to take one last chance with the hope that the treatment in the clinical trial may actually work, however infinitesimally small that chance maybe.

While the clinical trial for the "engineered T cells" with receptors that could identify and attack cancerous cell was a few months away, Joshua's parents urged Dr. Gupta to let him be the first patient and start dosing him with the experimental engineered T cells soon, as Joshua's days were numbered.

The risks of this experimental treatment were enormous. While the engineered T cells identified cancer cells in lab rats and killed the cancer as efficiently as white blood cells attack a common infection in the body, there was no guarantee that this would work in humans. Cancer cells in humans may be far more complex and may still evade these engineered T cells. Even worse, these engineered T cells could start attacking normal cells and tissues and could prove to be fatal for the recipient. The outcome was truly binary. If it worked, the cancer would be totally eliminated, but if it did not, it may kill the patient within forty-eight hours.

"His life is in my hands now, Rebecca. His engineered T cells look ready for the treatment but this still may not work. I wish I had more time to run some more tests."

"Steve, have faith. Everything has checked out so far. Joshua is fortunate to have found his way into our lab. If he has any chance to beat his cancer, this is it. I know you don't want to hear this but even if Joshua does not survive, someday you will figure out a way to make this work. Millions of children worldwide for generations to come will be thankful to you and young Joshua. We should start the procedure now. Joshua's prep is complete and he's ready. His parents are here too."

Small beads of sweat appeared on Dr. Gupta's forehead. "Is the priest here?"

Gustav was the one to respond, his voice lacking any emotion whatsoever. "Yeah, he's in the hallway. Don't think we want him in the room during the procedure though." For Gustav, science and math were languages of God for him, the method through which God communicated with his mortal creations. While he did not believe in the conventional Gods that everyone typically spoke of, he did not think of himself as an atheist. He believed there was a higher being that governed the universe.

Dr. Gupta started to fill the syringe with the engineered T cells, a miracle of modern science. The engineered T cells were prepared from immune cells taken from Joshua's own blood. He started to mutter in a soft whisper as the syringe was being filled up. "God have mercy on my soul. You've put young Joshua in my care and I've done all I can. I leave him in your just hands."

Dr. Gupta's eyes brimmed with tears for a few seconds. Rebecca found this strange that someone so steeped in science believed in a divine being or would pause to pray. He stopped and let the moment of weakness pass. As soon as it passed, he felt a surge of energy, determination and passion that drove him all his life.

Rebecca saw a noticeable change in his eyes as they turned from the gentle and compassionate eyes that she was used to, to cold and steely in an instant, lacking any emotion whatsoever. His face turned cold and distant, one that she had never seen before. It was like Dr. Gupta had turned into a different person altogether.

Rebecca felt a chill run through her body. Shivers ran down her spine seeing this twisted avatar of Dr. Gupta. She exchanged glances with Christy who looked equally perplexed by all of this but seemed to be taking it in her stride much better than Rebecca. Maybe this was his defense mechanism to deal with the pressure of having another human's life in his hands, she thought, as she tried to calm herself without understanding why this upset her so much.

Dr. Gupta held the syringe delicately in his hands and started walking towards the procedure room where Joshua lay in a bed with his parents near him. Rebecca, Gustav and Christy followed closely behind.

Christy walked next to Rebecca. Leaning closer to Rebecca, she whispered in her ear. "Do you think this is really going to work?"

Rebecca gave Christy a look of reassurance.

CHAPTER 8

DAY 5, MONDAY
I-95 SOUTH, OUTSIDE BOSTON

Dr. Matheus Faust pulled his Porsche to the side of the road to take the incoming call on his cellphone. He was driving down I-95 South to his summer home in Newport, Rhode Island. Matheus had first visited the area five years ago and fell in love with the idyllic beauty of the place. His house was a four bedroom neoclassical mansion and was a few minutes' walk from a private beach.

Matheus listened to Gustav's voice at the other end give him the news of Rebecca's no-show at the conference where she was slated to present the latest scientific data on the revolutionary cancer vaccine, ATCS-1010. Gustav also updated him about the rumors that the police were now involved and had started an investigation into Rebecca's disappearance and that they were looking into the likelihood of foul play.

Dr. Matheus Faust was the Founder and Chief Executive Officer of Faust Biopharma, a company that had "bought" the engineered T cell technology from the laboratory of Dr. Steven Gupta. Faust Biopharma was spending hundreds of millions of dollars on perfecting the technology and running large cancer-focused clinical trials across the globe in the hope of getting the therapy approved and commercialized globally.

At stake was the multi-billion prize of being the first true cure for cancer, something that had eluded mankind to this very day.

Humanity had solved major mysteries of the universe and even landed a man on the moon over forty years ago, but they yet had to solve the mystery that existed inside each one of us. Cancer was a mysterious and deadly foe that unexpectedly turned itself on inside us with the goal of terminating us, a sort of self-destruct mechanism, except that it turned on at will and was relentless in its goal of killing its host.

Matheus had tried to recruit all three of Dr. Gupta's protégés, Rebecca Chase, Gustav Henriksen and Christy Cassidy to Faust Biopharma soon after he acquired the engineered T cell therapy from Dr. Gupta's lab, but his archrival Julia got to Rebecca first and Christy followed Rebecca soon after. Matheus was able to recruit Gustav, the other leading cancer researcher in that lab. While Gustav was as brilliant as they came, Matheus knew he was a touch behind Rebecca whose scorching brilliance was self-evident. Rebecca was the ultimate prize and now she was missing with a police investigation into her disappearance underway.

Despite the initial setback of losing Rebecca to Julia, Matheus had held hope that he would be able to get Rebecca to come over and join him one day.

He was convinced that both Rebecca and Christy would join him after they saw what Matheus, Gustav and the rest of his team had done with the engineered T cell technology. He liked to think of having turned a promising Ford Model T into a modern day Ferrari, the Ferrari of cancer killing engineered T cells.

Rebecca on the other hand was working on her own version of engineered T cells, except that she was working on a 'universal cancer vaccine,' code named ATCS-1010, a single vaccine that could cure virtually any cancer. Faust Biopharma's current technology, for as advanced as it was, involved removing each individual patient's T cells, modifying them into engineered T cells and infusing them back into the patient. It was a slow and inefficient process compared to the concept of a universal cancer vaccine, a single vaccine that could be injected into any cancer patient.

ATCS-1010, a universal cancer vaccine would be a true game-changer. Was that even possible? Could cancer be conquered with a single vaccine? The idea sounded like medical alchemy to him. But then again, if Rebecca was right and Atticus Biopharma made that breakthrough possible, it would be probably belong in the pantheon with other game-changing discoveries such as the discovery of fire, the wheel or the steam engine.

ATCS-1010 was developed from the blood of a patient who had had a severe allergic reaction to an experimental cancer drug several years ago. The patient's immune cells developed a mutation that could attack cancer cells. Those cells were the basis of the treatment Rebecca was working on. While the mutated immune cells worked well against a couple of cancers, it was Rebecca's work that was instrumental in modifying those cells to attack any type of cancer in any patient, young or old, early-stage or late-stage.

Atticus Biopharma and Faust Biopharma were the Coke and Pepsi of the biotech industry. Each of them was trying to outdo the other in every which way imaginable. They fought tooth and nail to recruit bright young minds from medical schools across the country, poached each other's scientists, worked on competing therapies and even ended up building large corporate headquarter buildings right opposite each other across the street in Cambridge. The competition tore apart Dr. Gupta's team when Rebecca and Christy joined Julia at Atticus Biopharma and Gustav joined Matheus at Faust Biopharma.

Starbucks had to open two separate coffee shops across the street in Cambridge next to each company's headquarters. Atticus Biopharma employees would not go to the one next to the Faust Biopharma headquarters and visa versa. The same ended up being true of parking garages, pubs and restaurants in the area. They were either frequented by Atticus Biopharma employees or Faust Biopharma employees, but never both. The Atticus-Faust rivalry was the talk of the town in the Greater Boston area as well as the rest of the country.

Matheus was born and brought up in Brazil. After completing his medical education, he started his own private practice in a quiet suburb of Sao Paolo. The practice was humming along in a traditional boring fashion until fate intervened one day and changed his life forever.

Matheus encountered a patient, an eight-year old boy, suffering from Gaucher disease, an extremely rare genetic disorder that resulted in an enlarged liver and spleen. Matheus had read about a recently approved drug for the disease in the United States. The main drawback was that the drug was not approved for use in Brazil. To make matters worse, the cost of the drug was more than fifty thousand dollars per patient, a prohibitively expensive price in Brazil, and could only be bought with a prescription from a specialist in the United States.

Matheus knew an acquaintance that worked in a mid-level position in one of the company's factories. Matheus called his acquaintance and figured out that there were expired samples that were discarded periodically. He managed to convince him to ship some of the expired vials to Brazil. Matheus used the vial to treat his patient. The enlargement in the boy's abdomen subsided and the young boy's parents were immensely grateful for the miracle.

Word soon spread and Gaucher disease patients started to show up at his practice from all over Brazil. But there were only so many old vials that his acquaintance could siphon off from the factories in the United States without getting caught.

Matheus decided to take matters in his own hands. The parents of some of the patients were wealthy Brazilians. One of them was a notorious drug lord who controlled the drug trade in Sao Paolo. Two of his four children suffered from this horrific disease. With the help and generosity of these people, who were desperate for a cure, Matheus collected close to half a million dollars and flew to Boston all the way from Sao Paolo carrying hard cash with him in a duffel bag that he held on to through the entire trip.

Matheus knew that the odds of him being able to make it through United States customs with half a million dollars in a duffel bag, some of which could be traced back to South American drug money were slim, but he was bull-headed in his pursuit of the cure for his patients.

When Matheus reached the company's headquarters in Cambridge, security refused to let him in. But the iron-willed Matheus was determined not to return home empty-handed. He refused to leave without getting the medicine for his patients.

Before long, the Chief Executive Officer of the company, Jeffrey Crown, got a call in his office about this crazy doctor from Brazil who was waiting in the lobby downstairs with a half a million dollars looking to buy a large cache of the Gaucher disease drug for patients in Brazil. He was shocked and couldn't believe what he had just heard. He ran down to the lobby to meet this lunatic who had flown in all the way from the southern hemisphere for the cure.

What the CEO, Jeffrey Crown, learnt from Matheus was beyond his wildest imagination. There were more cases of Gaucher disease in Brazil that were referred to Matheus' practice than the combined total of all the cases of Gaucher documented in the U.S. currently.

Jeffrey recruited Matheus right away to represent them in Latin America and Matheus became a force to reckon with. He worked with governments of Latin American countries to get approval for several critical drugs, in some cases even getting the governments to bear the cost of drugs for rare diseases, which were typically in the tens of thousands given the small patient populations for each rare disease and the prohibitively high cost of finding a cure for each one.

After establishing the South American operations of the company, Matheus moved to the United States. He soon left the company to start Faust Biopharma. Faust Biopharma grew in leaps and bounds driven by Matheus' passion to provide patients with access to cutting edge drugs worldwide coupled with his proven organizational building skills.

Matheus first ran into his nemesis, Julia Fitzpatrick, a prolific scientist-turned-entrepreneur, when Matheus announced that finding a cure for cancer was going to be Faust Biopharma's primary goal. This was going to be Matheus' claim to eternal fame. But Julia was first at every turn and at every corner. He couldn't get his hands on the latest research, promising drugs or researchers without being outbid by her.

Not one to give up easily, Matheus raised the stakes and went even more aggressively after the building blocks for a top-notch cancer program at Faust Biopharma. Matheus nabbed Gustav from right under Julia's nose, who expected to sign all three of Dr. Gupta's most promising researchers to come work for her. The last minute defection of Gustav felt like a sucker punch in the gut and Julia was livid at losing one of the three protégés. Before long, the two companies were at each other's necks and word of their rivalry started to spread.

Rebecca was the trump card in the cancer treatment arms race and Julia had snapped her up. Matheus tried unsuccessfully several times to lure her over to Faust Biopharma with promises of money, the best researchers, access to unlimited resources and even a very senior position at Faust Biopharma with the opportunity to succeed him as CEO. But she never went for it. Until now. Matheus had set up a clandestine meeting with Rebecca at his home in Newport tonight. And now she was gone.

Matheus gripped the steering wheel of his Porsche and took long deep breaths. His heart was beating at a really fast rate and he felt as though it would burst out of his chest. He closed his eyes to calm himself.

His life's work was finally coming together. The ultimate prize was within reach, he thought.

CHAPTER 9

DAY 5, MONDAY
TETERBORO AIRPORT, NEW JERSEY

Nancy Mulligan stepped out of the Gulfstream G550 and walked down the steps. She quickly jumped into a black Mercedes that pulled up next to the plane on the tarmac. Attendants unloaded two bags and loaded them into the back of the waiting car.

As the car started to leave she dialed Julia on her cell. "Julia, I just landed at Teterboro. I'm headed into the city now. I'll see you in an hour or so." She hung up and went back to her thoughts.

Nancy had known Julia for over twenty years now. She knew Julia when she was still James, the brilliant yet extremely reserved researcher. With his brilliance and classic Irish good looks, James could've bedded anyone he wanted when he was younger, but his personality proved to be a huge impediment to social interactions of any sort.

She could still recall her first night with James. James looked lean and athletic but was extremely tender and passionate in bed. He knew all the right places to touch and all the right buttons to press on her body. While any other woman would have been thrilled to meet a man who knew the female body as well as James did, it was downright eerie for Nancy how well James knew her body. He knew what she was feeling and what she would enjoy next. In hindsight, when James finally admitted his true gender identity, it all made sense.

Over the years, even though the flame of physical passion between them had died, they had become the best of friends, trusting each other completely. She was the first person he called to join him when he formed Atticus Biopharma and it had been an exciting journey so far – up until Rebecca arrived on the scene. Nancy felt a strong surge of jealousy even at the thought of Rebecca.

Before Rebecca joined Atticus Biopharma, Nancy was an integral part of Julia's life. They met each other almost every day and worked hand-in-hand and spoke at least once, if not more, daily. But since Rebecca joined Atticus Biopharma she had become the center of Julia's universe. Nancy could not bear to see her bond with Julia weakening all because of Rebecca. She was taking over the place that Nancy once held with Julia, one of best friend and trusted confidant.

Despite how much she hated Rebecca, Nancy grudgingly acknowledged that Rebecca reminded her of the younger James but without all the social awkwardness and that thought enraged her even more. In some respects, Rebecca was like the child that James and she could've had, one who could've inherited their combined brilliance and Nancy's looks and personality.

She truly could've been their daughter, if they ever had one. Not that Nancy did not try. James never wanted any children and their relationship was on again off again and brief whenever it was on. His work was everything to him. Everything else was secondary. James did not even bother to address his gender identity till much later in life. He finally decided that he was done living in a man's body and started his gender reassignment journey, transitioning to become Julia.

Julia did not care that she still looked more like an aging Adonis rather than an aging Venus despite the aggressive hormone treatment. It did not matter, as long as she was not lying to herself and the world anymore.

Now that Rebecca was out of the picture, Nancy felt like she could restore the close connection she once had with Julia. Things would be back the way it was between them. She felt a huge surge of relief pass over her as she thought about Rebecca's disappearance. A small smile broke out on her face even though she wanted to hide that feeling from anyone. Not that it mattered. She was alone in the back of the car.

Nancy could now see the skyline of Manhattan as her car approached the city. She was looking forward to meeting Julia, consoling her, embracing her and maybe even reigniting the physical relationship that once was the bedrock of their early relationship. She still felt a physical attraction to Julia despite the gender change, maybe even more so now than when she was James.

CHAPTER 10

DAY 6, TUESDAY
UNKNOWN LOCATION

Nothing can fill the void.

Food does not fill it. Alcohol does not fill it. They only make the void want more. Drugs cater to the whims and fancies of the void. Sex fills the void but only temporarily. Then it comes back with a vengeance, replete with fury and rage.

Money is paper and means nothing to the void. A meaningless invention that cannot rein in a force honed and refined over millennia. Evolution created the void, sharpened its instincts and made it the perfect animal. Modern society with its iPhones, Twitter and fake Louis Vuitton bags did not even scratch the surface of the void.

Nothing can ever fill the void.

The void is deep and dark, dangerous and risky, yet exciting and full of dark adventures.

The void hides in plain sight. It is the plaguing emptiness that never leaves. It nurtures the soul, yet feeds on it, destroying it, slowly but surely. It is the disease without a cure that takes hold from the inside and never leaves. It keeps the host alive, manipulating, scheming and making the host hate itself.

The void loves sadness, nostalgia, pain and suffering. Not the violent kind but the dull ebb that never quite recedes completely, constantly reminding the host of its presence.

The void is a savage. The void is a beast. The void is a monster with its guard always up, ready to defend itself at a moment's notice. The void feeds on fear and thrives on adrenaline.

But then again, the void is the only lifelong friend who will stick around in good times and bad, hiding away some during happy times and embracing during times unhappy. The one true friend in a sea of loneliness. The only friend.

Nothing can ever fill the void.

The phantom stood facing the water, the mind clearer than ever. The sun had set, it was dark and there was no one else around. Thoughts and feelings all blended into one and re-appeared as if from a dark cave in the soul where they were forced into hiding, even if just for a few moments. The phantom started to walk away with near-nirvana calmness. It could hear the faint whispers of the void, telling it what to do next. It was all too clear now. The void needed to be fed again.

CHAPTER 11

DAY 7, WEDNESDAY
NEW YORK CITY POLICE DEPARTMENT,
6TH PRECINCT, WEST VILLAGE

"Okay, let's go over the details of the Rebecca Chase disappearance once more." Detective Timothy Burns was still sipping his morning coffee, waiting for the caffeine to kick in. Roberta Lopez, in contrast, looked sharp and ready, with her hair tied back and not a strand out of place.

"Rebecca Chase, 31 years old, is a cancer researcher at Atticus Biopharma. She lives in the Brentwood neighborhood of Los Angeles. Her father was the Head of Security at the Xerox corporate campus in Rochester in upstate New York. He was retired and lived in Buffalo. He died a couple of years back from pancreatic cancer. Her mother died when she was a teenager. Honors student throughout, first at Columbia University and then at Harvard University, where she worked in the research lab of Dr. Steven Gupta, a leading cancer researcher. She co-wrote several scientific papers, all of which sound like Greek to me, but it looks like she was working on some cutting edge cancer research.

"Rebecca was recruited to Atticus Biopharma personally by Julia Fitzpatrick, the CEO of that company.

She's one of the top scientists at Atticus Biopharma and close to the CEO, Julia. They were both featured in a cover story in *Forbes* magazine last year where they dubbed Rebecca as "the next-generation" with *Forbes* naming her as a potential successor to Julia as the CEO of Atticus Biopharma. Shortly after being featured in the *Forbes* cover story, Rebecca was engaged to a fashion photographer, Iain Thorpe, who was once named one of the most eligible bachelors in Los Angeles.

"Iain was a wild party animal and womanizer with all his escapades captured by every page six of every rag in the country. He was linked to several famous models until she put a ring on him. Since then, he's been getting much more favorable press. They've been showing up at charity events together and he's even held exhibitions and campaigns to raise money for cancer awareness and research." Roberta paused to make sure Timothy was listening to all the details. Timothy was now munching on a donut but she knew he was not one to miss even a single detail.

"So you're telling me she tamed a wild six foot five inch British photographer who was a party animal but still very well respected for his work?" Timothy asked. She realized he was very much on top of this investigation.

"It seems so. Not that he necessarily had bad press earlier. It was just the world he lived in. Young, tall and handsome photographer with immense talent constantly surrounded by beautiful models day in and day out in Los Angeles. What do you expect? She seemed to have changed him. He had an exhibition a couple of months ago that was well covered by the press and raised a lot of money apparently. He has virtually disappeared from the gossip pages since last year."

"Keep going." Timothy was now munching on his second donut, a chocolate glazed one.

"She came to New York City last week to attend a cancer conference in midtown. She was scheduled to present her latest research on a next-generation cancer treatment on Friday last week but did not show up. There were over four hundred scientists and pharma executives who showed up to hear her presentation. Atticus Biopharma had one of Rebecca's colleagues, Christy Cassidy, step in and present in her place. Christy previously worked as a junior cancer researcher in Dr. Steven Gupta's lab and joined Atticus Biopharma along with Rebecca.

"Christy tried to track Rebecca down on Friday after her presentation at the conference. Rebecca did not pick up her cell phone. Christy went to her hotel room and she wasn't there either. Rebecca is typically extremely responsive, replying to emails and texts almost instantly. She hasn't replied to any emails or texts since early Friday morning. Christy then reached out to her fiancé to check in. Iain called all her friends and then finally called in to report her missing on Friday evening."

"Good. Now let's go through the details of the last day she was seen."

"Sure. Rebecca had a busy day on Thursday last week. She started her day at six-thirty in the morning with back-to-back meetings with researchers from other companies. She attended a presentation at eleven for a company called Faust Biopharma, another cancer research company and the biggest rival to Atticus Biopharma. She grabbed a salad for lunch in the hotel lobby before heading back for a presentation by Dr. Steven Gupta at two in the afternoon. She apparently left around ten minutes into the presentation. She had a few meetings during the afternoon and then she was seen at an Atticus Biopharma-sponsored cocktail event at a lounge close to her hotel.

"Christy, among others, remembers seeing her until around eight in the evening. Next thing we know she was at the King & Duke bar in Greenwich Village around eleven-thirty. Her credit card was used there and we confirmed the time with the security camera at the bar. She left the bar with Ragnar around two in the morning. The bartender remembers the time they left and security cameras confirmed that time."

"What about where she was between eight and eleven-thirty in the evening?"

"We're working on that. Her credit card was never used during that time. She was probably still at the company cocktail event talking to folks. Maybe she was there but her colleagues don't remember her being around. There was lots of alcohol flowing at the event."

"No, I don't think so. She's hard to miss. From everything I heard, she was a beauty and had real presence that lit up every room she walked into. I think if no one remembers her being there after eight, she was probably not there." Timothy stated as a matter of fact as he finished his second donut. Roberta made a mental note to dig into this unaccounted time gap. Timothy was eyeing a third donut, trying to decide whether he should take the plunge with one or not.

"She leaves the bar around two in the morning with Ragnar and ends up at his place in the East Village, at a rundown second floor walk-up. Ragnar is a trader who used to work for Lincoln Myers till earlier this year. He worked with a group that lost a boatload of money for the bank and was fired. He is still under investigation by the Feds and the SEC. Ragnar used to live in an apartment in the upscale Gramercy Park neighborhood. He was over-leveraged and had to sell his apartment at a loss when he lost his job. Ragnar visits the bar regularly, which is close to his current rental apartment."

Timothy continued to nod, a sign that Roberta should continue going over the details.

"Rebecca and Ragnar go at it at night and..."

"Huh?"

"Okay. They ended up having sex that night, according to Ragnar. Next thing, according to him,

Rebecca took her things and was gone before he woke up the next morning. No security cameras in the building to verify what time she left. We canvassed the neighborhood yesterday. She probably left really early in the morning from his apartment because no one remembers seeing her leave Ragnar's building. We should not rule out Ragnar as a suspect. I think I saw something in his apartment that's been bothering me. I have a hunch but let me follow-up on that before we talk about it. She hasn't been heard from or seen since that night."

"So he's the last person to see her, right?"

"That's correct. For all we know, she could be stuffed in a suitcase in his apartment. Maybe he's a highly convincing psychopath who killed her. Or maybe she probably did indeed leave his apartment like he told us."

"And she did not check back into her hotel?"

"No, she did not. Hotel security cameras don't show her returning. Neither the night staff on Thursday night nor the staff from the Friday morning shift has seen her since. Her room key has not been used since. No credit card usage since Thursday night. No emails, no text messages. It's like she disappeared into thin air."

"What about Iain? What do we know about his whereabouts?" Timothy looked at Roberta to make sure she was thinking about all angles here.

"Iain was in New York City for a photo shoot at a studio in the Freedom Tower downtown on Thursday. We know he was not checked into the same hotel as hers.

We still need to question him on his whereabouts on Thursday and Friday." Roberta glanced at her notes and made another note about Iain.

"So a missing persons case so far, right?" Timothy was gearing up to poke holes into the story.

"Yes, that's right."

"Let's look into her cell phone records and where they show her last. Let's find out what she did between eight and eleven-thirty that night. Let's see if we can talk to Julia Fitzpatrick. Maybe she knows something and can shed some light on this case. Make sure you check her bank accounts to see if there were any cash withdrawals before she disappeared."

"Okay." Roberta was diligently noting down all of these.

"And let's get this Ragnar guy to come down to the station. I think we're missing something from that night, some small detail that only he knows. Or maybe there's something off about him. I want to question him again but only after you get some more background on him."

"What do you think happened here?" Roberta asked Timothy.

"You know me. I don't like to jump to any conclusions too soon. The possibilities are several though. She ran away and does not want to be found or was abducted by someone who either wants her for himself, to kill her or for ransom. There's always the possibility that something happened in Ragnar's apartment. Given the high-profile nature of the person who disappeared here, this could be work-related, either someone in the company or a competitor. Or it could be personal, someone who probably hated Rebecca for her achievements, maybe her fiancé, maybe a scorned lover, or maybe even an ex of the fiancé. The trick is to start broad and eliminate as many of the possibilities, as possible. But you can only do so if you collect enough evidence to reach the right logical conclusion."

She nodded in agreement.

"Let's start by bringing in Ragnar. We should also speak to Julia Fitzpatrick as well as Iain."

"Okay. In fact I got a call earlier today from Julia Fitzpatrick. She is going to come in today to meet us with another senior executive from Atticus Biopharma."

"That's good. Let's get this Ragnar kid down to the station. Let's also have Christy and Iain come down since they're both in the city."

"On it."

CHAPTER 12

DAY 7, WEDNESDAY
NEW YORK CITY POLICE DEPARTMENT,
6TH PRECINCT, WEST VILLAGE

Ragnar was sitting in an empty windowless room opposite the two detectives he had first met two days ago. He got a call from Detective Roberta asking him to come down to the precinct to answer some questions. He had inquired if he needed to bring a lawyer, not that he could afford one currently. She told him it was just for some questioning to go over the details from Thursday night last week.

A part of him felt like having sex with Rebecca on Thursday night was nowhere near the trouble he found himself in. On Monday, two detectives showed up at his doorstep investigating a missing person. Today he was at the precinct, probably a suspect in her disappearance, he thought. Since the visit on Monday, he googled Rebecca Chase and was fascinated by everything he had learnt about her. His heart ached even more now after learning about her. He saw pictures of Rebecca with her fiancé hand-in-hand at a cancer charity. She was beaming and looked genuinely happy with him. Was he just a one-night stand for her?

At the same time he wanted to help find her. Even though he could never be with her, maybe at least he could help find her.

"Ragnar, thanks for coming in today. We had a few more questions for you and wanted to go over some details that we did not cover on Monday." Timothy spoke first. Ragnar sensed a non-accusatory tone and felt he could relax a bit. Maybe they were just going over some questions after all.

"Ragnar, are you on Seroquel?" Roberta blurted out without any emotion.

"Huh? What? Whe… How did you know?"

"Answer the question please, Ragnar. Are you on Seroquel or not? I saw a prescription box on your counter when we were at your apartment yesterday. We spoke to your doctor who could not share your history, unfortunately." Roberta stated bluntly.

Ragnar swallowed and realized this was not going to be easy. "Yeah, I'm on Seroquel. Been on it for the last six months. It's mainly for anxiety…"

Timothy and Roberta looked at each other and then back at Ragnar.

"…and some, uhh, borderline, uhh, bipolar disorder. Well, my doc says it's schizophrenia and depression too, though I think he meant to prescribe it for my anxiety, mostly."

The two detectives did not react at all, which Ragnar read as shock. They were obviously shocked but tried hard to hide it, hence the robotic body language and lack of reaction.

"So can you tell us more about why you take Seroquel?" Timothy was the one asking the question, his interest level now piqued.

"Uhh, it's primarily related to anxiety and stress at work. I was getting irritable and once got into an argument at work. It got a bit, uh, violent. Just a little bit. I mean just a fist fight between me and another, uh, trader."

Timothy never liked to take notes on paper. He never wanted his body language to betray his thoughts. Timothy had an eidetic or photographic memory and he took extensive mental notes. They were not just answers, facts or numbers, but what the other person was wearing, what hand and eye movements accompanied the answers, whether the person started to sweat, whether he sat up or slumped down, the tone of the voice and other verbal and physical tics that you could not put down on paper.

Ragnar looked down and continued. "Honestly, it was just all the pressure. I was starting to crack. There were billions of dollars of capital at stake all being traded, some would say being gambled, based on my math. It gets to you, you know..." Ragnar went on to explain how he had helped create a trading strategy that made the bank lots of money in past years. But at the beginning of the year, the profits started to ebb and there was constant pressure from senior management to get the profit machine going again. The pressure of it all was just too much to handle and cracks started to appear in his demeanor.

"I'm feeling much better now since I stopped working. The stress has reduced dramatically. I feel like a new person now. I, uh, work out every day."

"But you're still under investigation, aren't you Ragnar? That's got to count, right? That must be pretty stressful, I'm guessing. Getting thrown under the bus and then having this investigation dragging out for so long with this cloud of suspicion hanging over you. You lost a lot of your own money too when you lost your job. You lost your fancy apartment in Gramercy Park. All of that must be stressful, right?" Timothy now looked at him with a watchful gaze.

"Yeah, I'm still under investigation but that's not a big deal in my mind. I was just doing my job. You gamble, sometimes you lose. You gamble large sums of money. Sometimes you lose those large sums of money. My bosses knew what I was doing and they still decided to roll the dice. If the Feds had to find something, they would've found it already. But they obviously haven't because I didn't do anything wrong. That's why I'm still here instead of rotting away in some prison. Anyway, what does this have to do with Rebecca?"

"Do you lose time, Ragnar? Have you ever woken up somewhere else and not known where you were? Schizophrenia is not an easy disease to deal with. Maybe she met you and was fooled by your meek demeanor. You both had a good time and then you realized you were just a one-night stand and that you could never have her. Maybe your paranoia kicked in. Did the two of you have a fight that night?" Roberta asked him with a stern face.

"No. Nothing like that happened, okay. I'm on my medication and I feel fine. I know it's been bothering you but she came with me on her own accord and yes, we had sex, okay. I didn't know she was engaged and she didn't tell me either. We had a one-night stand and then she left. That's all there is to it. I did not start planning a marriage, honeymoon, kids and a long happy life together in my head, if that's what you are suggesting. No Jekyll and Hyde here unfortunately for you to dig up.

"I have my issues, oh yes I do, but I'm not crazy or a killer. I'm just a guy, down on his luck, looking for a job, who thought he got lucky Thursday night last week, but apparently not." Ragnar slumped back. He could feel the adrenaline kicking in. He felt alive after a long time. Not since he lost his job did he feel this alive. It felt like he was back at his trading desk, battling his wits against an unseen army of traders.

"Who said anything about Rebecca being murdered? Why did you suggest that? Do you know something we don't Ragnar?" Timothy was now as alert as Ragnar, his sense tingling.

"Listen, I've studied math all my life. Correlation does not imply causation. Lots of people who've done horrible things are schizophrenic or bipolar. There is a high correlation but you cannot infer that every schizophrenic or bipolar person has done something horrible, is a kidnapper, or a killer, or whatever else you think I am."

"Yes, but here we have a person with schizophrenia, bipolar disorder, anxiety, as well as depression, which by the way I would label as a very mentally ill person. This person was the last one seen with a beautiful girl who disappeared into thin air. Wouldn't you say foul play was involved?" Timothy shot back. He stood up and gestured Roberta to follow him out.

Ragnar's mind started to race. He was feeling the same anxiety that he felt earlier this year when he saw the tide turn against him. Hundreds of millions of dollars of losses within hours at work.

I met her. I know I met her. She was wearing a black dress. We spoke at the bar. We spoke for a while. We went back to my place. She was so beautiful. Oh, so beautiful. We made love that night. Not sex, not a one-night stand. We made love. I made love to her. She was alive. She was breathing when I fell asleep all cuddled up next to her. I was angry. I was afraid. I was paranoid of losing her. I gripped her hard. Did I grip her too hard? Did she turn around and get angry? Did I lose my mind? Did I punch her like I do when I'm angry? Could I have killed her? Snuffed her with a pillow and then gone back to sleep? Oh God. No, no. I don't remember any of that. Or do I? What did I do? If I did, where would I hide her body? What if I did something to her?

Ragnar now closed his eyes shut tight as his mind struggled to make sense of the facts. Timothy and Roberta were still outside.

I probably proposed to her in my half-manic state. Maybe I said something about never wanting her to leave.

Maybe she mentioned her fiancé and I lost it. Did that really happen? Of course it did. Did I lose my mind? I felt a sense of loss the next morning. Maybe it was because I did something to her.

He could hear a distant sound calling his name. "Ragnar. Ragnar."

My pillows. No, couldn't have been my pillows. They could barely kill a fly, let alone Rebecca. What could've happened... the bra. The black bra. I strangled her with her bra. When she was naked. She writhed in pain and couldn't even scream. Nobody heard her. How come she was not there when I woke up? I mean, her body.

Where could I have...unless of course I carried her...

"Ragnar!" Timothy was shaking him hard now and he opened his eyes and came back to reality. "What were you doing? What happened to you? Are you losing it again?"

"Huh? No, I, uh, I don't know. I don't think I did it. I don't know. I don't think I...I, uh, I, uh, don't know. I can't remember. I can't...remember...what I did that night. I just can't be sure."

"Well, we're keeping you for questioning till tomorrow morning. Roberta is getting a search warrant for your place. I think you should call a lawyer."

"I don't need a lawyer. This is going to be an open and shut case. If I did it, I deserve to be locked away forever." Ragnar looked dejected and confused.

"She said she was at a cancer conference in town. She never told me what she did for a living. She did not give me her full name. And she never told me she was a famous and important cancer researcher who graced the cover of *Forbes* magazine. She basically lied to me." Ragnar kept going as Timothy listened. "But is that really surprising? I mean I'm just a stranger who met her at the bar and she probably wanted to blow off some steam with me, right? I honestly don't remember if anything sinister happened. I just don't."

Timothy kept listening as he waited for Roberta to come in with the search warrant.

CHAPTER 13

DAY 7, WEDNESDAY
NEW YORK CITY POLICE DEPARTMENT,
6ᵀᴴ PRECINCT, WEST VILLAGE

Raoul Perez was sitting outside the station in his car. Raoul was a detective with the New York Police Department for years. Raoul had built a reputation as a tough and intelligent cop. He was well liked by everyone who worked with him, above and below. Even the criminal underground in New York City had grudgingly admired Raoul for his work on the streets.

Raoul made a genuine effort to minimize crime in the neighborhoods he was involved in by addressing the problem differently than most cops. If he found drug dealing activity rising and there were teenaged kids involved, he would find the parents of those kids, visit them at their homes in the public housing projects, talk to them, organize an intervention and find a way to put the fear of god in the kids while encouraging them to re-focus on their education at the local public school. He would speak to the school, make sure the kids showed up regularly and take a personal involvement in those he tried to rehabilitate.

While not every case was a success, he felt that his methods, however dangerous and unconventional, worked often enough to keep him going at it. But the rules of the game changed on 9/11. The world was never the same again. New York City had decided to move on, build a memorial and build another tower to take the place of the two that went down that day.

Raoul could not live with the memories of all the colleagues he lost that day. Raoul decided to hang up his uniform a few months after the attack. He quit the force for good to start his own practice as a private detective but fate had other plans for him. At the recommendation of a former colleague who was then in Los Angeles, he flew out West to meet Julia Fitzpatrick who was looking for someone to be the head of her personal security team. Julia took an instant liking to Raoul's no nonsense and thoughtful approach to things and hired him.

Raoul had now returned to New York City to look for Rebecca. Julia sent Raoul as soon as she heard that Rebecca was missing. Find her no matter what it takes, were Julia's instructions. Don't come back to Los Angeles till you find her.

Raoul still had plenty of friends in the force. He got an update on the man Rebecca had spent the night with and for whom a search warrant was being processed. He saw detectives Timothy and Roberta jump into a squad car. He quickly started the battered, non-descript grey Toyota Camry he had rented to follow the detectives. He knew they were headed to the East Village apartment of Ragnar Johnson with a forensic team that would join them there.

"Julia, I'm tailing the detectives right now. They are headed to Ragnar's apartment. They have a search warrant for his place. I have a friend on the forensic team as well. I'll give you a call as soon as they find anything." He paused for a moment and then gave Julia the second piece of news. "Separately, I finally found someone who's been regularly hacking into all sorts of cell phone records. The kid's a genius. Seventeen years old but can get into any system anywhere. He's been tough to track down but I'm meeting him soon."

CHAPTER 14

DAY 7, WEDNESDAY
EAST VILLAGE, NEW YORK CITY

"Nothing? Really?" Roberta was getting more agitated.

The chief forensic investigator, Mike Moretti, started providing Timothy and Roberta an update after a long evening in Ragnar's apartment. "Nothing other than the black bra from the laundry hamper. We've swept the place for fingerprints and traces of blood. The fingerprints seem to be largely his. There may be a couple of other prints, which I suspect may be Rebecca and probably a handyman or someone from the building. This is a typical hermit apartment. A loner with few or no visitors. No traces of blood anywhere in the apartment. It doesn't even look like anything was cleaned up with bleach or any other chemicals. Let's see what the bra turns up in the lab, but my professional opinion, this is not really a crime scene and I've seen many."

"What about the forensics teams in the basement and on the roof? Anything? If he just strangled her or maybe poisoned her, it would be clean. Except for the body, which he'd have to hide somewhere in the building." Roberta replied.

"Nothing, Roberta. We've swept the roof, the basement, the stairs and every nook and corner of this building. It's always possible that he moved the body out but we don't have anything currently. Let's hope the bra turns up something. Other than that, we don't have any physical evidence of anything - kidnapping, murder or anything else."

"Let's get back to the questioning and bring in everyone we know so far. Did we get her cell phone records yet?" Timothy asked.

"It's expected this evening." Roberta replied. Roberta sighed as she thought about Rebecca.

Where are you, Rebecca? Why don't you want to be found? I'm looking for you. Who's got you? What did they do to you? I'm worried about you. Show yourself to us. Just a bit so I can help find you.

CHAPTER 15

DAY 8, WEDNESDAY
NEW YORK CITY POLICE DEPARTMENT,
6TH PRECINCT, WEST VILLAGE

Timothy was sipping his fifth cup of coffee as Roberta was going through Rebecca's laptop information and cellphone records with him.

"The forensics team has run through most of the important stuff on Rebecca's laptop. Nothing suspicious in her browsing history. They got access to her work email yesterday. The team is still combing through it but so far they've found nothing related to her disappearance. She did not have any real social media presence, just a dormant Facebook account. There was no activity on her Facebook account for a month or so. No Twitter, LinkedIn, Snapchat, Tinder or any other social media account." Roberta was looking straight at Timothy as she spoke.

"I've sorted through most of the incoming and outgoing numbers on her cellphone for the last month up until her disappearance. Most of them seem to be work-related calls. There were several calls with Julia Fitzpatrick, her boss, Iain Thorpe, her fiancé, Nancy Mulligan, one of the senior executives from Atticus Biopharma and Christy Cassidy, a subordinate researcher.

We've eliminated calls to restaurants and other similar calls." Roberta was looking at the computer screen as she sorted through the Rebecca's cellphone records.

"On the day of her disappearance, she had called and received a few calls from a number that is registered to a shell company in the Cayman Islands. We're trying to trace the ownership. Maybe that was one of Julia's companies or one of her private numbers. We don't know but we're trying to find out." Roberta calmly went through her findings.

"The very last call was from a prepaid number that was used only once early Friday morning. That one was probably from a burner cell. It was at 4:54 am on Friday morning." Roberta's eyes widened as she spoke about the details of the last call.

"So she probably got that call and it prompted her to leave Ragnar's apartment before he woke up. It was really early in the morning, which explains why no one saw her leave. The burner cell and the fact that it was only used once tell me there's clearly foul play involved here. Let's bring everyone who was close to Rebecca and rattle them hard. This is not a random kidnapping or disappearance." Timothy was feeling worked up thinking about Rebecca. It had been a long day. "I think we may need to let Ragnar go. Keep an eye on him to make sure he does not disappear till the forensic results on the bra come back. Find someone who worked with him at Lincoln Myers. I want to know for sure who Ragnar Johnson is before we let him completely off the hook."

CHAPTER 16

DAY 7, WEDNESDAY EVENING
WASHINGTON SQUARE PARK, WEST VILLAGE

Ragnar felt ambivalent when Timothy and Roberta let him out of his holding cell. They spoke to him about the search and warned him not to leave the city for a few days.

Ragnar was drained out. He could feel the exhaustion from the developments of the day. What was meant to be a simple questioning turned out to be a full-blown investigation, a short arrest and a forensic search of his apartment.

It was late in the evening and Ragnar was starving. He decided to walk back to his apartment. He figured walking through the Village would clear his mind. It always did. When Ragnar had to give up his apartment in Gramercy Park and downgrade his lifestyle, he decided East Village would be it.

As he was walking through the Village, Ragnar realized that he would be walking past the hotel that Rebecca stayed at when she was in New York. He knew he had to avoid that place but felt compelled to continue walking in that direction like a moth attracted to fire. As he got closer to the hotel, he realized it was quite late. It was dark and incredibly silent for New York. As he was walking by, he saw the King & Duke bar in the lobby. His heart skipped a beat. This was where he met Rebecca for the first time.

Something about the whole area struck him as odd. A nagging feeling overtook him. A detail simply did not fit. Something was wrong. He couldn't quite put his finger on it so he decided to stop right there. He took a deep breath and walked into the hotel.

Ragnar walked into the lobby and sat down on one of the lounge chairs. He closed his eyes and started going through the details of Thursday night in his head. The quantitative math genius side of his mind switched on as it went through the conversation trying to find something that did not fit the pattern. And then it struck him...

He opened his eyes, jumped up from his chair and ran outside the hotel. He circled the entire block until he was back at the entrance.

"This is going to sound a bit strange but do you mind if I crash at your place tonight? There's construction that starts at night just outside my hotel window. Kept me up most of the night."

That was it! There were no signs of construction around the hotel!

It was night time and incredibly silent. He ran back into the bar and grabbed a seat at the bar. The bartender knew him and gasped when he saw him there.

"Ragnar? What are you doing here? You know the cops turned this place upside down looking for that scientist who disappeared. They questioned everyone, man. I had to tell them about her leaving with you. They kept asking questions about you - how much you drink, how often you come here and whether you pick up women regularly from here. What is going on? Are you all right? Did the cops come by?"

"Has there been any construction around the hotel? In the last week? Any road, hotel walls or other buildings close by?" Ragnar was still thinking about the discrepancy.

"What are you talking about Ragnar?"

"Construction Joe. Has it been noisy at night this last week? Any construction that's been happening in the area of the hotel lately?"

"No man. Nothing going on around here. The last time there was something going on was last summer when the city was replacing some pipes along the pavement outside. Nothing since. Why?"

"Who was on duty the night she disappeared? I want to speak to them."

"Look man. I told you, the cops turned this place upside down. Everyone's a bit scared."

"Joe, listen to me. I think something happened on Wednesday night at the hotel before Rebecca disappeared. I just know it. I need to know what happened. You think these guys here are scared? I was at the station all day today. Cops turned my apartment inside out looking for her. You've got to help me." Ragnar pleaded to Joe. He knew old Joe well from his days as a student at New York University, right here in the Village.

"Paulie was there. I can speak to him. Do you want to wait while I go grab him or do you want to walk with me?"

"I'll come with you." Ragnar stood up to leave.

"Hey Kev, watch the bar. I need to go get something for my friend here."

CHAPTER 17

DAY 7, WEDNESDAY EVENING
THE GREENWICH VILLAGE HOTEL,
WEST VILLAGE

Ragnar, Joe and Paulie sat around a table close to the bar. "There was a lot of commotion on the floor Rebecca stayed on the night before she disappeared." Paulie was talking as the other two looked on.

"What was the commotion about? How was Rebecca involved?" Ragnar knew he had hit upon something.

"It's New York. People get drunk all the time and create a fuss, especially in hotels. It's a regular occurrence. It just happened to be on the same floor as that blonde scientist who disappeared."

"Paulie, what did the cops say?" Ragnar asked.

"I didn't tell them. They kept asking about Thursday night. They asked about you. Kept asking if we knew the guy she left with and whether she came back the next morning. I didn't think much of the incident on Wednesday night." Paulie seemed confused about why this detail was important.

"Okay Paulie. Let's go over this from the beginning. What exactly happened on Wednesday night? Run me through the entire sequence of events." Ragnar was trying to piece together the information.

"I was at the front desk and I got a call from a guest on the same floor as that lady scientist. There was a drunk old man who was screaming and shouting and freaking out all the guests on that floor. I left the desk and immediately went upstairs to get a handle on the situation. I saw this man standing close to her door, not directly outside, but close to it and screaming and crying about something that was stolen from him. He kept saying things like 'they stole everything I had.' Several guests had their doors open an inch or so and were peering outside at the commotion. I went to the old man and tried to talk to him. He calmed down and I told him that he was upsetting all the guests on the floor. I escorted him down. He was silent in the elevator ride down and till I walked him outside. I offered to hail a cab but he refused and then walked away mumbling the same stuff to himself." Paulie kept looking at Ragnar and Joe.

Ragnar pulled out his cellphone, typed a name and held up a picture for Paulie to look at. "Is this him?"

"Yeah, that's him."

Ragnar turned the phone back to see the picture again.

He had a million questions on his mind.

Dr. Steven Gupta! What were you doing drunk and upset outside Rebecca's hotel room the night before she disappeared? She was clearly scared of you showing up again the next night. Why were you there? Did you have something to do with Rebecca's disappearance? Where is she now?

. . .

As Ragnar stood up to leave, the person sitting at the table close by stopped pretending to be interested in the highlights of the game on the television. He pulled out a notepad and scribbled a quick note on it. He then pulled out his cellphone and typed a text message quickly using an encrypted messaging program, hit send and then walked out of the bar.

From: *Raoul Perez*
To: *Julia Fitzpatrick*

Message: *Still following Ragnar. Got a lead. Ragnar stumbled on it. Gupta was at Rebecca's hotel on Wednesday night. He was drunk and making a scene. It could be him.*

CHAPTER 18

DAY 8, THURSDAY
NEW YORK CITY POLICE DEPARTMENT,
6TH PRECINCT, WEST VILLAGE

"Iain, thanks for coming in to talk to us today." Timothy spoke first as Roberta looked on. She couldn't help but feel a bit weak at the knees. Iain was exactly as all the page six articles had described him. Tall, handsome and absolutely dashing. He had a gentle voice and a British accent that added to his charm. She straightened herself up trying to shift her focus back to the case.

"No problem, mate. I've been worried sick about Rebecca since Christy called last week. I hope you've found some leads. None of this makes any sense. She would never run away. Quite the opposite. She felt like she had a purpose in life and nothing could come between her and her mission. Who would want to harm her?"

"Look Iain, we're doing everything we can. We're leaving no stone unturned. We're going to find her. What we need from you is anything that may be related to Rebecca's disappearance. No detail is too small or insignificant. Can you do that? For Rebecca?" Roberta spoke in a kind tone betraying how she felt with Iain opposite her.

"Sure can. Anything for her. What do you want to know? Where should we begin?"

"From the beginning, Iain. Tell us how you met, what she was like, her friends, her likes, her dislikes, anything strange about her, any recent fights, any enemies she may have, everything. Start at the beginning and tell us everything."

Iain sat up a bit and started sharing his mind. "I had been in Los Angeles for just over four years. I had a heck of a social life but frankly I was bored out of my mind. I was working for hours and hours every day, traveling frantically and was surrounded by eighteen and twenty-year olds. All they wanted to do was to look good and all they talked about was what they needed to eat or not eat to keep their svelte figures. It was all very exciting when I started out as a photographer in the industry but it starts to get to you after a while. I decided to just accept things the way they were and go along with the tide.

"Rebecca and I, you see, we don't exactly move in the same circles. A mutual friend invited us to the same party and introduced us. I was just spellbound by her intelligence. She was really beautiful, too, but it was the combination of beauty and brains that I fell for. I had never met someone quite like her. We hit it off immediately. I called her two days later to ask if she would like to go out for dinner with me, waiting for the obligatory day before making the call. You know how she reacted? She said, 'I've been waiting for this call, Iain. Am

I like every other girl you've met before? Did you really have to wait for a day before calling me back? Why didn't you just call me yesterday?' I was just like, 'Wow! She is something.' We met for dinner that night and we dated for a few months before getting engaged."

"You were in New York last week for work. Why weren't you staying in the same hotel as Rebecca? Why were you living separately?" Timothy asked Iain as he leaned forward a bit.

Iain spoke with a hint to sadness in his voice. "We broke up recently."

"So why did you say you were her fiancé when you reported her missing?" Roberta looked at him with a question mark on her face.

"Look, I didn't mean to lie. The break-up only happened recently. And I hoped things would not stay that way, that we could mend our relationship and get back on track. I honestly do. I just want her back in my life."

"Iain, why did the two of you breakup? It sounds like you really liked each other." Timothy wanted to learn more.

"We did. We really did. While I love my work, it is not what I live for. All I really do is make some twenty-year old in a bikini or a designer dress look good. The right angles, the right light, the right background, the right expression and you have a beautiful picture. I'm not saying it doesn't require talent but then I'm not working on a cure for cancer, am I? But Rebecca, she was. She dedicated her life to finding a cure for cancer. Her work was everything to her. Everything else was secondary.

"She is an only child and when I met her, her father had passed away too. She had no family and no close blood relations. Her co-workers were her family. She was always in the lab, always at work. Even on weekends at home, she spent the entire day going through data, experiment results and scientific papers. I had to practically beg her to spend time with me. I really love her but it was tough for me."

Timothy and Roberta listened as Iain continued, "Everything seemed to revolve around her. Believe it or not, I was the one who was totally ignored in the relationship. I cheated on her and then told her about it, just to get her attention. This was as she was preparing for the conference in New York. She broke up with me. Told me never to show my face to her again."

"Did anyone at Atticus Biopharma know about your breakup? Is that why you took an assignment in New York at the same time she was here? It wasn't a coincidence, was it?" Roberta asked as she was taking notes.

"That's right, Detective. I came here to makeup with her. But she wouldn't have any of it. I really wanted it to work out between us."

"When was the last time you saw her?" Timothy asked.

"Thursday evening last week. She agreed to meet me at an Italian restaurant in midtown. We spent a couple of hours talking about our relationship but mostly it was her telling me it was over. She returned the engagement ring that night. Broke my heart. She left and that was the last time I was with her."

"Would you say this was sometime between eight and eleven-thirty on Thursday night?" Roberta asked casually with her eyes on her notes.

"That sounds about right."

. . .

Iain had left the precinct. Timothy looked at Roberta wiping his forehead. "Check on what he was up to after they broke up. Clearly there's more here to his story than he lets on."

"You're not going to believe this. I just got a message from the cop tailing Ragnar. He is on a train heading for Boston as we speak." Roberta looked annoyed.

"Make sure James is still tailing him. I want to know his every move. Don't lose him for a second."

"Yes. He's on his tail. He knows we can't lose him."

. . .

From: *Raoul Perez*
To: *Julia Fitzpatrick*

Message: *Iain was brought in for questioning. Likely to be a suspect too. On a train to Boston following Ragnar. He's probably headed to meet Dr. Gupta. A cop is tailing him too. The kid hacker I told you about is doing his magic. We'll have something soon from him as well.*

. . .

Iain dialed a number on his cellphone. A sultry voice answered the line at the other end.

"It's me, Iain. Do me a favor, will you honey?"

"Sure, anything for you. What is it?"

"If the cops call you about Thursday night, tell them I spent the night you." Iain glanced behind to make sure no one was close enough to hear him.

"But you did, didn't you?"

"Yeah, but just say I was with you from midnight onwards.

See you later honey. My hotel? I need you again."

. . .

Christy sat in a slightly dark room opposite Timothy and Roberta. Both of them could not help but be amazed at how Christy could've been Rebecca's younger sister.

Christy, for her part, wondered whether the two officers sitting opposite her would play the cliché good cop – bad cop part. She guessed in her mind which one would play which part and made a mental note to herself.

"Christy, we understand that you were the first one to realize that Rebecca was missing. Tell us about everything that happened on Friday morning." Timothy spoke first as Roberta looked down at a writing pad as if taking notes without making eye contact.

"Friday morning was a big day for Rebecca. We had made several breakthroughs in the lab working on ATCS-1010, our universal cancer vaccine. We had promising data that she was going to present. This was a closely-watched event in the cancer community. Everyone who was anyone was there. She was supposed to present and she did not show up on Friday. When it was half an hour before the presentation and I had not heard from her, I called her cell but it was turned off."

Timothy looked at Roberta who took the cue that Timothy wanted her to confirm the last statement against Christy's cell phone records.

"Why did you think something was wrong? Maybe she had a late night and would've turned up on time. What made you hit the panic button?" Roberta spoke this time in what Christy felt was a slightly accusatory tone. She told herself that she had guessed the good cop – bad cop roles correctly but was slightly irritated at the question.

Christy turned to Roberta when she spoke, making clear eye contact. "Rebecca is the most responsible person I've ever worked with. She is always on time. She is a total no nonsense gal. If she had a presentation in the morning, she would show up an hour early to practice and rehearse, and that was after she had invested hours practicing it already. She is a perfectionist."

"What happened after you realized that something was wrong?" Timothy couldn't get himself to stop thinking about the striking similarities between Rebecca and Christy.

"I called Julia right away. She asked security to try and track her down. Someone from Julia's security team even went to check on her in her hotel room. In the meantime, I had to present the data on the cancer vaccine at the conference. After the presentation, I called Iain to tell him that we could not get in touch with Rebecca."

Roberta spoke next. "We understand that you've been working with Rebecca for several years. Tell us about anyone or anything suspicious that may have something to do with Rebecca's disappearance."

Christy paused and took a deep breath. "Rebecca is one-of-a-kind. She is the strongest person I know. Despite her off-the-charts brilliance, she is the nicest person I've ever worked with. Rebecca treated me like a younger sister."

A smile broke out on Timothy's face when he heard the last sentence. It was as if Christy had just read his mind.

Christy continued talking. "Rebecca always attracted the wrong kind of men. It was just the very thing about her, her beauty and her brains combined made her a target. She was, she, uh…"

"What about her? Was there someone from her past that you think could be responsible?" Roberta sensed Christy was on the verge of giving them something.

"It's just…she was engaged to Iain. I never liked him. I never thought he was right for her. She is nothing like him and he is nothing like her. He has trouble written all over him. I sensed their relationship was not hunky dory. She never told me directly but I inferred that he was cheating on her."

"What about your relationship with Rebecca? How long have you known her?" Timothy still wanted to dig in to get a sense of how well Christy knew Rebecca.

"Of course, I know Rebecca for several years. We worked together at Atticus Biopharma since we joined there at the same time. Before that, we were both working as researchers in Dr. Steven Gupta's cancer research lab in Cambridge. Rebecca was a lead researcher and I worked with her, supporting her in everything she did. We got very close to each other. We are good friends. She treated me like a younger sister and was very protective of me. When Julia first offered Rebecca a job at Atticus Biopharma, I told her that I wanted to follow her there. She helped me get the job at Atticus Biopharma and I've worked with her since then."

"So you think Iain is involved in this?" Roberta cut straight back to the previous line of questioning. Timothy did not wince as Roberta interjected.

"I don't know. She is not one to run away or turn her back on her life's work. There are two others who might have a motive." Christy looked straight at Roberta as she spoke.

"Two others?"

"Yes. Nancy. She never liked the fact that Rebecca was close to Julia."

"Nancy Mulligan?" Roberta was flipping pages on her yellow legal pad to check something she had noted earlier.

"Yes. But I can't imagine she would do something like this. I mean, she would really have to…it doesn't make sense. I don't know."

"And who's the second one?" Timothy spoke as he made a mental note about following up on the last comment.

"Matheus Faust. He wanted Rebecca to join Faust Biopharma. He was relentlessly chasing her to join him. He would be high up on my list of suspects."

"Christy, thanks for taking the time to meet us. If you think of anything else please give us a call right away." Timothy stood up to leave.

"Of course. I hope we find her soon. If you need any help from me, anything at all, please don't hesitate to ask. I really hope we find her soon."

. . .

Timothy turned to Roberta once he felt that Christy, who was walking away, was far enough not to hear their conversation. "What do you think?"

"The wrong kind of men, she said. I would definitely put Ragnar in that bucket."

"Ragnar Johnson!" Timothy exclaimed as he started thinking about Rebecca and what might have happened to her.

CHAPTER 19

DAY 8, THURSDAY
NEW YORK CITY POLICE DEPARTMENT,
6TH PRECINCT, WEST VILLAGE

Roberta came running towards Timothy trying to catch her breath and speak at the same time. "Tim, the press got wind of Rebecca's disappearance. Philbrick called from the Daily Post. He's asking for a comment. This is going to the press tomorrow."

"That jerk. Let's call him back. See if we can get him to hold off the story. Try to get ahead of it."

"The press leak is the least of our problems right now. We may finally have our crime scene. A runner on the West Side Highway stopped to catch his breath and was kneeling when he noticed a shiny object in the bushes. He reached out to grab it when he noticed an expensive black dress. He has a diamond bracelet and a black dress with holes and what looks like blood. He called it in."

"Let me guess, a black Valentino dress?" Timothy asked.

"That's right. A couple of other detectives are there now and forensics is headed over too. We should get going." Roberta said as she grabbed her cellphone and started walking fast towards the exit with Timothy.

. . .

HUDSON RIVER PARK, NEW YORK

Timothy and Roberta arrived at the scene. The area was blocked off with yellow crime scene tape. The runner who found the dress and bracelet was sitting on the side as another cop was taking his statement.

Mike Moretti, the chief forensic investigator, who was also at Ragnar's apartment previously, walked up to Timothy. "This is not a crime scene, just where the dress and bracelet were dumped. Both the items are on their way to my lab. I briefly inspected the dress. There were a few tears that looked like knife stabs and blood on the dress. It is a strange place to drop evidence like this. I can think of a thousand places in Manhattan that are better for dumping evidence."

"Maybe whoever it was dumped her body into the Hudson River after removing everything that could be used to identify the body. Maybe that person dropped the dress and bracelet in the bushes in a hurry. Maybe it was careless or maybe someone was close by and this person panicked and quickly dumped the dress and the bracelet into the bushes." Timothy's mind was working overtime. He was no closer to solving the case as it took one giant turn. This was officially a murder investigation now. And the press was on their heels. This was going to get crazy really fast.

"We need to find the body now. Let's get police divers to start searching the waters here. Put out an alert for all the coastal places for a body that may have washed up in the last week. Let's call Philbrick and use this to our advantage. We need the press here. Someone knows something." Timothy's mind was racing.

"Tim, Julia Fitzpatrick will be at the precinct later today." Roberta said putting her cellphone back into her pocket.

"Moretti, get me results on this as well as the bra you picked up earlier as soon as possible. We need to nail the bastard that did this to her." Timothy was putting his pad away. "Let's go."

CHAPTER 20

DAY 8, THURSDAY
NEW YORK CITY POLICE DEPARTMENT,
6TH PRECINCT, WEST VILLAGE

"Julia, Nancy, Christy, thanks for coming in. There's been a development in the case today. I want you to brace yourself." Timothy and Roberta were sitting across Julia and Nancy. The room was small and Christy was sitting on a chair behind the two of them. If Timothy knew any better, they could've been all members of one happy family. Julia and Nancy could've been Rebecca and Christy's parents, from when Julia was James, he thought.

"She's gone, isn't she?" Julia said closing her eyes and holding her face in her hands as she felt a deep sense of loss. Nancy put her hand on Julia's shoulder. Christy was silent but tears started to stream down her face as she tried to sit there without breaking down completely.

"Unfortunately, that's what it looks like Julia. We found her dress from the night she disappeared with what looks like multiple stab wounds. There's blood on the dress and forensics confirmed a few minutes ago that it matches Rebecca's blood group. We still don't have a body but I suspect it's only a matter of time. I'm really sorry. I know how much she meant to you." Timothy spoke in a sympathetic tone.

Julia was now sobbing dramatically. Timothy stood up and walked over to Julia. "Can I get you some water, Julia? Are you alright?"

Julia looked up and had a crazy look in her eyes. "Matheus, that bastard. He killed her. He could not have her, so he killed her. I'm going to kill him. I'm going to kill him myself with my bare hands. I'm going to strangle him in front of everyone for what he did to her." Julia started howling ever louder.

Nancy was shocked to see this reaction. She started rubbing Julia's back with her hand, trying her best to console Julia, letting her know she felt her sense of loss. Christy had a look of disbelief in her eyes. She was the next to speak, "Are you sure about the dress and her blood type?"

Timothy shook his head with a grim look on his face. He waited for Julia, trying to let the moment pass.

Julia composed herself after a few minutes and wiped her face with her hands. "Rebecca was working on cutting edge research. She was developing a universal cancer vaccine that I had started working on but could never make a real breakthrough with. I spent years and years of my life in a backbreaking effort to make it work but just couldn't. A single vaccine to cure any cancer."

Julia paused to take a deep breath. She realized that she had to be the beacon of strength for the others in the room. She turned around and put her hand on Christy's leg as if to console her. Julia then turned back and spoke in an authoritative tone. "We had code- named the vaccine ATCS-1010. Our firewalls and security software showed that her lab computer was most often the target of hacking attacks. Her house in Brentwood was broken into a couple of times last year. Papers have been stolen from her car on one occasion when she stopped for coffee. She felt threatened and scared but continued her work without fearing the consequences. We all know Matheus is behind all of this. He tried several times unsuccessfully to hire Rebecca. He's wooed her with everything imaginable - money, status, power, even a CEO position at Faust Biopharma."

"Why didn't she leave? Why did she decide to stay back with you?" Roberta asked.

Christy spoke up this time. "We are all like a family. We love Rebecca and she loves all of us. It's a complicated history though."

"So let's go through it. We have time and it's important we know. Why did she not leave for Faust Biopharma?" Timothy asked, knowing this was going to be a long day.

Nancy spoke up next motioning to Christy to let her tackle the next question. "Julia, Dr. Steve Gupta and I worked together years ago when we founded Atticus Biopharma. We ran several clinical trials together in the early years of the company. Dr. Gupta had left academia and was working as the Chief Scientist at Atticus Biopharma. We worked on several trials in a drive to accelerate bringing new drugs to market, drugs for diseases for which there were no cure before then. We did some truly pioneering work in those early days. But after a failed clinical trial for one of the drugs that we were working on, Steve felt that he was better suited for doing basic research.

"He dedicated himself to discovering treatment options to develop an understanding of how our body works at the cellular level rather than working with us on discovering promising new drugs and getting them approved. He left us years before the IPO of Atticus Biopharma, selling most of his stock back to Julia and me for a modest sum. He then headed back to academia."

Roberta was taking notes as Nancy continued to speak. "Despite the separation, we have always been on good terms. We've stayed in touch over the years and exchanged notes periodically. We've regularly recruited the best talent from his lab with his help. That was up until he made his breakthrough. Steve finally cracked the code and figured out how to make "engineered T cells" to attack cancer cells." Nancy was looking at Julia, who signaled she was ready to continue.

Julia started filling in the details. "When Steve made his big breakthrough, there were three bright researchers who were instrumental in the discovery, Rebecca and Christy here, who work with us. There was another fellow named Gustav Henriksen who went to work for Matheus instead.

"Rebecca was clearly the brightest and was instrumental in the breakthrough. Following the discovery, Rebecca pushed Steve to license the technology to a larger company to accelerate development. She even convinced him to present the case to the university board, unwittingly setting in motion a chain of events that led to Steve losing the rights to his discovery, his life's work. The university and the lab had received large sums for money for several years by an anonymous benefactor. Little did Steve, Rebecca, Christy and the others know how indebted the university was to Matheus and his company or how he had filled the governing body of the university with his own cronies.

"The University invited proposals from various companies but it was obvious that Faust Biopharma had the inside track here. They were the winning bidder and they even managed to remove Steve from the whole process. Steve had a defined role according to the licensing agreement, but in reality, it did not amount to much. We fought tooth and nail to prevent the technology from falling into Matheus' hands but lost that battle."

Christy, who by now had wiped her tears and managed to compose herself, spoke next, "Julia tried everything in her power to recruit all three of us. Rebecca and I were close and we understood who the good guys were. I convinced Rebecca to join Atticus Biopharma to work with Julia. But Matheus corrupted Gustav's head and he ended joining the evil empire – he joined Faust Biopharma. He wanted to be where the original technology was. He did not want to start from scratch with us."

Timothy and Roberta looked at each other and then at the others sitting across them. It was certainly strange to see how the three of them were like one elite unit. They completed each other's thoughts and spoke in turns as the conversation progressed. They were also stunned to learn that this situation was much deeper than what they originally suspected.

Julia continued with the Dr. Gupta's history. "Rebecca figured Steve would team up with us and they would find a way to replicate the technology without violating the University's patents. Steve, exhausted after losing the long battle to keep his technology in our hands and have control over it, decided not to join us. He blamed Rebecca for losing his life's work. He was bitter and angry. He never forgave her after that. Rebecca, handicapped by the absence of her mentor, dove head first into the challenge. Within eighteen months she had replicated a new method of creating engineered T cells, which was entirely unique from what Steven had achieved. She combined that with my unsuccessful ATCS-1010 program and made critical breakthroughs, something that even I failed at, despite trying for years."

Julia looked at Nancy as her cue to go through the rest. "Rebecca theorized that each person's cancer was unique and the mutations that caused that cancer were also unique. These mutations, or neoepitopes, could be identified and used to create a vaccine for that person. The process of identifying the neoepitopes and creating individualized cancer vaccines could be harnessed using the current technology she developed. She theorized that a set of immune cells could be made to identify neoepitopes over successive generations of cancer treatment in a test tube to create a body of immune cells that recognized all the common neoepitopes existent in 99% of cancers, thus creating a universal cancer vaccine."

"Her work was truly revolutionary. Way ahead of anyone else. And then all hell started to break loose. Julia and I are convinced we have a mole in the organization. Bits and pieces of Rebecca's work started to show up in papers published by Faust Biopharma. Like Julia mentioned earlier, Rebecca's computer has been the target for several hacking attempts."

As if on cue, Christy spoke next. "She felt like she was being followed everywhere. It started to take a toll on her. She was always looking over her shoulder everywhere she went. She was increasingly distrustful and irritable."

Nancy motioned for Christy to stop and finished her earlier thought. "We know Faust Biopharma has been behind the hacking attempts as well as the leaks but we just can't prove it. We've tightened our security considerably and it has worked somewhat over the last few months. Matheus probably figured that they were better off eliminating Rebecca after all. After stealing Rebecca's work, he could always have Gustav replicate it for him. I have no doubt in my mind that Matheus is behind Rebecca's death. No doubt at all."

Timothy leaned back and took a deep breath.

■ ■ ■

TEN YEARS EARLIER
CAMBRIDGE, MASSACHUSETTS

Dr. Gupta peered at the slide through the microscope. "I can't believe this. How is this even possible? This sample is cancer-free now. Where did you get these cells, Julia?"

"It's a miracle, isn't it?" Julia was smiling as Nancy stood with her hands on her waist and a broad smile across her face. "It's the result of a mutation. This is an old sample, several years old. I recently stumbled upon it from Atticus Biopharma's archives when I was reviewing some old patient data. One of my patients had developed a severe allergic reaction to some medication. We stopped the medication immediately but there was a mutation. The patient's cells developed a mechanism to identify cancer cells."

All three of them standing in this room understood the profound implication of this unique mutation. Cancer cells multiply uncontrollably in the human body. The reason they are able to do this is because the body's natural defense, the immune cells, are fooled by cancer cells into not detecting them. Cancer cells "pretend" to be normal cells and multiple uncontrollably.

However, the blood that Dr. Gupta was looking at under the microscope had immune cells that were able to detect and then attack several types of cancer cells. There was no fooling these cells.

Julia continued explaining what they were looking at. While the blood was able to wipe out cancer cells in a petri dish, the activity in the body did not look as promising. "These cells work great in small numbers but they get outnumbered in the body. They grow weak and eventually die attacking the cancer."

Nancy who was up to speed on this new project spoke next. "We need to be able to give these immune cells more potency. They should be able to turbo-charge and multiply when they encounter a cancer, create an army of cancer killing cells."

Julia had a twinkle in her eye as she explained her sweeping vision. "Those are baby steps and I'm sure we'll get there. I see something more fundamental here. These cells can be modified to fight any type of cancer in any patient. This can one day become a universal cure for cancer, a cancer vaccine."

Dr. Gupta shook his head in disbelief. "Julia, the technology to make the cellular modifications that you are thinking about is years away. We just don't know enough about what happens at the cellular level, let alone play God with someone's cells."

"I'm in this for the long haul Steve. I'm going to put Atticus Biopharma's resources behind this treatment. I'm calling it ATCS-1010. I want the best minds in the field to work on this. I need you to consult part-time on this project." Julia put her hand on Dr. Gupta's shoulder.

Dr. Gupta gave her a reassuring smile. "Of course, Julia. I know you can crack the code on this one day. You will have my support. Are you sure this is the Holy Grail for curing cancer?"

"I can feel it, Steve." Julia had a fierce look of determination on her face. "I've stared at cancer in the face day in and day out since I first stepped into a lab. The answer to curing cancer is right there in that sample. It's staring at us in the face, challenging us to explore its full potential."

"We're going to be fabulously rich when we do this." Nancy spoke with a cocky expression on her face.

Both Dr. Gupta and Julia looked at her in a bewildered fashion. They wondered whether she could fathom the enormity of the potential discovery that awaited them. Alexander Bell did not invent the telephone to become rich. Louis Pasteur did not discover the vaccines for anthrax and rabies to become rich.

Julia held up the vial containing a portion of the sample against the sunlight streaming into the lab. "ATCS-1010, the drug that will one day eradicate cancer. One day in the future, humans will get a vaccine shot of this, like any other vaccine, and their cancer will disappear, just like a common cold."

Nancy held up her hand as if she were holding an imaginary champagne glass and toasting the beginning of an eventful journey. "To ATCS-1010." She toasted looking at the others in the room.

Dr. Gupta smiled and held his imaginary champagne glass up, "To ATCS-1010. To a cure for an ancient and cruel disease."

Julia just smiled as she thought about the cells in the vial.

No matter how long it takes, no matter how much money I need to pour into this, I will crack the code. I will find the brightest minds to work on this. I will never give up. I will keep fighting.

CHAPTER 21

DAY 8, THURSDAY
NEW YORK CITY POLICE DEPARTMENT,
6TH PRECINCT, WEST VILLAGE

Otis Philbrick sat across from Timothy and Roberta. "Look, I already have most of the story. I don't need more from you. A beautiful, young and intelligent cancer researcher disappears right before her big presentation. She's been missing for a week now and there are no real leads other than a bloody dress. Add to that the corporate rivalry between Atticus Biopharma and Faust Biopharma and the whodunit element. Am I missing anything?"

"You've got great sources, Otis. I've got to give you that. We have some suspects but it's still early for us to bring charges against anyone. The investigation is still going on. Add to that we don't have a body yet. Chances are we will find a body soon but it's not a full-blown murder investigation before then. Look, here's the deal. You give us a heads up on anything that's likely going to hurt the investigation or make us look bad and in return you will be the first to get updates on the story, before other papers. Deal?" Timothy looked at Otis, who had a hipster Brooklyn mustache that was well waxed and perfectly in place. Not a single hair was out of place. Even his name, Otis, was hipster and cool. His parents probably knew what he was going to look like growing up.

"Look, I have my own leads and I'm heading my own investigation into some of the people involved. I can't always promise to share it with you unless you agree to confirm my facts before I print. If you agree to that, then this can be a two-way street. How does that sound?"

"Sounds like we have a deal. At this stage, can you stick to the basic facts without any speculation of whodunit? There will be ample of opportunity for that. Something tells me this is not a straight one and you don't want to blow the entire load in the first five minutes here. You need to keep this alive for some time to sell papers. We have a suspect. Someone unstable she spent the night with just before she disappeared." Otis's eyes widened. Clearly, he did not have all the right sources at the precinct. "We'll share the details with you at the right time. I promise you. I just wanted to mention that as a good faith gesture."

"Okay. That sounds good. I'll send you a copy of the story before I send it to print. Look, I still need to do my job. You can have a say but you can't go all censor on my story." Otis put his notebook away into his satchel. So very hipster, Timothy thought.

"I think we understand each other well."

■ ■ ■

"So what did you think about that?" Timothy asked Roberta, feeling a bit better about his day. At least one thing seemed to be going all right.

"I wouldn't trust that snake for a second. He's just going to use us." Roberta had a disgusted look on her face.

"The feeling is mutual. I'm not planning to share everything about this investigation with him. Only enough to make him feel like he has an in with us."

Timothy was holding his hand on his forehead trying to think through this vexing case. "Call Moretti for the detailed forensics. We need those as soon as possible."

CHAPTER 22

DAY 9, FRIDAY
DR. STEVEN GUPTA'S RESEARCH LAB, CAMBRIDGE

"Thanks for meeting me at short notice Dr. Gupta. I'm a friend of Rebecca's. You've obviously heard about her disappearance. I'm extremely concerned about her and I'm looking for her. I wanted to ask you a few questions about your relationship with her and your meeting with her in New York during the conference last week." Ragnar sat opposite Dr. Gupta in his office. He looked worn out first thing in the morning. Sleeping on an old friend's moldy couch in a small one-bedroom apartment in South Boston can do that to a person.

"How do you know Rebecca again?" Dr. Gupta looked at him strangely suspicious.

"I'm a quant and I've been helping Rebecca with some statistical analysis related to her research for the last few months. We became friendly through work. I helped her with complex data analysis related to the research at Atticus Biopharma as an external consultant. We socialized a few times. I've had a long week since she disappeared. I know I don't look like someone who she would even talk to but you have to believe me." Ragnar tried his best to bluff his way with Dr. Gupta. He knew the one-night stand truth would get him nowhere. He gave Dr. Gupta a "concerned friend" look and could see him dropping his guard a bit. Ragnar always knew the right things to say when it was required. How did he become so good at lying, he wondered to himself.

"We haven't spoken for some time. There's not much I can tell you that will help you find her. She worked in my lab a few years ago. She left to join an old colleague's company, Atticus Biopharma. She's been doing phenomenal work there but we haven't kept in touch. I went to hear her presentation on Friday but someone else was there. I heard the rumors about her disappearance and then I called Julia, who confirmed it." Dr. Gupta looked unfazed and emotionless.

"Look, I was really fond of her when she worked for me. But then she left, like most of my researchers. They leave when they find a great opportunity to make money with one of the biotech firms. We did not keep in touch."

"Then why were you outside her hotel room on Wednesday night last week, banging on her door? What were you doing there? She disappeared on Thursday night, you know." Ragnar changed the tempo of the conversation with a direct hit.

Dr. Gupta's face turned ashen white. He stood and started talking in an animated fashion with his arms swaying wildly. "Who the fuck do you think you are, coming in here making these accusations? Who do you think you are? I had nothing to do with her disappearance."

"I'll leave but at least answer that question. Were you there outside her hotel room on Wednesday night? I have at least one person at her hotel that places you there. The cops can probably pull up the security tapes from that night. It's a simple question."

Dr. Gupta looked perplexed and defeated. He sat down on his chair. "Yeah, I was there. I had a lot to drink that night. I was emotional. My work, my baby, was snatched away from me. I spent years and years toiling away in my lab working on a cancer treatment while no one in the scientific community paid attention to it. I've traveled to conferences where I've seen my peers present to packed rooms with no standing space. And when it was my time to present, do you know how many people were in that room? Four people. Maybe. That's what people thought of my work."

Ragnar listened as Dr. Gupta continued, "Rebecca was one those bright people you see once in a lifetime. I met her when she first came to campus. I explained what I was working on and she volunteered to join my lab. We worked on refining the technology and it finally started to gain traction. We've had our fair share of setbacks though. Not everything worked the way we had imagined. And then she came up with the plan to pursue some deep pockets to accelerate the development of this technology. She prepared the development and financing plan and we presented that to the board of governors at the university. Before I could fully understand what we set in motion, I lost the rights to my work to Faust Biopharma. Rebecca left soon after to join Atticus Biopharma. We haven't been on speaking terms much since then. I just went to her hotel room drunk and emotional and wanted to tell her what I couldn't say when I'm sober. That it was all her fault. That she led me down the path to my destruction."

Ragnar listened trying to pick up as much information as he could and analyze it in his head as he weighed the various probabilities and outcomes. Dr. Gupta continued his side of the story, "I never got to speak to her. Someone called security and I was escorted out. I woke up the next day with a bad hangover and a tremendous sense of embarrassment. But I did see her the next day. I did not speak to her, I just saw her. She was in the audience when I was presenting. She was there for a few minutes in the beginning and then she was gone. That was the last time I saw her."

"Did you go back to meet her on Thursday night again? I know she was scared of you showing up again the next night." Ragnar asked in a polite manner.

"I may be old and bitter but I'm not a fool. I made a fool of myself on Wednesday night – let alcohol get the better of me. I wasn't going to make that same mistake twice."

"Thank you Dr. Gupta. You've been very helpful, really. Is there anyone else from her years here in your lab that might hate her? Anything that you can think of?" Ragnar believed Dr. Gupta's side of the story. He could almost feel his pain. Even though Ragnar had a different setback in his professional career, he knew exactly how Dr. Gupta felt. How many times had Ragnar drunk himself into a hysterical maniac and wanted to show up unannounced at the door of the people were really responsible for firing him and give them a piece of his mind? Too many to remember.

"So you don't know about that one, do you?" Dr. Gupta asked.

"No, please tell me."

CHAPTER 23

DAY 9, FRIDAY
NEW YORK CITY POLICE DEPARTMENT, 6TH PRECINCT, WEST VILLAGE

Timothy was furious as he flung the newspaper across the room. Roberta looked at him sympathetically. "That scumbag, Otis. He was here just confirming his story about Ragnar."

The *Daily Post* had published a front page story about Rebecca's disappearance. They had somehow found a younger picture of Rebecca from her days as a part-time fitness instructor. There were two pictures of her on the cover, one of her younger self in a blue sports bra accentuating her toned body and the second of her sitting on a chair in her lab with a warm smile across her face. The story profiled in detail all the characters involved, including Julia Fitzpatrick, labeled as "the Boss and Mother Figure," Nancy Mulligan as "the Mother Figure," Christy Cassidy as "the Sorority Sister and Colleague," Matheus Faust as "the Rival," Iain Thorpe as "the Fiancé," Dr. Gupta as "the Former Mentor," Gustav Henriksen as "the Former Lover" and a blank body outline which was a placeholder for Ragnar as "the Mystery One-Night Stand."

There were four pictures around Iain linking him to four fashion models that Iain had previously dated. The article mentioned Rebecca having a volatile relationship with Iain and rumors that he had even fathered a child with a model he had a brief fling with. There was a mention about a shouting scene at Rebecca's hotel with Dr. Gupta being involved. There were details about the one night she spent with a stranger who was described by the paper as a pathological liar, basket case and "probably the most mentally disturbed person in New York." The article had a leaked picture of the dress that was recovered along with suggestions that the police had few, if any, leads so far.

"I have Ragnar's colleague from Lincoln Myers here today." Roberta said trying to make him feel better. She was carrying a large Dunkin Donuts iced coffee for Timothy.

"Did you know that Rebecca dated another researcher from Dr. Gupta's lab who now works with Matheus Faust?"

"No, I don't think it ever came up in any of the interviews we've conducted so far."

"That makes this even more suspicious, don't you think. You have Julia strongly pointing a finger at Matheus. And now we find out that his chief cancer scientist is an ex of Rebecca's. Maybe she broke up with him, dumped him."

"Not everyone who's dumped kills their ex."

"But we have a missing girl here who is likely dead. Let's not rule him out. Let's keep looking at everyone till we start ruling them out." Timothy took the coffee from Roberta, made a thank you gesture with his head and started walking towards the room where Ragnar's former colleague was waiting.

. . .

"Thanks for coming in today, Ms." Timothy paused as he was mentally assessing Ragnar's colleague sitting opposite him.

"Ruby. Ruby Vohra. Happy to meet you and talk about Ragnar." Ruby was a stunning black-haired Indian girl. She wore a grey business jacket with a matching grey skirt. Timothy had expected another nerdy male quant.

"I'm Timothy Burns and this is Roberta Lopez. We have some questions about your former colleague, Ragnar. How long did you know him? How closely did you work with him? What was he like? What happened at Lincoln Myers and why was he fired? I know I've thrown a lot your way, so please go ahead."

"Ragnar. Hmmm. He's a pathological liar. You can't trust anything he says. He's just plain crazy." Ruby looked upset.

"Can you provide additional color please? We need to know what sort of person he is." Roberta asked in a gentle tone, the way two women would confide in each other, even when they didn't know each other well enough.

"Okay. It's been a wild journey and I've tried to forget it. I never talk about it with anyone anymore." The two detectives kept looking at her with bated breath.

"Ragnar and I worked on the same desk at Lincoln Myers for a few years. We reported into the same person. Our boss was a lifer at Lincoln Myers, having worked there all his life. It was the only job he ever had. Ragnar was his mentee and they were both very close. Our boss set up some complicated trades more than a year before Ragnar was fired. The trades went sour almost immediately and the desk was looking at huge losses. Rather than come clean right away and let the boss take the rap for his mistakes, Ragnar took it upon himself to right the wrong. He created an even more complex set of trades that managed to hide the loss very effectively. Behind the scenes, he was trying to buy time and let our boss trade his way out of the previous losses. Ragnar was manipulating accounts, valuation models, valuations, portfolio marks, you name it and he managed to bust it."

"Why didn't you say something?" Roberta coaxed. "Mind you, I came to understand all of this only after the fact. That man is a criminal mastermind. He knew how to manipulate systems and people to hide this massive loss for as long as he did. Even after it was discovered, he made it look like it was a recent loss from the trades he set up and not a cover up job. I can't tell you how mad I feel at myself. All the signs were there and I never caught it.

"It's not as simple as changing a program. People ask questions. We were heavily scrutinized. There were middle office accounting folks, back-office folks, internal auditors, external auditors, external consultants who scrutinized our books, regulators from the Fed and even the SEC sometimes. He fooled them all. No one can lie like Ragnar can. If he wants something gone, then it's gone. If he wants something hidden, then it's hidden, never to be found again."

"Then how come he was discovered if he was so smart?" Roberta glanced sideways at Timothy who now clearly looked like he was breaking into a sweat.

"That was our stupid boss. He compounded his losses and made them so large that they just couldn't be hidden any longer. Even then, the whole episode has been made to look like an innocent well-intentioned trade that worked for a while, made good money and then blew up when the markets turned making $2 billion in losses. Nothing could be further from the truth. I can't believe they both got away with it." Ruby looked mad and she was fidgeting now with the large diamond ring on her finger.

"Why didn't you report it?" Roberta asked a bit confused with Ruby's body language.

"I left the group shortly before the whole thing blew up. I was transferred to another division within the bank. Last thing I needed was to implicate myself in any which way in that scandal. I was fortunate not many people questioned me about it. I told everyone that it was someone else's trade that blew up, which by the way is the truth. I had nothing to do with the original losses, the cover-up job or the subsequent losses."

"Then why talk to us about it now?" Roberta nudged her again.

"When you called me asking me to talk about him, you said something about a missing persons case. I can't let that bastard get away again. Don't believe anything he says. He is a pathological liar and a master of deception. No one can set up smoke and mirrors like he can. He is a master magician and he holds all the cards. If he wants a person to disappear, you'll never find that person. He is one determined bastard. That's why I want to help. I want you to know what he is capable of, so you can catch him this time. He is a set-up artist. He'll show you want you want to see and it will be exactly the perfect cover, the perfect alibi." Ruby was fidgeting with her diamond ring even more.

■ ■ ■

Roberta hung up the phone at her desk and walked over to Timothy's desk. "The forensic results just came in. Our tech team confirmed that a bra of the same size and model was purchased by Rebecca earlier this year from a boutique in Beverly Hills. That is the only outlet that makes the brand that was in Ragnar's apartment.

Forensics confirmed that the only thing they really found on the bra is semen. There's no blood or anything else on it. They are still working on the dress and bracelet."

Timothy spoke out aloud. "The perfect cover, the perfect alibi..."

CHAPTER 24

FOUR YEARS EARLIER
CAMBRIDGE, MASSACHUSETTS

Dr. Steven Gupta stood next to Joshua Nelson's bed as he was checking his IV. Gustav and Rebecca were monitoring his vitals on the computer next to the bed. Christy ran in with an iPad in her hand, which had the readouts for Joshua's latest blood tests. Christy Cassidy, a tall leggy girl with blonde hair, looked like an Olympian in training rather than a cancer researcher.

Joshua had started responding to his treatment for the first day or so. But after the first twenty-four hours, his body temperature spiked. He developed a high fever and felt extremely unwell, a classic case of "cytokine release syndrome" or in layman's term, his body was fighting back the medicine, in this case the engineered T cells, which were given to him to fight his cancer. Even though Joshua received his own T cells back, his body treated them like an alien or any other infection and fought back causing severe internal inflammation.

Christy, the young cancer researcher, had tears streaming down her cheeks. She knew what this meant. Joshua's time was limited. His last treatment was failing, miserably and he would die even sooner than if they had let his cancer consume him. She had also run into his parents in the hallway on her way in and that made her even more emotional.

Gustav and Rebecca tried to maintain their calm as they were trying to figure out ways to suppress this immune reaction as best as they could. Dr. Gupta was back in his Mr. Hyde demeanor. He looked emotionless as his miracle treatment was failing this young boy whose life lay in his hands. Dr. Gupta was mercilessly ordering the three of them to administer various drug combinations to the boy. Gustav, Rebecca and Christy would look at each other and then proceed to do as instructed, knowing that none of this would really work at the last minute. Joshua's body was not going to give up attacking the T cell and the T cells in turned attacked healthy cells.

They all knew the damage was irreversible. It was only a matter of time before Joshua's internal organs would start to shut down one by one.

After a couple of hours of trying unsuccessfully, Joshua's heart rate monitor flat-lined. Everyone in the room was stunned and at the same time relieved that Joshua was free from his misery. Everyone except Dr. Gupta.

"Double the antibiotic and combine it with the anti-inflammatory again. Now." Dr. Gupta barked.

Christy was now crying loudly. Rebecca had tears streaming down her cheeks, as she could not bear to see Dr. Gupta in his state of denial. Gustav walked up next to him and put his hand on Dr. Gupta's shoulder. "Steve, he's gone. Joshua is gone. We should talk to his parents now. I can do that if you'd prefer."

"No, Rebecca should do it. It was her design. She needs to talk to Joshua's parents." He gave her a look that an angry parent gives a child when they've broken something.

Christy, seeing the cracks in the team, ran out howling even louder. Gustav looked at Rebecca blankly. She tried to decipher his expression. It was not love, not hate, not anger nor confusion. It was just blank.

Rebecca wiped her face defiantly. She channeled this defeat into a beacon of strength. "I'll do it Steve. I'll speak to them." With that, she started walking out of the room.

CHAPTER 25

DAY 9, FRIDAY
DR. STEVEN GUPTA'S RESEARCH LAB,
CAMBRIDGE, MASSACHUSETTS

"And after Joshua died, we took a long break, most of us. I let them go and told them not to come back. It was three months before we were all back in the same room." Dr. Gupta still looked disturbed by Joshua's death. "We all took it really hard. Even though Joshua's ultimate fate was already decided when he came into our lab, we tried our best and we could not save him. Joshua died an excruciatingly slow and painful death here in this very lab. It lasted around forty-eight hours and it was bad. None of us slept during those forty-eight hours. I suspect I did not sleep for a week after that. I was in the lab going through every data point, every report and every last detail."

"I'm sorry. I truly am. What does this have to do with Rebecca's disappearance?"

"Joshua's parents blamed us for his death. They did not consider the fact that Joshua was going to die anyway. They felt we were to blame for killing him even earlier and making his death horrible. Most terminal cancer patients are on a regimen of meds to manage their pain, make their passing more peaceful and calm. Joshua died in the exact opposite way.

"We traveled to Michigan to attend his funeral. Joshua's parents did not allow us in. They went as far as to blame us for his early death. Joshua's mother cursed Rebecca saying she hoped she would die a horrible and painful death." Dr. Gupta looked straight at Ragnar as he spoke about the curse.

"Thank you, Dr. Gupta. You've been tremendously helpful. Any chance you still have their address?"

CHAPTER 26

DAY 9, FRIDAY
JULIA'S APARTMENT, 15 CENTRAL PARK
WEST, NEW YORK CITY

Julia was sitting on the terrace of her duplex apartment at 15 Central Park West, one of the most coveted addresses in New York City. The building was designed by the noted architect Robert A. M. Stern. Julia's neighbors in the building included actor Denzel Washington and the musician Sting, who dined with Julia every few months when she was in New York City.

Julia was sitting opposite Nancy and Christy browsing the news on her iPad Pro. Julia had just completed reading the *Daily Post* story about Rebecca. She switched over to her Bloomberg Professional App. Atticus Biopharma stock was down more than 20% on the news of Rebecca's disappearance. The financial community was speculating on the future of Atticus Biopharma with the disappearance of the heir apparent to Julia as well as the tilting of the scales in favor of Faust Biopharma. The salacious manner of Rebecca's disappearance did not help either. Billions of dollars of market value evaporated within minutes.

Julia was calm. She really did not care much about money. Her mission in life was to find cures for diseases.

Money or no money, company or no company, she would forge ahead no matter what. Not knowing what happened to Rebecca and why was the most painful aspect of the current situation.

Nancy, on the other hand, looked extremely distraught on the developments of the morning. She sounded more upset today than when she first heard about Rebecca's disappearance. Nancy had made it quite clear in the past that she was not a fan of Rebecca. Christy, on the other hand, still looked upset over the disappearance.

"Have you heard anything else from the cops about Rebecca?" Julia spoke softly. It was obvious she had been crying and was still upset about Rebecca's disappearance. "Julia, wake up. She's gone. She's probably dead.

We're all still here. Thousands of people and millions of patients depend upon what we do from this point on. I know you loved Rebecca like a daughter but now is not the time to get soft. We need to face this head on. You still have me. You still have Christy."

Julia did not say anything. She kept listening as Nancy continued. "Christy and I have been fielding calls from our largest investors all morning. They are all upset about the stock. They want to know what we are planning to do in the aftermath of Rebecca's disappearance. We need to put out a statement. We obviously need to be respectful and sympathetic about the whole Rebecca situation but we need to let the markets know that we continue our mission, no matter what. You need to name someone heir apparent. I don't want to sound insensitive, but in this situation, it should probably be me."

Julia looked at Nancy trying to read into her last comment.

"Look, our collaboration partners are also worried about all the clinical trials Rebecca was supervising. Without her, those trials could go awry. Years and years of hard work all down the drain. I need to take the reins here, help you navigate the ship. We cannot lose everything we've built here. This media shit storm is not going away, Julia. This has just started. What do you think happens when they find her body?"

Julia felt a sharp pang of pain like a knife was stabbed through her heart. Despite these years, she still found it difficult to express her emotions. She listened to Nancy and put her head down, closed her eyes to think. Nancy saw that as a sign to stop and let Julia now weigh the pros and cons.

Julia looked up. "Let's put out a statement today naming you co-CEO and acting Chief Scientific Officer. We need to word it appropriately and make sure it shows deference to Rebecca. She was not just another employee. I have faith in you, Nancy."

Julia then turned to Christy and spoke gently. "Christy, please set up a telephonic board meeting for today. I need to speak to the Board. Tell the Board I am proposing Nancy become co-CEO of the Company given the recent developments."

"Okay, I'll do this." Christy quickly made her way from the terrace into the apartment.

"What did Raoul find out in Cambridge?" Nancy asked, after she saw Christy leave and felt convinced that she was alone again with Julia.

"I don't know. Nothing new since he called yesterday about following Ragnar to Cambridge."

Nancy stood up, sat next to Julia and put her hand on hers. "We'll find her, Julia. I honestly think we will."

"I don't have any more tears left, Nancy. I've shed them all. I've never been an emotional person but this has broken me."

"You have me by your side, Julia. I'll always be there." Nancy put her hand on Julia's face, gently caressing it. "I still love you, Julia. I never stopped. I won't let you break. You have me by your side. You always will." Nancy caressed Julia's face and gently started to lean forward to kiss Julia.

Julia deftly stood up and started walking in. "Put out the statement today. I have other things I need to handle."

■ ■ ■

Julia dialed Raoul's number as Nancy was leaving her apartment.

"What's going on Raoul?"

"I'm at the airport. He just bought a one-way ticket to Chicago. I will be on the same flight as him. He left Gupta's lab and went straight to the airport."

"Why Chicago?" Julia blurted out loudly. She noticed Nancy stop cold in her tracks and turn around to look at Julia with a look on her face. She made eye contact for a second and then turned around again and left.

"He's obviously chasing some lead that Dr. Gupta gave him. Must be related to something or someone Rebecca knew in the past. I don't understand why he cares so much but it seems like he may be on to something. I'm going to continue tailing him. He's obviously really smart."

"Okay. Keep me posted. What else do you have so far? Do you know if the police have found a body?"

"Nothing yet, Julia. They have her description out to various departments around the water where these bodies typically wash ashore. I wouldn't rule out the possibility that whoever it was dropped her body with weights tied. If she's dead, it's possible her body may never be found. I know that's not what we all want to hear, but if foul play was involved, my money is on her body never being recovered."

"Find me whoever did this Raoul. I need to know what happened and who did it. Chase down Matheus and Gustav too. They had something to do with this. I just know it."

"I will. I'm following up on some other leads too. I'll let you know as soon as I know something. I've got to go. My plane is boarding shortly."

■ ■ ■

Ragnar was sitting with a cup of coffee in the boarding area. He pulled out the slip of paper with the Nelson family's address. He stared at it again and then put it back in his pocket.

Raoul peered up from his newspaper briefly. He saw Ragnar put the slip of paper back into his pocket.

Raoul also recognized James Lin from the 6th Precinct. James and Raoul did not overlap but he knew who James was. So Timothy and team were also on to Ragnar. That was interesting, he thought.

Where are you going Ragnar? What ghost are you chasing from Rebecca's past? Why are you really doing this? Why do you care so much about her?

■ ■ ■

Julia dialed a number she had not dialed in a while.

"This is Dr. Steven Gupta. I'm away from the phone. Please leave me a name, number and a detailed message after the beep and I will get back to you."

Julia hung up. She looked up another number on her iPhone and hit "Call."

"You have reached the research lab of Dr. Steven Gupta. You have reached us after hours. Please leave a name and number and someone from the staff will reach out as soon as possible."

Julia hung up and dialed another number. "Christy, it's me. Ragnar is on his way to Chicago for some reason. Do you know what it maybe about? Did Rebecca ever mention Chicago to you?"

Christy paused for a moment and then replied, clearly sounding confused. "Chicago? No, I can't imagine what's in Chicago. Maybe she had some old acquaintances but no one who really mattered to her. That's really strange."

"Hmm. Okay, let me know if you think of someone. I called Steve but could not reach him. Could you please call him? Tell him I need to speak to him."

"Okay."

"Did you speak to the Board yet?" Julia was starting to feel misty-eyed at the thought of delivering the bad news to the Board. Julia always thought of Rebecca as the daughter she never had. Parents were not supposed to outlive their children.

"I did. We're setting up the meeting soon. Anything else from the cops?" Christy sounded genuinely concerned about her sister-figure.

"No. Nothing yet. They're still waiting for a body to turn up." Julia hung up shortly after and disappeared into her thoughts about Rebecca.

Where are you Rebecca? Are you at the bottom of the Hudson River? Will I ever see you again my dear? I hope you did not suffer. Know that I still love you very dearly. I will move heaven and earth to find you and punish the person that did this to you.

CHAPTER 27

DAY 10, SATURDAY
STATEN ISLAND, NEW YORK CITY

Timothy woke up to the incessant ringing of his cell phone. His wife moved next to him kicking him gently under the covers nudging him to pick up his phone. She still had her eye mask on. Timothy sat up in bed and picked up his cell phone.

"Roberta, what's going on?"

"Tim, campus security found Dr. Gupta's body last night."

Timothy almost jumped up. "What? How? What happened? Where is James? Didn't Ragnar meet him yesterday?"

"Yes. They found his body last night in his lab. He was incapacitated with a blow to his head. Then he was injected with some biological materials most likely from his lab. He died a horrific death. They found him bruised and bleeding from everywhere. There was blood coming out even from his eyes."

"Where is Ragnar? Where is James?"

"Ragnar was on his way to Chicago yesterday. James is still tailing him."

"Okay. As soon as possible, I want James to bring him back in. He's the last one with Rebecca and now it seems he may have been the last one to meet Dr. Gupta before he's been killed."

"Okay boss."

"The press is going to have a field day with this." Timothy now jumped out of his bed. "Call Cambridge PD. Let them know we'll meet them there. We should both head over there." Timothy looked down at his wife, who pulled up her eye mask from one side to peer at him with one eye. She was still sleepy but hardly looked surprised.

Timothy hung up his phone. He looked at his wife. "Sorry hon, I need to be in Cambridge today. I'll make it up to you tomorrow. I promise."

All she said was "go" before she slumped back in bed. "I love you." Timothy ran towards the shower.

■ ■ ■

Timothy was sitting next to Roberta on the train. Both of them were on their phones conferenced in with Mike Moretti.

"We have the results from the dress and the bracelet. The bracelet is an expensive diamond bracelet that Rebecca purchased from Graff last year in New York City. They customized the bracelet for her and it matches the description from her purchase, so it definitely belonged to Rebecca. There was some blood on the bracelet. The dress is another matter altogether."

Both Timothy and Roberta held their phones closer to their ears as they tried to block out the noise of another train passing them in the opposite direction. "The tears on the dress are consistent with stab wounds with a hunting knife given the tear patterns. There were eight stab wounds in total, all to the front torso. She was most likely lying down when the killer stabbed her. The blood on the dress matches Rebecca's blood type. We're running a DNA analysis with hair that we recovered from her hairbrush. We should have the results by end of day tomorrow. The blood on the bracelet matches the blood on the dress. It looks like the dress was removed soon after she was stabbed.

The train passed and Timothy and Roberta could now hear Mike much better. They looked at each other, none of this surprising either of them much. "There was a lot of blood but we did not find enough, so the dress was probably removed before she bled out in it. The killer probably did not want any identifying items on her body before dumping it in the water."

"Was there any semen on the dress?" Timothy asked as Roberta winced at the question.

"No, none. If we haven't found a body washed up somewhere yet, I would suggest getting police divers check the waters around the area where the dress was found again."

"We already did. We spent hours and hours scouring every inch of the waters around there. It's likely she was weighed down to sink but could have drifted out to the sea rather than settling at the bottom of the river. We're still hopeful we'll find a body. Let's see. Did the techs get more information from her cell phone?"

"Yeah. It was a task getting access to the cell tower data. Our techs scoured the information the best they could. They triangulated Rebecca's position around the hotel where the conference was taking place most of the day. There's a change in position to another place in midtown. We were only able to triangulate her position to a block plus or minus one block for triangulation errors in the evening. That block is actually the same block where Iain said they met when they formally broke up. The remaining evening is clearer. We were able to triangulate her at the bar she met Ragnar and then his apartment early the next day. Her cell phone then disappears from all records around 5:05 am the next morning."

Timothy flipped a few pages of his small pocket book and looked at his notes. "So the last call on her cell was at 4:54 am. That call lasted four minutes. That gets us to 4:58 am. Her cell is switched off at 5:05 am. So something happened in those seven minutes either in Ragnar's apartment or as soon as she left his apartment."

"Are the techs sure there are no other records of her cell phone?" Roberta asked.

"No. That was the last of her cell. Whoever took her removed the SIM card right away. What about Dr. Gupta? What does Cambridge PD have?" Moretti asked.

"About that Mike, you should come down to Cambridge today. You need to look at the crime scene. We now have one likely murder and another definite one with a gruesome body. This is going to be become a high-profile case. The top brass is already going crazy demanding answers. Pack up your stuff and start heading over. We need you in Cambridge."

"Okay. I'll start heading over now. Ask the Cambridge forensics team to wait for me before they start clearing anything there. I want to see the scene firsthand. Maybe there's a connection to the dress or something else that we know of from this case that Cambridge PD may not be aware of."

"I'll see you there, Moretti." Timothy hung up the phone and turned to Roberta.

"I have a theory now, Tim."

"Okay. Let's hear it."

"The theory is that Ragnar is responsible for the deaths of Rebecca and Gupta. Ragnar meets Rebecca at a bar. He falls for her. The guy is down on his luck and finds himself with a knockout at the bar. He probably hasn't had a steady relationship in a while and suddenly he finds himself with this beautiful and smart woman. He's a schizophrenic suffering from bipolar disorder. Maybe he's been off his meds for some time. Rebecca goes with him to his apartment. Maybe she gets there, sees his dump of an apartment and gets cold feet. Next thing you know, she wants to leave but he just wants to have sex with her, maybe own her. His crazy side takes over and he kills her.

"He returns back to his self and finds himself with Rebecca's body. He decides to cover it up. He creates an alibi about having sex with her. He removes her bra and masturbates on it. Throws it into his laundry hamper. He creates enough of an electronic trail to escape suspicion. He probably has a burner cell tucked away from earlier. He calls her cell from that number at 4:54 am and keeps the call on for four minutes. Then he lets a few minutes pass to make it seem like she left his place in a hurry and then at 5:05 am, he switches off her cell, removes the SIM card and destroys the phone.

"He proceeds to dump her body in the water and drops her dress and bracelet in the bushes. He's got an alibi. His story checks out with the physical evidence and he's a free man."

Timothy was impressed. "That would make sense. If he killed her and she bled to death, where is the physical evidence of that? There was no crime scene in his apartment."

"Maybe he was in his crazy state. Maybe he killed her in cold blood somewhere else in the building. Maybe a stairwell, the basement or the roof. This is a mentally disturbed man that hid hundreds of millions of dollars and later billions of dollars of losses from an army of auditors and regulators for over a year. Again, this is my theory."

"Okay, let's talk about Dr. Gupta. Ragnar kills Rebecca, he gets grilled by us. Even though he's not arrested yet, he is under constant suspicion. If he is as cold and calculated as we think he is, why would he meet Dr. Gupta and kill him shortly after?"

"Well, that's simple. He thought he was off the hook. We turned his apartment upside down and we let him go. Maybe Rebecca told him something about how Dr. Gupta and she were not on talking terms. Maybe there was some more bad blood between them. He feels like he needs to settle some score with him. He heads straight to Cambridge and kills Dr. Gupta too." Roberta looked at Timothy for his feedback.

"Simple and elegant. We need to bring him in. Let's get an arrest warrant for him. What other theories could we consider?"

Roberta knew Timothy had already thought of all of this. He just wanted to check if she was thinking that too. "My next suspect would be Iain. She breaks up with him. He is clearly upset. He follows her after their last meeting. He sees her with another guy. He follows them to Ragnar's apartment. He waits there all night and he's fuming. He decides to take matters into his own hands. He has a burner cell from his bachelor days that he uses to call her. He kidnaps and kills her."

"What about Dr. Gupta. Why does Iain kill him too?"

"Maybe Dr. Gupta knows something that can tie Iain to Rebecca's death. Unlikely, but possible."

"Let's find out where he was yesterday. And let's check his alibi on Thursday night when Rebecca disappeared."

Roberta had a small smile on her face. "I spoke to the techs on my way here. Iain was in Cambridge yesterday. He flew to Boston and stayed at a hotel in Cambridge."

"What else?"

"Well, another suspect is Gustav Henriksen, her former boyfriend from Dr. Gupta's lab. We don't know much about him other than the fact that they dated when they worked together and then they joined rival companies. Probably broke up over that. They were probably bitter rivals. Matheus, his boss, tries recruiting her but fails. He sees her pull ahead in the field they're working in at Atticus Biopharma. He's jealous and bitter. He tracks her down before her big presentation, kidnaps her and then kills her. His master plan includes anyone else that could be a threat to his work at Faust Biopharma, so he needs to get rid of Dr. Gupta. The perfect opportunity presents itself when Ragnar, a suspect, shows up at Dr. Gupta's lab. He uses that as cover and gets rid of Dr. Gupta, knowing Ragnar will be framed for it."

"So we have three male suspects who were involved with Rebecca at some point?" Timothy asks.

"Four actually. I would not rule out Matheus. In his case, it's just corporate rivalry. He tried to recruit Rebecca and fails. He hires someone to kidnap and kill Rebecca and make it look like a disappearance. He learns that one of the suspects is someone Rebecca spent a night with. He's tracking Ragnar and when he learns that Ragnar is meeting Dr. Gupta, he uses the opportunity to get rid of him too."

"You're missing one more suspect, one other possibility which is also simple and elegant." Timothy remarked and looked like he just pulled out a trump card.

"What is that?"

"Dr. Gupta killed Rebecca, Ragnar learnt about it and he killed Dr. Gupta for revenge. How about that one for simplicity and elegance?"

Roberta shook her head. "Yes, that could be one too, in which case it comes back to Ragnar."

"Let's bring him in as soon as we can. We can't have him out there while this case remains unsolved."

CHAPTER 28

DAY 10, SATURDAY
EVANSTON, ILLINOIS

Ragnar pulled up at the address Dr. Gupta gave him in a cheap rental car. The house was a beautiful white three-bedroom house in a tree-lined neighborhood. There was a small lawn and a paved walkway in front of the house. The house had a bright red door. There were a couple of chairs in the lawn. The house had one story and an American flag hung above the patio. There were two windows on the top floor facing the street and the curtains were drawn in on both.

Ragnar swallowed hard and stepped out of the car. He did not notice the other car that pulled up further behind him on the same street and stopped. James Lin put on his sunglasses as he pulled over and stopped. James did not notice the third car that pulled up even further behind him, the one with Raoul.

Ragnar walked up the stairs and rang the doorbell. There were a few children playing on the lawn in the house immediately next door. The kids were running around with water guns spraying each other. An old lady opened the door.

"Hello, I'm looking for Mr. and Mrs. Nelson." Ragnar asked. The woman who opened the door looked too old to be Joshua's mom.

"Who's asking?"

"My name is Ragnar Johnson, ma'am. I am the father of a five-year-old boy who is suffering from cancer. I understand the Nelsons had a young child who underwent the same treatment my son is about to undergo. I wanted to speak to them about it. I got your address from someone who knew about Joshua's treatment." Ragnar was surprised how the lies flowed so easily.

"Come in." That was all she said as she ushered him in.

The Nelson house was sparsely furnished inside. There was a fireplace with several family pictures around it. There were pictures of the Nelsons in happier times. The father, mother and Joshua enjoying a day at the waterpark, pictures of the family in Disneyland and even a picture of Joshua in a local soccer league for young children.

"I'm sorry for your son…" the old lady paused, as she could not recall his name.

"Ragnar. Rag, uh, Ragnar Johnson."

"Ragnar, I'm sorry to hear about your son. I can answer any questions that you might have but I don't think I can be very helpful. I wasn't there during his final treatment. Joshua died in a horrible manner in a lab hospital outside Boston."

■ ■ ■

Raoul pulled out a computer that he did not like to use often. This was his special computer for limited use only. He used the computer to log into the NYPD's servers remotely using a dormant user and password that was created specifically for his use and that only he knew about. He ran the address in the search bar.

He could immediately see the owners of the house. There was a police report attached to that address from three years earlier. He clicked on the report and opened it. He quickly browsed through the key items in the report and his jaw dropped.

He looked up from the computer screen at the house.

■ ■ ■

James got off the phone with the precinct. He was all clear to arrest Ragnar as soon as he came out of the house. James started the car and drove closer to the house and parked right behind Ragnar's rental car.

■ ■ ■

"Joshua's mother, Marge Nelson, was my daughter. Marge was my only daughter and Joshua was my only grandson." The old lady spoke as she wiped a tear.

"What happened to Marge?"

"Marge and David committed suicide a year after Joshua's death. They both decided to end their lives together. Joshua was everything in their lives. They were devastated after his death. They could literally not see themselves living a life without him. Joshua was born ten years after they married. They tried for years and years unsuccessfully before they had Joshua. He was the apple of their eye."

"I'm really sorry about Marge and David. I truly am. I did not, uh, know…about…"

"They made a suicide pact, bought some poison and drank it together on the first anniversary of Joshua's death. At least they are happy now. They're reunited with their son." She wiped another tear but the dam had broken. She was crying profusely.

"I'm sorry, ma'am. I better be going. I did not know and didn't mean to, uh, mean to upset you. I know it can't be easy, losing your family. Is there anyone else who may have known about his treatment that I can speak to?" Ragnar stood up awkwardly to leave.

"Why don't you leave me your number, Ragnar? I'll call you if I can think of anyone who knew about Joshua's treatment. All the best. May God bless your son."

"Thank you ma'am. I, uh, I appreciate it." Ragnar pulled out an invoice from a recent purchase at the airport and scribbled his cell number behind it and handed it back to her. "Thank you."

■ ■ ■

"Ragnar Johnson?" James stood outside the house as Ragnar stepped out gingerly and closed the red door behind him.

"Yes?"

"You need to come with me. I'm Detective James Lin of the NYPD. Did you meet with Dr. Gupta in Cambridge yesterday?"

"Yes, I did."

"Then you need to come with me Ragnar. Dr. Gupta was found dead yesterday. Killed in his lab."

"What?" Ragnar froze and his mind just went into quant mode calculating the new outcomes. The lead that Dr. Gupta gave him was a dead end. And now Dr. Gupta was also dead. Killed according to this detective who was obviously tailing him from when he left New York. It didn't take a genius to realize that he was linked to two disappearances and would be the top suspect in any investigation.

What happened when I asked Dr. Gupta for the address? Did he say no? Did I lose my mind? Did I torture him to get the address and then kill him? Do I really not remember anything? How could I have done something so horrible? When did I last have my pills? Did I even carry them when I left for Cambridge? Did I refill my prescription last week? Was I off my pills when I met Rebecca?

Ragnar held his head down, his mind struggling to understand the events as they were unfolding but at the same time accepting the cold reality of his situation. "I'm ready to go, Detective. You can read me my rights now."

"Ragnar Johnson, you have the right to remain silent..."

■ ■ ■

"Julia, Raoul here. The NYPD have arrested Ragnar. You are not going to believe who he came to meet in Chicago. Do you remember Joshua Nelson?"

Julia winced when she heard the name.

CHAPTER 29

ONE DAY EARLIER – DAY 9, FRIDAY
DR. STEVEN GUPTA'S RESEARCH LAB,
CAMBRIDGE, MASSACHUSETTS

The void plunged a needle into Dr. Gupta's chest. Dr. Gupta winced in pain, which only excited the void. The void's eyes lit up.

The void plunged the second needle into his chest and emptied the contents into his body. Then a third, then a fourth, on and on again till the void lost count.

The blood, the pain, the writhing, the inevitable cocktail playing havoc in Dr. Gupta's body made the sensation peak. The void gave out a muted scream, still sitting on Dr. Gupta's chest, a near orgasmic scream of relief, joy and exhilaration.

The void sat next to the body. The wave from joy and excitement passed quickly and was replaced with a deep sorrow, an emptiness that could not be filled. The void gave out a second scream, one of pain emanating from a deep, old wound, a wound that refused to heal, a wound that constantly reminded the void of its existence.

The pain started swelling until it took over. The void stood up, sighed at the anti-climactic end and walked off.

Nothing can fill the void.

...

PRESENT DAY – DAY 10, SATURDAY
DR. STEVEN GUPTA'S RESEARCH LAB,
CAMBRIDGE

"This has to be one of those dead bodies that haunt you for years to come. What exactly happened to him?" Timothy asked as he looked at Dr. Gupta's body. Dr. Gupta had collapsed and was lying on his back. There was a pool of blood behind his head that was caused due to the blunt trauma to his head. There was a statue of a laughing Buddha covered in blood on the floor close to Dr. Gupta's body. The extremities of his limbs were horribly swollen and his face was swollen too. His eyes were pushed out quite a bit due to the swelling and there were lines of blood next to both his eyes.

The image of Dr. Gupta with his eyes open, staring at the ceiling and his mouth open as if he died screaming, was quite disturbing to look at.

"So what do we know so far?" Roberta asked the forensic team from Cambridge PD.

"Well, the assailant first hit Dr. Gupta really hard on his head with a statue of the Buddha, which was a piece from his own office. It looked like he was running away from the assailant when he was hit on the head, really hard. He collapsed on the floor and was kind of incapacitated or maybe even passed out. The assailant then removed all sorts of experimental injections from the refrigerator and injected Dr. Gupta, while he was still on the floor, one by one with all of them. The vials included modified rat immune cells, modified human immune cells of different types for various experiments.

"Whoever did it was probably a very angry person. The assailant injected him with everything they found in the refrigerator. His body is filled with a deadly cocktail of experimental cells that probably attacked his internal organs and ultimately killed him. That would explain the state of his body and the blood oozing out from everywhere, including his eyes and ears."

"What about the security tapes?" Timothy asked. "Friday was a slow day. There was not much planned.

Dr. Gupta wasn't expecting anyone. He was virtually almost always in his lab according to his lab assistants." He handed Timothy a picture printed from a frame in the security video. "This is the last person who entered and left his lab before security found his body later that night."

Ragnar Johnson, there you are again, Timothy thought. He stared at the picture for several moments. At least there was a body this time and not just a bloody piece of clothing.

"Okay. Please leave the crime scene as is. Mike Moretti will be here soon from New York. We'd like him to scour the crime scene as well. As you guys know, this is related to the disappearance of Rebecca Chase, who used to work in Dr. Gupta's lab."

"Of course. We'll wait for Moretti. In fact I just spoke to him. He's ten minutes away."

Timothy heard Roberta's cell phone ringing. She picked up the cell phone, spoke for a couple of minutes and then hung up. "James has Ragnar in custody. He voluntarily surrendered when James confronted him. They are both on their way back to New York."

"Good. We should also head back once Moretti gets here."

...

Mike Moretti had spent several hours going over the crime scene with the forensics team from Cambridge PD, Timothy and Roberta.

Mike was now standing next to Dr. Gupta's body in a sterile post mortem room at the Medical Examiner's office. He wanted to be present for the post mortem examination.

The coroner made a Y incision in the chest of the corpse. He opened Dr. Gupta's torso and started the examination. Moretti couldn't help but think about Dr. Gupta, who probably did these procedures on lab animals and maybe human beings thousands of times. Never must he have imagined that he would be here undergoing an autopsy for a horrific death caused by the very agents that were stored in his lab as potential medicines of tomorrow.

The coroner carefully performed the autopsy, weighing the various organs and examining the internal damage to all the tissues. It was obvious that the biological agents wreaked havoc inside his body, liquefying some of his organs while hardening some others.

It was getting late on Saturday evening. Mike Moretti hoped this was not how he would be spending his Saturday night. He really needed a beer. Thankfully, he was almost done here. As he was reading through the findings, something jumped out at him. He grabbed the coroner's shoulder. "Are you sure about the time of death?"

"Of course, it's a wide band but that is fairly accurate."

Moretti was staring at the conclusion. Dr. Gupta's time of death was Friday evening. Ragnar had met with Dr. Gupta in the morning and had left the lab by ten-thirty. There was video evidence of that. He was already on his way to Chicago at the time of death with James Lin tailing him. That meant that it was someone other than Ragnar. But there was no one in the video.

Moretti ran out of the building and jumped into his car. He quickly turned around to head back to Dr. Gupta's lab.

■ ■ ■

AMTRAK TRAIN
BETWEEN BOSTON AND NEW YORK

"Are you absolutely sure?" Timothy grunted as he spoke to Moretti at the other end of the line.

Roberta looked at Timothy as he hung up. "That was Moretti. The time of death does not match the time period Ragnar was at the lab. Gupta died several hours later. In fact, Ragnar was on his way to Chicago at the time of death. He has the perfect alibi. Again. James Lin, a detective, was tailing him and can vouch for Ragnar being nowhere close to the lab when Dr. Gupta was murdered. Fuckkkkk."

"What about the surveillance video?"

"Moretti went back to the lab. He examined all the videos and the placements again. He thinks there are several blind spots from the entrance all the way up to the lab. Someone who is familiar with the lab and the cameras could've gotten in and out undetected. The security cameras are fine but they just aren't set up to cover every square inch. Whoever it was, either the attacker knew the lab or was a professional who knew how to evade security. Moretti counted at least six cameras the killer would've had to evade to get in and out without being noticed."

"Someone could've hacked into the security system and rigged it, right."

"That's a possibility too." Timothy was wiping his brow and looking beaten.

"Matheus is coming in tomorrow to the precinct."

"Good. Let's talk to him too. Get his whereabouts during both the crimes. We need to move quickly. The press is going to be on our heels and the pressure is going to get real."

CHAPTER 30

DAY 11, SUNDAY
NEW YORK CITY POLICE DEPARTMENT,
6TH PRECINCT, WEST VILLAGE

"Look, Ragnar. We don't think you did it." Timothy was sitting with Roberta and James Lin in the precinct. Ragnar was sitting across them looking dejected.

"Are you sure? How do you know I didn't just do it and forget it?"

"You were on your way to Chicago when Dr. Gupta was murdered. That's all we can tell you right now. We know it wasn't you. We just want to ask you a few questions and then you'll be free to go."

Timothy wanted to know what Ragnar was doing in Boston and then in Chicago. Ragnar ran through the entire series of events from the night when he found out that Dr. Gupta had been at Rebecca's hotel the night before to his meeting with Joshua Nelson's grandmother, which turned out to be a dead end.

Roberta leaned forward as Ragnar finished his story. "Did you hear Rebecca's cell phone ring on Friday morning around five?"

"No, I would've told you if I remembered that. I woke up and she was gone."

"Try to remember, Ragnar. She spoke to someone for four minutes before she left your apartment."

"No, I did not. Like I said I would've told you."

"Like you told us about Dr. Gupta being at the hotel?" James Lin asked in a tough voice.

"Look, I'm sorry. It was something that came up after I had spent the entire day with you. I wasn't sure what I was going to find. It turned out to be nothing after all."

"Except you probably stirred up something that you shouldn't have, someone got upset and killed Dr. Gupta." Timothy joined the bad cop wagon.

"It's a free country. I spoke to someone from Rebecca's past, trying to learn more about her. That's not a crime. How would I know that someone would kill Dr. Gupta over this information? And why is that even relevant? It turned out to be a dead end."

"He probably knew something else that could've exposed Rebecca's killer. Probably spooked that person and they killed him just to be safe." Roberta commented.

Ragnar was just shaking his head. "You're free to go Ragnar, but the next time you come up with a hunch, let us handle it. Don't go chasing ghosts again."

"You bet I will."

Okay. Now I know what time she left my apartment.

Ragnar's mind was already running ahead on what the most logical next steps here would be.

■ ■ ■

"Thanks for coming in today, Dr. Faust." Timothy and Roberta were sitting opposite Matheus.

"Please, call me Matheus."

"Matheus, thanks for coming in today. Getting right down to business, please tell us how you knew Rebecca."

"Rebecca. Well, she was something."

"Was?"

"I read the papers too officers, especially when my name is plastered all over them."

"That was an unfortunate story but there's only so long that we can contain an explosive story like this one. The press was sooner or later going to get wind of it and twist it in every which way." Roberta spoke calmly.

"I know. It's really sad. Rebecca did not deserve it." Matheus looked up as if deep in thought. "I met Rebecca four years ago. She was a brilliant researcher in Dr. Gupta's lab. Rebecca and Gustav, they were both working for Dr. Gupta. Rebecca was working on engineered T cells at that time, the foundation of the technology that would explode onto the biotech scene over the next few years. The technology was revolutionary in its conception. The basic idea of the technology was to remove a cancer patient's immune cells and add a molecule to the cells that can stick to cancer cells similar to how a lock and key operate. The engineered T cells would then be reinfused into the cancer patient.

"Some say Rebecca conceived the approach at Dr. Gupta's lab, though she never officially took any credit for it. Did you know that Einstein once said that anyone who had not made a great contribution to science before the age of thirty would never do so? Einstein himself wrote his seminal work on special relativity before his thirtieth birthday. Rebecca was one of those - young, brash and brilliant with a few more world-changing discoveries in her. As we grow older, we gradually lose our imagination, our appetite to take risk and settle into the mundane activities of life.

"When I met Rebecca, the early experiments in the technology had flopped when the cells turned out to be inactive with a failed human trial as well, a five-year old cancer patient. Rebecca was frustrated with the results and planned to leave the lab and join Faust Biopharma to continue her research. It was at that time that I introduced Rebecca and Gustav to research in our lab where the engineered T cells needed an additional signal, a molecular tail jutting out of the cell that stimulated the engineered T cells to attack the tumor. This idea married to the work they were doing in Dr. Gupta's lab was what resulted in the ultimate success of this technology.

"Dr. Gupta and his team including Rebecca, Christy and Gustav applied this technology to treat a little girl, Cienna Boyle, whose cancer disappeared rapidly. Her heartwarming case was covered in several news articles and even a documentary on revolutions in cancer. As I got closer to recruiting Rebecca and the others to Faust Biopharma, Julia showed up, following all the press coverage and the highlights of the case. She talked Rebecca and Christy out of joining Faust Biopharma with her pseudo-story about how she cares about changing the world and how I was a greedy capitalist. Gustav saw right through Julia's bogus story. He ended up joining Faust Biopharma but Rebecca and Christy were lured by what they thought was a noble goal and they both joined Atticus Biopharma."

"You must've been pretty upset at Rebecca for joining Atticus Biopharma. After all it sounds like you were the man behind some of the early successes and she repaid it by ditching you. How did that feel?" Timothy was searching for some change in Matheus' body language, anything that he might slip if he had anything to do with Rebecca's disappearance.

"If I want to talk about my feelings, I'll speak with a psychologist, thank you. I don't need you." Matheus immediately snapped after the last question. "Of course, I was upset but this is a competitive field. We try, we lose, we move on to the next goal. Anyway, I kept a tab on Rebecca's work at Atticus Biopharma. I know she wasn't happy there. She was going to leave Atticus Biopharma and that would've been a huge blow to Julia and Atticus Biopharma. I'm not saying I know anything specific but Julia had the most to gain from Rebecca's death. Her leaving for Faust Biopharma would've been a deathblow for their cancer programs. Everyone important in the cancer research department at Atticus Biopharma would've followed her to Faust Biopharma. If I were you, I'd look into that."

"You know Julia thinks that you had something to do with her disappearance."

Matheus smirked. "Of course she would take my name. In reality, Julia had the most to gain from Rebecca's disappearance and I had the most to lose. Rebecca would've left Atticus Biopharma to join Faust Biopharma. Can you imagine the message that would send to everyone? Her disappearance caused Atticus Biopharma stock to drop over 20% but her defection would've been catastrophic for Atticus Biopharma."

"When did you last speak to her?" Roberta was toying with a small notepad in her hand flipping some pages.

"On the Thursday she disappeared. We spoke a few times and we had a low-key meeting set up on Friday night at my home in Newport to discuss her move to Faust Biopharma. She obviously never showed up. Julia probably got to her first. She has her tentacles everywhere. Don't be fooled by her demeanor. She is a ruthless person and she will do whatever it takes. Both she and Nancy. You should look into their pasts. They have blood on their hands. They're not as innocent as they want everyone to think they are."

"When you say blood on their hands, what do you mean?" Timothy was looking at Matheus trying to decipher his body language for any obvious signs of guilt.

"They never had any issues sacrificing a life if they thought it could advance a cure that could save others.

Dr. Gupta's technology was not ready to be tried on humans but Julia pushed him behind the scenes. Gupta reluctantly took on the case of a young boy who died a gruesome death in the quest for a cure. For Julia, that was an acceptable loss in the pursuit of her grand vision of curing cancer. She is blinded by her goal. You should look into her. She has the resources to pull off something like this."

Roberta looked at her notes and thrust one of the open pages in front of Matheus. "Do you recognize this number?"

Matheus did not look surprised at all. "Yes, that's a number I use for confidential discussions. I called Rebecca on Thursday several times to set up the meeting in Newport. You probably got that off her cell phone records, I'm guessing."

"Yes, we did. Is this number registered to a company in the Cayman Islands?" Roberta pulled the pad back and started making some notes on it.

"Yeah, that's the one. It's meant to be registered in the name of a shell company that cannot be traced back to me."

"Then why share it with us?" Timothy was ambivalent and could not judge how much Matheus candidly shared with them versus sandbag the investigation.

"I have nothing to hide."

"And where were you on Thursday night when Rebecca disappeared?"

"I was in New York for some meetings on Thursday but headed back to Boston on Thursday night. I was on my way to Newport on Friday when I heard about her disappearance. I tried calling her but her cell was switched off."

"Tell us about Gustav. He's the Chief Scientific Officer of your cancer programs and he used to date Rebecca." Roberta changed gears to the next suspect on her list, mentally making a note to re-visit and verify everything that Matheus told them.

"Gustav? What about him? He wouldn't ever hurt Rebecca. They dated when they were at Gupta's lab but that was a long time ago. They were colleagues working in close quarters day in and day out and ended up dating. They broke up before they joined Atticus Biopharma and Faust Biopharma, respectively. Gustav is the most balanced and calm person I know. He could never harm another human being."

"How did he take the break-up? He couldn't have been happy about it?" Roberta continued to probe Matheus.

"If he wasn't happy, he never showed. Like I said, they broke up before he joined Faust Biopharma. I don't think they had spoken in a while. I don't know if he's single or seeing someone. We don't discuss our personal lives."

"Is there anything in his manner or his behavior that was odd in the last couple of weeks?"

"So you think he's a suspect? Is that where this is going?"

"Matheus, we're just asking about an employee of yours who dated Rebecca. Was there any bad blood between Gustav and Dr. Gupta?" Timothy chimed in trying to push Matheus and rattle his cage a little bit. "Anything that he would hold against Dr. Gupta?"

"You've got to be fucking kidding. Do you know how ridiculous you sound?"

"Answer the question, please." Timothy was glad to see some reaction out of Matheus but it was not what he was hoping to see from someone who was guilty.

"No, I don't think there was anything funny between Dr. Gupta and Gustav. Gustav worked for him and held him in high regard. You should seriously look into Julia and Nancy. The skeletons in their closet will overwhelm you. No one becomes as rich as she is without steam-rolling innocent people."

"You're pretty rich too! What do you have to hide?" Timothy tried to push his buttons.

"I have my skeletons, but I don't have blood on my hands. And definitely not Rebecca's. I told you, no one had more to lose than me when she disappeared."

"We'll be in touch, Matheus. Thanks for coming in today."

■ ■ ■

Timothy was proud of Roberta complementing him so well. They worked great as a team.

"So what do you think?" Timothy wanted to see if he missed something.

"I don't know if I completely believe him. He's hiding something. I can feel it."

"Wasn't it ironic how both Julia and Matheus named each other as the culprit? They're so blinded by their hate for each other, they can't see beyond it."

"It's almost like they don't care about Rebecca. All they want to do is nail each other over her death." Roberta was momentarily sad at the thought.

"Well, Julia looked like she was shattered."

"It could all be an act."

"It could be. We won't know till we get to the bottom of this. Tell me, what ties Rebecca to Dr. Gupta? Who would want them both dead? Why? And what about the timing? He was killed shortly after Ragnar met him. Why then? What is the killer thinking?" Timothy was testing Roberta again.

"That's a simple one. Whoever kidnapped and killed Rebecca hated her and had their reasons for killing her. When Ragnar spoke to Dr. Gupta, it spooked the killer. Dr. Gupta knew something that could connect the killer to Rebecca. He was probably killed because of that."

Timothy shook his head in approval. "For that theory to work, it would've had to be someone who kept close tabs on Dr. Gupta, like someone who worked in his lab currently, or someone who was keeping close tabs on Ragnar. Given what a loner he is and the fact that he is somewhat of a pariah in New York City, he was probably being followed. It could also be someone who worked for Julia or Matheus. In either case, it's obvious Ragnar is on to something and dredging up secrets someone does not want found."

"I'm not ruling out Ragnar as a suspect though. At least for Rebecca's disappearance."

"That's fair. Gustav will be here shortly. Let's see what he has to say."

. . .

Gustav was a tall and lean blonde man. He had soft blue eyes and classic good looks. He had blonde hair that was stylishly combed back giving it a casual yet measured look. Gustav had a dimpled chin and a two-day stubble that added to his look. Timothy and Roberta could see why Rebecca would be attracted to him.

"Gustav, we appreciate you coming in today to talk to us." Roberta kicked it off.

"No problem. I want to help Rebecca. Whatever I can do to help find her."

Timothy and Roberta glanced at each other.

"Could you tell us about your relationship with Rebecca and why you broke up?" Timothy asked as he glanced at his watch. It had been a long day with no end in sight. He was craving for some coffee. Black.

"Rebecca and I met each at other at Dr. Gupta's lab. We worked together on a new approach to cancer, one that did not involve killing cancer cells but stimulating the body's immune system to learn to attack cancer cells, much like how your body would fight a common cold or an infection. Rebecca and I were on the same wavelength. We both loved to work for hours at an end and we both loved to spend our nights painting the town red despite the long hours. We hit it off soon after we started working together."

"How long did you date Rebecca? Why did you two breakup?" Roberta glanced at Timothy whose eyes looked red and weary.

"That depends on what you define as a breakup?"

"What do you mean?" Timothy promised himself he would run out for coffee as soon as this ended.

"Rebecca and I broke up just before we joined Atticus Biopharma and Faust Biopharma. For the world we never spoke to each other again after that. In reality, we kept in touch as friends secretly. We could not let Julia or Matheus know that we were friends. They would never tolerate that. We had to keep our friendship a secret."

"So the two of you were friends after you started working. Big deal. Why not just do it openly?" Roberta looked genuinely surprised on why someone would let something like a job dictate how they should live their lives.

"You won't understand. Atticus Biopharma and Faust Biopharma are archenemies. It's a strong characterization but its close. Rebecca was fiercely independent and so am I. That's what attracted both of us to each other to begin with. When the dice was rolled, I chose Faust Biopharma and she chose Atticus Biopharma and there was no turning back. She never faulted me for joining Faust Biopharma nor I her for joining Atticus Biopharma. I respected the fact that she followed her heart. We just couldn't be successful in our careers if we were seen as having an ongoing friendship. So we made our break-up appear acrimonious but continued talking to each other."

"She was engaged to Iain last year. So did you break-up before then? What happened?"

"A lot. A lot happened. See after Rebecca and I parted ways to join rival companies, we both started working on the basic technology that we developed in Dr. Gupta's lab and started taking it forward in a different direction. I started perfecting the engineered T cell therapy. My work involved making the immune cells more efficient in attacking cancer. However, what I did involves individualized treatment. Each person who has cancer gets his immune cells removed from his body, modified in our lab and reinfused. Rebecca, on the other hand, decided to leapfrog the next stage of development to work on a universal cancer vaccine, a set of cells that could be injected into anyone's body to fight cancer. You see, cancer is a generic name for a diverse set of diseases. Cancer could take multiple forms. Each person's cancer is unique. How do you develop a universal cancer vaccine? That is the Holy Grail of cancer medicine.

"A few months after I joined Faust Biopharma, I got a few pages from Matheus on a new suggested approach to curing cancer. It was pretty obvious that the pages were prepared from Rebecca's ongoing work though they couldn't necessarily be traced back to Atticus Biopharma. At first, I figured someone in her lab leaked a few papers. I decided to keep it from her. Three months after leak, I received another set of papers from Matheus, which was revolutionary. I did the same thing again, did not mention anything to Rebecca. When I received a third set of papers from Matheus, it finally dawned on me that we were slowly but surely stealing work from Rebecca to develop the same universal vaccine in our labs.

"I met Rebecca one night in a hotel outside Boston and told her about the leak in her lab. She went ballistic on me. She was angry and upset that I did not mention the leak to her when it first surfaced. As much as she liked me, she loved her life's work even more. She was hurt. She was already under a lot of pressure from Julia to develop the universal vaccine, ATCS-1010. That night marked the end of our friendship as well."

"You knew this would drive a wedge in your friendship and yet you decided to tell her? That's odd, wouldn't you say?" Roberta asked as she checked on Timothy again who was surprisingly silent today evening.

"That's correct. I knew how she would react when I told her but I had to come clean. I really liked her and did not want to see her hurt. I didn't want to see her work brazenly stolen from her."

"So the leaks stopped?" Timothy looked sharp and back in his form. Roberta wondered how he found the energy to recharge again.

"No, that's the surprising part. After I told her, I presumed there would've been a total overhaul of their security protocols. That they would've really clamped down hard and nothing confidential would ever leave the lab. And it did seem that way for some time. I did not get anything from Matheus for several months. And then they re-appeared again. I've received two sets of documents from Matheus since I broke up with Rebecca. The weird thing is that the papers from the two latest leaks were more extensive and detailed than the three sets of papers that were leaked previously."

Timothy's mind was racing. This new information added a whole new paradigm to an already complicated case. Add to that none of this had anything to do with Dr. Gupta. How did that piece of the puzzle fit in? Who was this mystery person leaking all this information to Matheus? And why did Matheus not mention anything? Of course he wouldn't. This was a classic case of corporate espionage.

Timothy paused and then spoke. "Why are you telling us all of this? Wouldn't this jeopardize your standing with Faust Biopharma?"

"All I care is about Rebecca. I don't care about anything else at this stage. I wanted to tell you all of this so it could help you find her. And the person that did this to her."

"Where were you on Thursday night Gustav? The night she disappeared?" Roberta had her pad open as she made some notes while Gustav spoke.

"I was in New York for the conference. I did not meet her though. I had dinner with an acquaintance and then I went back to my hotel. I attended a few seminars on Friday and then headed back to Boston on a late afternoon flight. Nothing exciting, unfortunately."

"When was the last time you met her?" Roberta was flipping her pad to check something else.

"The night we ended our friendship. We haven't spoken or met since."

"Any thoughts on who may be responsible for her disappearance?" Timothy was now craving a hot cup of black coffee again.

"I don't think she had any enemies. I don't know Iain so I can't say whether it could be him or not. I personally think this had something to do with Dr. Gupta's death. It's just a hunch."

"Well, that's certainly some hunch. Thanks for coming in today. If you think of anything else that may be helpful, please call us." Timothy stood up to shake Gustav's hand, the promise of a cup of coffee was just around the corner.

"I will."

■ ■ ■

"What do you think?" Timothy undid the cover of his black coffee and was stirring it to cool it down. He could never have a hot cup of coffee. It needed to be lukewarm for him to be able to sip it.

"Something tells me his alibi is going to hold up. Credit card receipt and a couple of security cams at the restaurant and the hotel."

"Maybe it's an elaborate cover. Dig in deep to make sure this really checks out." Timothy was visualizing all the moving pieces and the cast of characters in his head. He knew he was missing something.

Someone was clearly lying. But who? Where is Rebecca? Is she alive? Is she dead? Where is her body?

CHAPTER 31

DAY 11, SUNDAY
MOTT STREET, CHINATOWN, NEW YORK CITY

Raoul Perez was standing over the shoulder of a fat, nerdy teenage kid who had eight monitors set up in front of him. Other than the lights from the screens, the room was totally dark, yet this kid was wearing a pair of sunglasses as he typed furiously on his keyboard.

"Come on kid. Tell me you have more than what the cops have on the cell phone records."

The kid did not look up. "Do you want to find out who killed JFK?"

"Stop the drama and get back to the subject, will you?

Did you find anything on the cell number I gave you?" 'The kid' was a legend within the hacker community.

No one knew his real name. He only went by his handle 'the_kid_1618' online. He was known to hack into government agency websites just for fun. Rumor had it that he hacked into an Iranian nuclear power plant and shut it down for weeks. Like everything, this was a rumor that could not be verified.

"Did you know that George H. W. Bush's favorite dessert was made by a small street shop in Baghdad? During Operation Desert Storm, a refrigerated container full of those goodies was smuggled across the border into Saudi Arabia and then flown clandestinely by private jet to the United States. Did you know how much each piece of that dessert cost in taxpayer dollars?"

"Come on kid. Enough with the bragging. I don't care what you pulled off CIA or NSA's database. Get a real girlfriend, will you? Impress her with all your stories. Tell me you were able to find something."

The kid turned back to his screen and took a deep breath. "Do you know what Stingrays are?"

"Yeah, it's a portable device that mimics a carrier cell tower and forces all closeby cell phones to connect with it. It's basically a spying tool."

"Did you know that the NSA has more stingray cell towers across the country than AT&T, Verizon, Sprint and T-Mobile combined?"

"Again with your conspiracy theories. Do you ever get out of this room much? When did you last speak to another living person?"

"Not all those cell towers are actual towers. Some of them are virtual ones. Look, the short answer is that there is a whole other secret cell network that exists in this country for surveillance purposes. It's not for civilian use. Here, look at this map." The kid pulled up a map of Manhattan and its boroughs. "Look, this is the map of the city on the morning Rebecca disappeared."

Raoul gave him a disapproving look.

"Come on, you give me a number and you don't expect me to look up who it belongs to? By the way, next time you rent a car, you should get a non-descript car. The Ford you got in Chicago is statically more likely to stick out there. Next time try a black Chrysler..."

"Cut the crap, okay. Let's talk about the map."

"You see, I hacked into the NSA Stingray network and got a history of the pings that this cell number registered across the network. I plotted all the pings with the times and see what you get."

The map showed Rebecca's cell phone in the East Village. The next tower showed up as a red dot close to 23rd Street and 1st Avenue with a time stamp a few minutes from the East Village dot. The next dot showed up around 34th Street and 1st Avenue. The next one was close to 42nd Street and FDR Drive. The next dot was time stamped several minutes later around 51st Avenue in Brooklyn. The dot continued to pop up on the map, each a few minutes apart clearly showing a route taken on the I-495 East. The last dot on the map was on I-495 East in Flushing just where it crossed a small body of water connected to Meadow Lake.

"You know what this means right?"

"You're a genius kid. So Rebecca's cell phone traveled from the East Village into Brooklyn. The time stamps suggest that the cell was clearly in a moving vehicle. So someone kidnapped her, switched off her cell phone and removed the SIM card so the cell did not register on the regular networks, but the NSA network continued to ping all cells, with or without SIM cards and irrespective of whether they are on or off."

"Correct."

"So whoever took her, they headed on the I-495 East into Long Island and not west towards the Hudson River."

"See you're learning. Stay with me for a few days…"

"And I'll never get laid. So whoever took Rebecca probably broke open and threw her cell phone into the water as they were driving over Meadow Lake. Seriously, you're a genius. I have a niece that I can introduce you to. She's plump but charming. She definitely gets out more often than you do. What do you say?"

"Did you know that every time Rihanna starts getting ready for a shower, she…"

Raoul's mind was racing as he started to run towards the door.

"Don't you want to see the vehicle she was kidnapped in?"

Raoul stopped in his tracks and turned around. "Of course. Of course."

"But it's going to cost you."

"You greedy little pig. What do you need all that money for?"

"You'd be surprised. I'm collecting the moolah to buy an asteroid space resort in *Entropia Universe*. Ever play that one?"

"You're saving money for a video game?"

"No Grandpa! I'm saving money for an asteroid space resort in the virtual game. The seller is asking for 400 g's but I think I can get him down to 300."

"Whatever, Revenge of the Nerds! I'm going to add an extra five thousand. Nothing more."

"Seven."

"Six. And I don't want to hear your Rihanna shower story, ever."

"Deal. It's your loss though. You're not going to believe what she does just before…"

"Wasn't I clear? I don't want to know. I don't care if you have a stolen video of Kanye West face banging Taylor Swift."

"Ewwwwwww. You're sick man! Give me a few minutes. I'll pull up all the videos along that route."

The kid was furiously typing at his keyboard.

"So how short are you? How much do you still need to buy that game thingy?" Raoul asked curiously.

"294 g's."

"What about all the money I gave you earlier?"

"I got needs, man."

"Jesus. Can't you just download all the money you need from some bank? Just hack a bank to get your money."

The kid stopped typing and looked up at him. "I'm one of the best hackers in the world, not a common thief. It's an art form. You won't understand."

Raoul had a grin on his face. He liked the kid. As eccentric as he was, there was a likable quality about the kid.

"Here we go D-O-T." The kid pulled up traffic camera videos of an old maroon cargo van driving up 1st Avenue. The next video was at a different angle showing the van enter the Queens Midtown Tunnel. The next few videos showed the van moving east on the I-495 East. The next video tracked the van at it took exit 22A-E towards Interstate 678. There were no videos after that.

"Keep looking, kid."

"You don't get it do you? I wrote an algorithm that can track a fly's ass as it moves across traffic cameras. Whoever took Rebecca drove the van into Mount Hebron Cemetery and had another car there. He probably changed cars and waited for some time before driving off again. This is probably how far you're going to get with electronic surveillance."

"Can you pull the plate and any markings on the van?"

"Already did. The plates match with the plates of a Jeep Cherokee for someone who lives on the Lower East Side. The plates were either stolen or purchased from another car thief. The side of the van has some faded lettering."

The kid pulled a sheet of paper from the printer under the table, close to him on his left. "Here you go. I made the letters as clear as I could. It says 'H A R D B E'. That must be what was left over. Could be Hard Beer, Hard Beaver, Hard Beach, Hard Bed, Hard Bear, Hard Beard, Hard Belt...."

"Thanks kid. Give me that printout. Keep looking and call me if you find anything else. I'll make it worth your while. An artist needs a patron."

"Indeed."

The kid turned around, pulled up another screen, put on a pair of headphones and started playing a multi-player video game that he was clearly playing with other players who were probably just like him.

Raoul gave the kid's shoulder a gentle squeeze and headed out of the door.

■ ■ ■

From: Raoul Perez
To: Julia Fitzpatrick

Message: Rebecca might still be alive. Kidnapped on Friday morning. Kidnapper used a maroon van. She might probably be somewhere in Long Island. The kid turned out to be a genius.

CHAPTER 32

DAY 11, SUNDAY
SOMEWHERE IN LONG ISLAND, NEW YORK

The void kills. The void destroys. The void rejoices. Nothing can fill the void. The void keeps demanding for more. More blood, more bodies, more pain.

Time does not heal the void. Seasons do not change the void. Wounds cannot distract the void. The void craves. The void cringes. The void tortures the soul. The void has complete control. The void is the puppet master, holding all the strings.

The phantom stood outside the door as screams continued to come from behind the door. They were screams of sheer horror. The door was reinforced with an iron frame and had multiple locks on it. The door had a small rectangular mail slot at eye level.

The phantom walked over to the slot, slid it open and peered inside.

■ ■ ■

Rebecca was on the floor on her back. It was dark save for the weak daylight that made its way through the outline of the door of her cell. Her cell had stone walls and a rough stone floor. There was a small toilet in one corner of the cell.

Rebecca was rolling on the floor and screaming. Her hallucinations were vivid and felt real. She knew she had been drugged but couldn't help herself. Her skin was on fire and she felt like she was in a pit covered with scorpions that were crawling all over her body, stinging her on her body, her face, each sting more painful than the previous one. The scorpions all emitted a vibrant blue-green glow in the darkness as they crawled over her body. She was holding her face and screaming in sheer horror. Rebecca was naked except for a pair of white cotton panties that was dirty with dark stains from dirt in the cell. She continued to roll on the floor trying to get away from the scorpions.

She stopped rolling and lay on her back and looked up to see all the scorpions on her body form a circle around a small exposed spot in the middle of her stomach. All of them had their tails in the air ready to strike in unison. She stared at them in disbelief as all of them froze for a few seconds. Suddenly, without warning, all the scorpions started stinging together as if trying to tear a hole in her stomach. Rebecca saw blood spurting out of her stomach and the scorpions stung and stung together like a coordinated evil opera. She screamed even louder than before.

. . .

The phantom was starting to feel a rush of blood to the head seeing a near naked Rebecca writhe and thrash in pain. Even though the phantom did not expect it, the sight of Rebecca naked, except for a pair of panties, seemed to sexually excite the phantom.

The void needed to see pain. The void needed to see suffering. The void would make her pay. Dearly. Very dearly.

■ ■ ■

Rebecca was still screaming, but her mind was trying to rationalize the ferocious hallucinations and pushing her to calm down. "Keep calm. Take deep breaths, Rebecca." Her mind was guiding her to relax. Even though the drugs continued to play havoc with her senses, she started breathing deeply, closing her eyes, trying to distract herself from the sensation she felt all over her body and the fear that rushed through her nerves.

She opened her eyes and the scorpions were still stinging away at her stomach but there were fewer now. There was no blood anymore.

She looked at the door to distract herself and was shocked to see a pair of eyes peering at her through the slot in the door. The eyes were red and on fire as if the devil himself was behind the door. She knew it was the chemicals circulating in her blood and in her head that was distorting the image, but they really did look like two small balls of fire staring at her.

. . .

The phantom turned away and walked into what was a makeshift kitchen with a small stove in one corner. The stove was on and there was a long bread knife in the fire. The knife was gleaming red now. The phantom pulled up a skull facemask that hung around the neck and pulled the hood of the sweatshirt on so that only the eyes were now visible. The phantom wore a thick leather glove and picked out the red-hot blade by the wooden handle and started walking towards the door.

. . .

Rebecca saw the devil's eyes disappear as the scorpions slowly started to crawl off her skin and disappear into the darkness of the cell. There was an eerie silence that permeated in the cell. She continued to lie on her back, clutching her stomach with her eyes tightly closed wincing in pain.

Rebecca did not hear or see the door open. She did not see the phantom quietly walk up to her and kneel. With all the mayhem of sensations in her head and body, she barely noticed the phantom gently opening her legs and caressing the soft skin of her inner thigh.

. . .

The phantom was caressing Rebecca's inner thigh. Her skin felt soft and tender. The phantom was breathing faster as the excitement made the phantom's heart beat even faster and a rush of adrenaline gushed through the phantom's body. The phantom took a deep breath and touched the flat surface of the blade to Rebecca's skin.

■ ■ ■

A searing pain ran through Rebecca's leg as she felt a red-hot metal object come in contact with her inner thigh. Rebecca let out a hoarse scream as the knife seared her flesh and the smell of burnt flesh filled up the small cell.

■ ■ ■

The phantom started to scream over Rebecca's screaming. "Biittttchhhhh... how does that feel, huh? Does that feel good to you, you fucking biiitttchhhhhhh..."

The phantom pulled the knife away, stood up, quickly paced out of the cell and shut the door behind. The phantom pulled back the hood, pulled down the pants and started to masturbate vigorously while staring at Rebecca. The rush of blood from scorching Rebecca definitely helped. The phantom gave out a scream and held the door with one hand for support as it reached an orgasm. The phantom stood there without moving for a few minutes as the intense sensation gradually ebbed and then started sobbing. First gently and then it got louder and louder until the phantom gave out a loud painful scream.

■ ■ ■

Rebecca was in intense pain. She was in shock and was starting to lose consciousness. Just as she was about to faint, she heard a guttural wild animal-like scream at the door and her blood froze hearing the phantom shriek.

■ ■ ■

Nothing can fill the void.
Nothing can ever fill the void.

CHAPTER 33

DAY 12, MONDAY
EAST VILLAGE, NEW YORK CITY

Ragnar's head was spinning with all the possibilities after his conversation with Timothy and Roberta. He wondered how it could have slipped his mind. It was so obvious.

Ragnar put an alarm for 4:00 am on Monday morning. He went to bed dressed for the morning. As soon as the alarm went off, he quickly washed his face, used a mouthwash and sprinted down the stairs of his building.

Of course no one would've seen Rebecca leave his apartment. If she left at five in the morning, only someone who was there at five routinely might have seen her leave. If the cops canvassed the neighborhood during regular business hours, it was highly unlikely they would fine someone who was also there so early. It was so basic.

He walked around his block to see if there was anything open or anyone who would have a reason to be there. He came back to the entrance of his building and checked his watch – 4:17 am.

Ragnar stood there with his hands in his pockets and waited. There were a few cars that passed but nothing or no one there that looked like they needed be there. And then it happened.

A refrigerated delivery van pulled up outside the Chinese restaurant diagonally opposite his building. His street was narrow and due to scaffolding and the layout of the street, there were few available parking spots. The van pulled up in what looked like the only spot there on the street. The driver, a Chinese man, who was smoking furiously and had a cigarette hanging out of his mouth, hopped out from the driver's side and went towards the back of the van and opened the doors. The man was delivering fresh pork. There were several freshly slaughtered pigs in the back of the van.

Ragnar walked up to the deliveryman. "Sir, are you here delivering pork every day at this time?"

The deliveryman stopped, looked at him with a confused expression and replied in Chinese.

"Do you understand, uh, English?" Ragnar made an expression with his hands as if trying to ask if he understood Ragnar's words.

The deliveryman replied again in Chinese.

"Crap. Of course you don't know English. Here." Ragnar pulled out a twenty from his wallet and handed it to the deliveryman. "Wait here. I'll be right back."

The man took the twenty and spoke in Chinese again, expressing his disapproval at the small payment. Even with the language barrier, he made it quite obvious that he was not happy and that he wanted more.

"Here, here." Ragnar pulled out two more twenties for the deliveryman. "Wait here. Wait. I'll be right back.

Here. Right here. Don't go anywhere." Ragnar made several gestures with his hands as he spoke so it was amply clear that the deliveryman should not leave. The deliveryman smiled and nodded. His teeth were crooked and stained from years of smoking.

Ragnar started running back towards his building. He ran up two flights of stairs and started knocking on one of the doors on the third floor.

"Mr. Gao. Mr. Gao. Please open up. I really need your help. Mr. Gao."

Ragnar heard some rumbling inside the apartment. It was obvious that Mr. Gao was not happy about the commotion at such an early hour. He heard some loud phrases in Chinese that sounded like curses. Mr. Gao opened the door partly. He still had the chain lock on.

"What is it? What's going on?"

"It's me Mr. Gao. Ragnar. I helped you with your groceries a few weeks back."

"Once! You helped me once with my groceries. So you think that gives you the right to barge into my apartment at this hour? What time is it?"

"Mr. Gao, please. I'm, uh, I'm really sorry but I need your help. There's a delivery man outside who may have seen the person who kidnapped my girlfriend last week. He only speaks Chinese. I need your help. I need to speak to him and ask him a few questions."

"So just because I look Asian and my last name is Gao you think I'm Chinese? That I speak Chinese? Is that what you assumed? You know I was born here, in America."

"Uh, I'm, uh, sorry. I thought you were... so you don't speak Chinese?"

Mr. Gao sighed, his previous statement was meant to throw Ragnar off. "Of course I do. You said your girlfriend was kidnapped?"

Ragnar nodded. "Yes, she's been missing for more than a week now. I've been going crazy looking for her."

"Let me get my glasses."

■ ■ ■

Ragnar watched as Mr. Gao spoke to the delivery man. Every few sentences, they would both look at Ragnar as if they were sharing some juicy gossip about him.

Mr. Gao turned to Ragnar after conversing with the delivery man for a few minutes. "Yeah, he remembers his delivery from last Friday morning. This was his last delivery on Friday morning and he wanted to drive out to New Jersey to his sister's place. He said there was another van parked in his spot. There was a person sitting inside with a hood and some mask covering most of the face. Our man here, Xiao Jun, knocked on the window and signaled that person to move but the driver of the other van flicked him the middle finger. Xiao Jun was really upset and angry. He's gotten tickets before for double parking, sometimes even at these unearthly hours. He had to park a block away and haul the pork from there to the restaurant."

"Does he remember what the driver of that van looked like?"

"No. He says he took a picture of the van though. He said if he ever saw that van anywhere in New York, he was going to go terminator on it."

"He has a picture?"

"Yes, the beauty of cell phones. Everyone has one now."

"Can he message the picture to me?"

"Yeah, I asked him that as well. He thinks you are rich. How much did you pay him? He's asking for another twenty for the pictures."

Ragnar pulled out another twenty and handed it to the deliveryman.

"Thank you." He smiled with his crooked teeth again. "So now you know English, huh?"

"That's probably the only English he knows." Mr. Gao commented.

Mr. Gao helped translate Ragnar's phone number. Ragnar heard his phone beep. He unlocked his phone and looked at the pictures.

The deliveryman had taken quite a few pictures. Some of them were blurry but there were a couple that provided some clues.

The first picture was of the side of the van with some faded letters on it. The second picture was of the driver of the maroon van. The window was rolled up and the picture was taken without the driver's knowledge. The driver was looking sideways as if peering at Ragnar's building. He had a hood on and what looked like a skull face mask covering the bottom half of his face. The only thing that was really visible were the eyes. The kidnapper clearly did not want anyone to see his face.

Ragnar looked at the first picture of the van and saw the letters 'H A R D B E' followed by two faint I's. He looked at it again.

'H A R D B E I I'

What the heck is Hard Beii? Where did you take Rebecca? Who are you, masked man? What do you need from her? Why did you harm her?

CHAPTER 34

DAY 12, MONDAY
JULIA'S APARTMENT, 15 CENTRAL PARK WEST, NEW YORK CITY

"So Rebecca is alive. A bloody dress is dumped on the west side to throw the cops off. The cops stop looking for her and start looking for a body instead. What else?" Julia had a look of relief on her face. She looked at Nancy and Christy, both of them looked confused.

"That's right. Whoever took her wanted everyone to think she was dead, which makes me feel even more certain that she is alive and is being kept alive for a reason. Have you received any ransom requests since she disappeared?" Raoul was sipping on a green juice that Julia offered him as a "healthy alternative" to coffee. He sipped on it slowly trying hard not to throw up. He couldn't understand how someone who could afford the finest coffees in the world would settle for this horrendous green juice. Kale? Seriously?

"No, nothing. You can leave that if you want. I just offered it to you as an alternative." Julia had a calm grin on her face.

"No, no, this is great. Healthy. I need this. I do. It's a great, uh, what do you call it, a cleanser, a great system cleanser?"

Julia signaled the butler who was waiting across the hall. "Please get Raoul a black coffee, lukewarm, no cream. Maybe Dunkin if we have some in the pantry. Or do a quick coffee run, please? I'll get a Starbucks, large, black, unsweetened, no cream. A double espresso for Nancy. What will you have Christy?"

"I'll have a medium decaf latte." Christy adjusted her glasses as she spoke in a rather meek tone in Julia's presence. The butler nodded and walked off.

"Who am I kidding? I hate this green thing. I'm just not a cool Kale-muncher." Raoul put down the juice and quickly wiped his mouth.

Julia gave out a short laugh. She felt like it had been a long time since she felt this relieved and gave out a smile. At least there was a chance that Rebecca was alive. Nancy looked surprised but relieved while Christy was expressionless.

"We should definitely let Timothy know about this. I know we can't disclose your source but Tim is smart. He will understand he needs to change gears and look for her in the right places now that they don't necessarily need to look for a body. The more people looking for her the better. Maybe even leak this to the press."

"I agree wholeheartedly about sharing this information with Timothy and Roberta. They are turning over every stone to get to the bottom of this, but right now unfortunately they're looking for a killer and a motive, not for a kidnapping victim or a kidnapper. But I don't think leaking this to the press is a great idea. Timothy will know it came from us." Raoul flipped open his notebook and was going over his notes.

"What else do you have?" Julia asked as she leaned back again on the sofa.

"Ragnar's story checks out. He is looking for her and he ran into a dead end. He had a sketchy past. I'm presuming you saw the articles I sent you and the police report of their interview with his colleague?" Raoul still had many friends on the precinct. If there was one person in New York who could get his hands on police documents from an ongoing investigation, it was Raoul. Even though he could, he used his privileged access on rare occasions. It was a useful tool if one did not use it willy-nilly.

"Yeah. He's a sly fox. Hiding large losses for that long, that's something. I don't understand how something like that could've gone unnoticed. I don't understand how these banks could be that irresponsible. You don't think he could be involved?"

"No, I'm pretty certain it's not him. His actions suggest otherwise. But Iain on the other hand...," Raoul paused to see Julia's reaction.

Nancy shot Raoul a surprised look. "What about Iain? Did he have something to do with this? How? Why?"

"I checked out the video surveillance at his hotel. He was not at the hotel on Thursday night, the night Rebecca disappeared. He met Rebecca for dinner in midtown and then his whereabouts are unknown after then. He came back to the hotel on Friday morning at around nine wearing his clothes from the previous day. He got ready and left the hotel again around ten."

"What else?" Julia was making mental notes in her head.

"No credit card use or cash withdrawals on Thursday night after the dinner with Rebecca. If he were out partying, there would've been heavy use of his credit card. That's what his credit card records look like. He typically parties hard, racks up large bar tabs and tips lavishly. Either there's an innocent explanation or he was up to something, especially since he had an unpleasant dinner with Rebecca. This does not add up. In either case, I think we should share this information as well with Timothy and Roberta."

Raoul had known Timothy for a long time. They had worked together on a gruesome ritualistic murder case that took a heavy toll on their mental health but brought them closer. They had remained friends even after Raoul left the force.

Timothy was not the source of the documents from the precinct, but Timothy knew that Raoul had access and he tolerated it since he knew Raoul well and knew that he was judicious in using his access to NYPD documents. He was also a team player and shared information with the department and that in Timothy's book was the definition of a trusted friend.

"Do you think we should confront Iain? Dig in some more, find out where he's keeping Rebecca?" Christy asked.

"Yes, but let's also get the information over to Timothy so he can start looking in the right direction. He can be an ally on this case." Raoul was now craving that cup of coffee.

As if the butler had read his thoughts, he walked over with a four large mugs of coffee. The mugs had the Atticus Biopharma logo emblazoned on it. The butler walked over and handed Raoul his coffee.

Raoul smelt the freshly grounded coffee and took a sip trying to wash away the remnants of the green kale drink that he had tried earlier. The butler walked over and handed the drinks to the others in the room.

"One more thing I learnt. The leaks did not stop after we revamped security. According to Gustav, Matheus received two sets of research documents *after* we made the big security overhaul changing all the passwords and adding new access authorizations across the company. It appears that the newer documents were even more detailed than the previous leaked documents."

Julia was red in the face as soon as she heard this. "That just drives me crazy. There's no saying how low Matheus will stoop. Dammit. Let's change security protocols again, bring in a new outside cyber security team. I want the leak plugged. And I want to find out who is sharing our secret documents with Matheus. Put a cyber team on it. Review all the logs, all video footage since the last overhaul and every print log."

Nancy immediately jumped in. "Julia, that's going to be several million dollars, if not more. These enterprise software teams are not cheap. As co-CEO, we should probably discuss…"

"I don't care about the cost. The existence of our very company is at stake here. Everything we've worked for is being stolen from us right under our noses. Nancy, we have to do this. We have no choice. Speak to the Board if you need to, but this needs to be done."

Raoul put his coffee cup down. "Nancy may be right. An overhaul may not necessarily plug the leak."

"What do you mean it won't plug it?" Julia looked even more confused.

"This brings me to another theory. It's just a theory, but the biggest threat you have right now is Rebecca herself. She is missing and the kidnapper wanted all of us to think she was dead. Why?"

Julia also put her coffee down and looked out of the window with a pensive look on her face. It was a gloomy day in New York. The city looked dull under a cloudy sky. It was going to rain later that day.

Raoul continued explaining his latest theory. "So, now the kidnapper has Rebecca. But there are no demands for ransom, no proof of life, nothing. Why? What would someone want from Rebecca?"

Julia was still staring out of the window. "Our research. You don't need to snoop into our system anymore if you have Rebecca."

Raoul continued. "That's the biggest threat to the company right now. Taking Rebecca away was a blow but getting all her research out of her would be devastating."

"But Rebecca would never just give her work away. She would have to be..." Julia's eyes widened at the thought. It made her sick to the stomach. Nancy put her hand on Julia's thigh as if trying to console her.

"Tortured. That's right. They would need a lot of time and someone who knew what to ask, someone who was as steeped in the science as she was." Raoul glanced at the butler, picked up his mug and made a gesture asking for more coffee.

"So, someone like Matheus?" Nancy asked.

"Matheus would never get his hands dirty. It would be someone below him, someone who worked in the same cancer research, maybe someone who even worked in the same lab as Rebecca."

"Gustav? He worked with us in Dr. Gupta's lab. He's with Matheus now. You think it could be Gustav?" Christy asked as she exchanged confused glances with Nancy and Julia.

Raoul nodded. Christy saw tears brimming in Julia's eyes and she started getting teary-eyed as well.

Christy had a sparkle in her eyes and she spoke up. "What if we're all on the wrong track? As much as I hate to say this, what if Rebecca faked her disappearance? What if she is cooperating with her kidnapper? I don't know why she would, but what if?"

Raoul sighed heavily. "That is something that I thought of. I wouldn't rule it out. I don't have a good theory of why she would do something like this, but you're right Christy. Did you have any reason to think that?"

Christy looked at Nancy wondering whether speaking up about the strained relationship between Rebecca and Nancy might be badly received in the room. Nancy gave a quick but noticeably stern look in Christy's direction and that was enough for Christy to not speak up about it. "Nothing in particular. Just a thought given the strange circumstances."

Nancy, as if taking control of the situation spoke up. "Thanks Raoul. Please speak to Timothy and give them the information on Iain and your theory on Gustav." Nancy was clearly angry with Christy at almost bringing up her relationship with Rebecca in the context of her disappearance in front of Julia. Christy was the only one who sensed the anger.

"Let's get the security measures in place too. We'll find Rebecca as well. We're going to be back in control." Julia stood up and started walking off, totally unaware of the tense and unspoken confrontation in the room between Nancy and Christy.

■ ■ ■

NEW YORK CITY POLICE DEPARTMENT, 6TH PRECINCT, WEST VILLAGE

Timothy and Roberta were on the phone for over half an hour. They asked questions as Raoul gave them the lowdown. Roberta was taking notes furiously. As the call ended, both of them looked at each other, slightly stunned by the developments and the twist this case had just taken.

"So Rebecca is probably still alive and some genius underground hacker, who we can't get access to, verified this." Timothy was perplexed but knew he had to follow the lead.

"So Iain and Gustav seem to be our prime suspects."

"Yeah, at least for the Rebecca kidnapping. We know Iain was in Cambridge when Dr. Gupta died and now we know he lied to us about Thursday night." Timothy was trying to work the story and eliminate other possible explanations in his head.

"So jealous boyfriend kidnaps ex-girlfriend, kills former boss. Why is she still alive then?" Roberta was trying to poke holes in the story.

"Let's bring Iain in again. And I want Gustav tailed."

. . .

GANSEVOORT HOTEL, MEATPACKING DISTRICT, NEW YORK

The Gansevoort Hotel in New York City is located between 12th and 13th Streets in the Meatpacking District, a serious contender for the most glamorous neighborhood in the city.

With cobblestone streets and a rich industrial history alongside facades of former meat lockers, the Meatpacking District is known for its nightlife that attracts insomniacs from all walks of life. In addition to the exclusive night clubs and bars littered all over the neighborhood, the area had also started to turn into a high-end shopping mecca with several luxury brands such as Diane von Furstenberg and La Perla having opened up shop around there.

The Gansevoort Hotel, the first of its kind in the area offered a year-round pool, a fabulous rooftop bar with amazing views of the city, lots of eye candy and frequent celebrity sightings. The hotel was also just a short walk to the art galleries of Chelsea.

The Gansevoort Hotel is close to the Hudson River and the rooms facing the river had beautiful panoramic views of city.

It was cloudy and gloomy in the city. The curtains in the room were open. The young aspiring model in the room was completely naked and was standing facing the window, both her hands against the glass, slightly bent and pushing her hips back and forth into the man having sex with her. Her eyes were shut and she was moaning. There was another naked woman, her roommate, and another aspiring model from Eastern Europe completely naked sitting on the bed. She held a mirror in her hand and was snorting a line of cocaine using a twenty-dollar bill.

Iain held on to the hips of the young woman close to the window as he continued to thrust into her. He looked at the city and all the cars pass by on the West Side Highway. He was sure if someone looked up, they would see the sweaty outline of the young woman he was having sex with. He grabbed her hair and started to thrust even harder. She seemed to be enjoying the feeling of giving him control. After a few minutes, she gave out a loud moan as she climaxed and collapsed on the floor where she was standing.

Iain looked at her, gave her a smile, bent down and kissed her on her mouth. He stood up and walked over to the other young woman on the bed. "Turn around."

She put down the mirror and positioned herself. Iain started having sex with the second young woman thrusting from behind. He knew exactly what he was doing and knew that he could make a five thousand year old mummy come from behind. Soon after the second young woman started moaning louder as Iain continued from behind. The first woman stood up and walked over to the bed. She held Iain's hair from behind and started kissing him on the mouth. Iain kissed her back as he continued to pleasure the second woman from behind.

"Go slow. Go slow. I don't want to…" With that, the second woman climaxed mid-sentence and gave out a moan and collapsed on the bed.

The first woman was giggling now and she pushed Iain on the bed on his back. Her friend lay next to him, still recovering. The first woman started to climb on Iain when his cell phone rang. She pulled Iain's face with both hands as he started to reach for his phone. "No, don't," she urged him as she started to position herself on him and in one quick move she had him inside her. Iain picked up the phone and answered.

Iain spoke for a few minutes while the woman continued to ride him. She made a few soft noises while Iain gestured her to keep quiet with his finger on his lips. Beads of sweat broke out on his forehead as he heard Timothy at the other end of the line asking him to come in to verify some minor facts.

Iain understood what that meant. They thought he had something to do with it and they had dirt on him. He hung up the cell phone, chucked it across the hotel room in disgust and turned his attention back to the woman on top of him as he tried to push the thoughts on what would happen to him next out of his head.

■ ■ ■

EAST VILLAGE, NEW YORK CITY

Ragnar had his phone pressed to his ear. His laptop was open in front of him and there were numerous equations and puzzles scratched out on several blank pages of paper on his desk. They all had various forms of 'H A R D B E I I' on it.

"Hey Ruby, it's me Ragnar. I was wondering if you still had access to the beta version of PatRec…"

. . .

PatRec was the code name for pattern recognition software that Ragnar's group was developing at Lincoln Myers. The bank had hired cryptographers, experts at breaking codes and speech recognition software experts to develop the software to detect hidden signals in market information to predict whether securities were heading up or down. In theory, the software would identify patterns and opportunities, trade securities and make sure profits. The cryptographic and speech recognition algorithms were being incorporated into PatRec to analyze trading patterns. The software had multiple inter-layered algorithms that helped with the identification of the trading patterns.

Several members of the PatRec development team were older cryptographers who had worked at the Department of Defense during the Cold War years having worked on deciphering encrypted Russian communication signals. These code breakers had decades of experience in analyzing and breaking codes using manual methods, specialized code-breaking machines and computers. Some of the developers had even worked on the Verona project, a counter-intelligence program dedicated to intercepting and decrypting messages transmitted by various Soviet intelligence agencies including The People's Commissariat for Internal Affairs (NKVD), the KGB and the military intelligence unit, GRU.

PatRec had broader applications in the real world including university admissions - identifying the students that would be good fits for particular universities and prioritizing their applications over others; drug development - identifying the most promising molecules for research earlier through large data sets rather than doing endless animal studies to find the right molecules to advance; and crime fighting - using incomplete crime scene information to make links to other crimes, likely suspects and other possible links.

Ragnar worked as the finance and math expert with the team in the development of PatRec. PatRec performed brilliantly using historical trading data. In various test runs using historical data streamed as if it were occurring live. PatRec was able to predict Black Monday and create strategies for selling securities in advance and setting up trades to profit from a dramatic collapse. In other test runs, PatRec was able to recognize the technology bubble in the run up and created trades to profit from the run up and sell shortly before the sell-offs. PatRec was a trader's wet dream, the perfect trading machine.

PatRec was plugged into the bank's trading system and was slated to go live on a Monday morning at the beginning of a trading week in August, a relatively slow month in the markets due to the summer slowdown. The entire department and everyone that worked on PatRec gathered around the terminals with bottles of champagne in ice buckets on the desks at around nine in the morning. All the systems checks were good to go. They turned on the live feed at nine-twenty and the software was analyzing all the pre-market moves.

At 9:30 am, the trades started to flow through. The system was live and PatRec started trading. There was a live P&L on one of the terminals and most of the non-tech folks in the room had their eyes glued to that. For the first thirty minutes or so when the market is most active, PatRec made some modest gains of around seventy thousand dollars. And then suddenly the unthinkable happened. PatRec lost those gains within minutes. The P&L turned red quickly and as the minutes passed by, PatRec was racking up larger and larger losses. Within minutes, the losses were close to one million dollars. Within the next few minutes, losses were closer to ten million dollars.

All hell broke loose. There was screaming and shouting in the room. It was sheer panic.

"Shut it down. Right now. Shut it down." The head of the group that developed PatRec was screaming his lungs at the programmers.

"I'm trying. We need to halt the trading module and then disconnect the settlement system and then log out of the…" One of the junior programmers was replying as he was typing furiously. "Let me check what's wrong. The system should have tripped with the losses. It looks like PatRec is making larger and larger bets to recoup the losses. Maybe it's a simple fix."

"Didn't you hear me? Shut it down you, nincompoop. How long?" The group head was now barking into the programmer's ears. The programmer could feel the breath on his ear.

"Five minutes. Seven minutes max."

The group head looked around. "We don't have five minutes. This system is a drunk and reckless gambler." He ran to the back of the terminals and started pulling all the wires himself. He was ripping out power and the broadband connections. Sparks flew out as he pulled out the wires erratically. The terminals started to shut down one after the other.

The whole event was a massive disaster. Within forty-five minutes, PatRec lost close to fifty million dollars for Lincoln Myers. The entire project was moth-balled and the team that worked on it were either re-assigned or unceremoniously fired the very next day.

. . .

"Ragnar? You mean Ragnar Johnson?" Ruby could not believe he had the nerve to call her.

"Yeah Ruby, it's me. It's, uh, it's good to hear your voice as well after, uh, so long." Ragnar was trying to make it up as he went along.

"What do you want, Ragnar?" Ruby did not even try to mask her derision on the phone.

"I wanted to run a few trading simulations on, uh, PatRec. On an offline version, of course. Do you, uh, have a login to the PatRec version on the Lincoln Myers server? I really need this. I would not be, uh, asking if this wasn't important."

"Ragnar, I was called in by the NYPD because of you. What have you been up to? Did you know they called my desk? Dana, our old shared admin, picked up the call. You know what a big mouth she is. She told everyone in the group that the cops asked me to come down to the precinct. Do you know how difficult it is at Lincoln Myers once the rumors start? Dana told all the other admins and then they told their respective bosses."

"Listen, this is a life and death matter really. I, uh, need to help a friend who's been, uh, kidnapped. PatRec could help with finding where she is, you know. Pattern recognition to solve a crime. I have a clue that I need, uh, to run through the…"

"What new crime did you commit this time Ragnar? Kidnapped someone? Making the body disappear and making it look like you're trying to help? You're never going to change are you? You know when..."

Ragnar hung up midsentence while Ruby was ranting. The conversation was going nowhere. Ruby was the senior most person he knew who might still have access to PatRec.

Ragnar did not like what he knew he had to do next if he wanted to access PatRec. Ragnar walked up to a drawer, pulled it out and turned it over. The bottom of the drawer had a tape that was painted over to match the color of the wood. It was nearly unrecognizable to a casual observer. Ragnar used his fingernails to scratch the edges of the tape.

Once he was able to scratch up a corner of the tape from one end, he grabbed it and pulled the tape out completely. Under the tape was a flat access employee key card. It was a working key card he had stolen from a co-worker and made sure it was not deactivated with the help of a junior employee in the IT department at Lincoln Myers. He had stolen the card when he was still at Lincoln Myers.

Ragnar stared at the card. He had intentionally chosen this person because he looked similar to Ragnar, same facial features and bone structure. Alex Leslie, the person whose picture was on the card, wore a pair of glasses. That seemed to be the only real difference.

Ragnar was nervous as he fiddled with the access card in his hand.

What if Alex Leslie has already left and all his cards are now disabled? What if someone recognizes me? How am I going to access PatRec? Is it even accessible anymore? What if PatRec was wiped out and the entire investment written off? What if Rebecca is dead?

Ragnar paused at that last thought and felt dejected.

And then another thought crossed his mind.

What if Rebecca is still alive?

Ragnar was going to be Alex Leslie for a few hours and walk into the Lincoln Myers headquarters to access PatRec.

I'm coming for you, Rebecca. I'm going to find you.

CHAPTER 35

DAY 13, TUESDAY
GLOBAL NEWSWIRE

Press Release

Faust Biopharma Announces Top-Line Results from a Phase 3 Study of Glovir in Patients with Advanced Non-Small Cell Lung Cancer

Glovir did not meet trial primary endpoint of progression-free survival in patients

Faust Biopharma announced today that a trial investigating the use of Glovir as monotherapy, did not meet its primary endpoint of progression-free survival in patients with previously untreated advanced non-small cell lung cancer. The company will complete a full evaluation of the trial data and work with investigators on the future presentation of the results.

Dr. Matheus Faust, M.D., Chief Executive Officer, Faust Biopharma, commented, "Glovir has become a fundamental treatment that is transforming cancer care across multiple cancer types. While we are disappointed at these results, we remain committed to improving outcomes through our comprehensive development programs, including...."

■ ■ ■

FAUST BIOPHARMA HQ, CAMBRIDGE

Matheus' cell phone started to ring as the press release of the recent failure hit the newswires at seven in the morning Eastern Time. He knew his large investors would call him immediately about the press release. For months, Matheus touted Glovir as a drug that would change the paradigm on cancer treatment. Glovir's global sales were in excess of four billion dollars. Faust Biopharma had worked hard to expand the applicability of Glovir to multiple cancer types. Despite that, Faust Biopharma had several trials in progress for expanding the use of Glovir for different cancers for which it was not approved.

Matheus had constantly expressed confidence that the ongoing trials were a slam dunk and Glovir would one day be one of the highest selling drugs with applicability across virtually all cancer types. The failed Glovir trial for non-small cell lung cancer was a huge blow to that vision that Matheus' investors had bought into.

The failure of Glovir was the top story on CNBC within minutes. The Wall Street Journal picked up the news instantly showing the failed Glovir trial as a "Breaking News" story as reporters tried to back fill a whole story. Reporters in financial television channels speculated on how much Faust Biopharma would drop in pre-market trading as well as when the markets opened.

Faust Biopharma was one of the larger biotech companies and traded on both the New York Stock Exchange as well as the tech-friendly NASDAQ.

Matheus saw the caller ID and knew he could not ignore this call. The call was from Ranjeet Kapur, the rock-star biotech investor who ran one of the largest biotech-focused funds in the country, the $20 billion Formidable Biotechnology Fund.

Ranjeet had joined Formidable Management over fifteen years ago and had become the portfolio manager of the Formidable Biotechnology Fund nine years ago. Ranjeet's fund produced outsized returns and that in turn attracted more capital to the fund, growing to the current twenty billion dollars. Ranjeet was one of the earlier investors who recognized the promise of Atticus Biopharma as well as Faust Biopharma. He even theorized that the competition between the two companies would bode well for both. Atticus Biopharma and Faust Biopharma were his two largest holdings in the fund. Formidable Management, a fund management company based on Boston that had multiple funds under its umbrella, held Atticus Biopharma and Faust Biopharma in other funds as well.

"Matheus, Ranjeet here. I'm on a speaker phone and I've also got Michael Weintraub here as well."

Matheus swallowed hard. Michael Weintraub was a legend within investing circles. An unassuming person, Michael single-handedly ran the largest actively managed fund in the world at approximately one hundred and five billion dollars. Michael along with Ranjeet were early supporters of Faust Biopharma. Michael had been a cheerleader of the company internally at Formidable Management and made sure portfolio managers purchased Faust Biopharma stock every time they were there to raise capital. Between Weintraub's Formidable Columbus Fund and Ranjeet's Formidable Biotechnology Fund, they held close to ten billion dollars of Faust Biopharma stock. And today was going to be a rough day for all three on the call.

"Hey Michael, how are you doing?"

"I'm good, Matheus. I saw the Glovir press release. Stock is down 20% in pre-market trading. I'm down around a billion dollars in my fund and Ranjeet is down around the same. You've always come through. What happened this time? Have you finally run out of steam? Is there any more of that pixie dust left at Faust Biopharma?" Michael Weintraub sounded calm, but having known him for over a decade, Matheus knew he was coldly calculating whether to hold on their stakes or dump them.

Formidable selling their stake in Faust Biopharma would be a vote of no confidence in Matheus. The stock would fall considerably more and Matheus would probably be fired as CEO. The Glovir results were bad and a rude shock for investors who were used to only good news from Faust Biopharma. But that would be nothing compared to what would happen if Formidable pulled the carpet from under Matheus.

"Michael, Ranjeet, this is a small set back. The market is overreacting. We are strong as ever. Our pipeline of cancer drugs has never been stronger. We're firing on all cylinders. Glovir is not even on the radar when I think about what we're close to." Matheus was hoping Michael and Ranjeet caught the bait.

"Explain yourself Matheus." Ranjeet sounded a bit confused.

"Look, you know we've been working on the universal cancer vaccine much like Atticus Biopharma's ATCS-1010. We think we're miles ahead of where Atticus Biopharma is right now in their research on the universal vaccine. We've managed to replicate what they've done and taken it much further than them. They've lost their chief researcher recently, Rebecca Chase. She worked on that vaccine and they don't have a good replacement for her. We, on the other hand, have Dr. Gustav Henriksen who worked with Dr. Steven Gupta and Rebecca in the same lab. Gustav has performed miracles in catching up to them and leaving them behind."

"Come on, Matheus. Let's talk about Glovir. You're always beating Atticus Biopharma up." This was not the first time Michael Weintraub had heard Matheus trying to beat up his rival from across the street in Cambridge.

"Guys, you have to trust me on this. Glovir is based on old technology. It was bound to succeed in most trials and fail in some. And we're going to set up a new trial and protocols and probably go after lung cancer again with Glovir. I'm telling you, now is the time to buy, not sell. Buy the dip. Once we get to a point where we have tangible results to announce for the universal vaccine, we'll be worth much more. Much much more. It'll be like having Faust Biopharma and Atticus Biopharma under the same umbrella. If you sell my stock and hold on to Atticus Biopharma, you'll be doubling down on a serious mistake. Atticus Biopharma will be left in the dust. If nothing, you need to hold us as a hedge."

"Why can't you release the universal vaccine data? You should've included a note on the progress of that along with this press release." Ranjeet sounded clearly frustrated. He was definitely the one from the two fund managers who did not hold back how he felt. Matheus could feel his emotions through the call.

"Ranjeet, this is going to be a huge one when we announce it. Why would I want to dilute that by making it a side note in the Glovir trial results? It would sound defensive and wouldn't really register with investors. When we announce the universal cancer vaccine results, we are going to do it with huge fanfare. Mark my words it will be a deathblow for Atticus Biopharma. You will thank me for making you hold on to Faust Biopharma. But if you don't think you want to wait for that, you should just sell. Buy more Atticus Biopharma now. Load up on that instead. Maybe Faust Biopharma is not really for your fund."

Matheus was desperate but he had been in the game long enough to know that showing desperation was never a good strategy. "I'm happy to buy some of your shares back. You can dump the rest in the market."

"Atticus Biopharma has not hired anyone to replace Rebecca. What if they hire Gustav? What are you going to do then?" Michael was sharp as ever, thinking of every possibility.

"I have Gustav handcuffed. His contracts are pretty solid. Unless he wants to give up everything he ever worked for, he will never go to Atticus Biopharma. I can guarantee that. His employment contract is ironclad. He's going nowhere." Matheus was glad at least this part was true.

"No more hiccups, Matheus. I like you but I am responsible for hundreds of thousands of retirees. Even more people have trusted me with their children's college funds. I cannot let them down. I need to protect them. One more whiff and we'll sell every last stock we own. You need to make this right and steer the ship around."

"Understood. I need to be back in the lab, guys. Hang in there. This will be a blip when you look back on it."

"No more blips either, Matheus. Get in the lab. Get to work." Ranjeet hung up abruptly.

Gustav had made significant progress on the universal vaccine technology using the papers he had passed along to him but they were still behind Atticus Biopharma. Matheus was drenched in sweat. He had dodged a bullet with this one.

Matheus picked up his cell phone and dialed a number he had memorized. "It's Matheus…"

CHAPTER 36

DAY 13, TUESDAY
NEW YORK CITY POLICE DEPARTMENT, 6TH PRECINCT, WEST VILLAGE

Iain was sweating profusely sitting in front of Timothy back at the precinct. Iain was feeling the urge to snort a line. His body was craving the kick.

"Iain, come on. You know how guilty this makes you look. We have the videos from your hotel. Where were you the night Rebecca disappeared?" Timothy ran Iain through the evidence from Raoul without mentioning him. Timothy was trying hard to make Iain talk but he was sandbagging them. Roberta was not sitting in on this session.

Iain's mind raced trying to sort through facts he could share and those he could not without severely compromising himself. "Look, I'm telling you it wasn't me. That is all you really need to know. So what if I wasn't at my hotel. You don't have anything on me."

"Yet, we don't have anything yet but we will. If you're hiding something, we will dig and dig till we find out what you are hiding. Come clean now, Iain. Rebecca is missing and Dr. Gupta is dead. You were also in Cambridge when he died."

Iain froze when he heard that. Timothy caught his expression and realized he just found an opening.

"Coincidence, right? You were with Rebecca a few hours before she disappeared and then again you went to Cambridge and Dr. Gupta was found dead. Brutally murdered. Someone he knew. Maybe that someone was you. You've probably been to his lab before, right? With Rebecca? You probably knew how to get in and out, didn't you?"

"I'm telling you it wasn't me. You don't understand. This is much larger than you think it is. Julia and Matheus are at each other's throats. Rebecca was caught between them. I loved her. I still do. I would never hurt her."

"Then what are you hiding, Iain? Why can't you come clean?"

Iain put his head down, clutched his hands together, closed his eye tightly shut and barely whispered, "Because she left me. You wouldn't understand but I've never been rejected. Never. She broke up with me. I begged her to stay. You don't understand how hard that was for me."

"I followed her that night after our dinner. She went to a bar at her hotel. I spied on her. She was talking to a stranger for several hours. I was burning with rage and jealousy. And then she left with him. I followed them to the guy's place in the East Village. I couldn't believe it. She went to a rundown building with him. I waited outside for a couple of hours across the street till it was obvious that she didn't just go there for a cup of coffee.

"I was heartbroken, totally shattered. Here she was, my ex-fiancé, who I tried winning back and failed. And she was now with this stranger, a one-night stand. I left and ended up at another bar, drank for the next couple of hours." Iain looked up at the end.

"Where were you after that? You must've been quite angry at her? Did you go back?"

"No. I went back to my hotel."

"That was at nine-ish. Last call for drinks is four in the morning in New York City."

"I don't remember. I was at the bar all night. I went back to my hotel in the morning."

"Iain, you need to come clean. You did not use your credit card all night after the dinner."

"Haven't you heard of cash? I used cash all night." Iain was clearly making up his story along the way. It was difficult for Timothy to make out what was true and what was made up.

Roberta opened the door, walked in and dropped a folder on the table, perfectly timing her entry. Timothy and Roberta had discussed this strategy before Iain showed up.

"Can you explain these large deposits in your bank accounts?" Roberta shot him a look and then looked at the folder as she sat down next to Timothy.

Iain pulled the folder closer, opened the flap and looked at the first page. He recognized the bank statement, it was one he had set up at a non-descript bank in Curacao, an island country in the southern Caribbean Sea a few miles north of the Venezuelan coast.

"I'm not talking any more without a lawyer. We're done here. I need a lawyer." Iain shut down completely. Timothy and Roberta looked at each other. They had pushed this as far along as they could.

"Make your call, Iain. Call your lawyer. We'll get you." Timothy stood up and held the door open for him.

Iain stood up and started walking out. Timothy noticed his fingers and hands shaking as he was leaving the room to make his call. Timothy had seen this before with drug addicts, a classic withdrawal symptom. "We're not done, Iain. Let's sit down again after your lawyer shows up."

■ ■ ■

"I'm afraid we're not going to get much out of him anymore. Not without concrete physical evidence tying him to Rebecca or Gupta." Timothy stated his thoughts to Roberta.

"We knew this was a possibility. Either he would come clean completely or shut down. Do you think he did it?"

"I wouldn't rule him out. He is involved in some way. I can feel it."

"But do you think he was directly involved with her kidnapping or Dr. Gupta's murder?" Roberta was straightening her hair watching Iain on his cell phone talking to a lawyer.

"I wouldn't rule out anything. He could be our guy."

. . .

Iain was sitting opposite Ira Edelstein, a prominent and expensive New York lawyer. Iain had met Ira at a mutual friend's party in Los Angeles. Ira had represented a model Iain had worked with during her divorce from her rich real estate magnate husband, thirty years her senior. She retired from modeling altogether following the divorce, having become fabulously wealthy thanks to Ira.

Ira, though, was famous for fighting a custody battle for Joseph Kahn, a billionaire financier based in New York City, whose wife was demanding forty thousand dollars a month as well as custody of their five-year-old son. Ira successfully argued against the extravagant ask and even showed that the wife was unfit to be given custody of the young boy. She ultimately lost custody and was awarded a much smaller settlement. Again, thanks to Ira.

While high profile divorce cases brought in the fees, Ira's true love was criminal law. He fought tough cases for his wealthy clients with passion and rarely lost. Ira was on his way for some rounds of golf with some friends and clients at Winged Foot Golf Club in Mamaroneck, New York. The golf club had two eighteen-hole golf courses designed by A.W. Tillinghast, a noted golf course architect and one of the most prolific architects having worked on or designed over two hundred and sixty different courses during his lifetime. Both the courses at

Winged Foot are ranked among the top hundred golf courses in America, with the West Course being ranked in the top ten.

As soon as Ira got the call from Iain, he apologized to his golf buddies and headed back to the city.

Iain was taking Ira through his story at Ira's request. Ira wanted to make sure he knew everything there was to know before he put his client in front of the police. Iain walked him through his evening with Rebecca and how she refused to get back together with him, how he followed her to her hotel and spied on her there, how he followed her to Ragnar's apartment building and waited across the street for two hours or so.

"Then what happened, Iain?"

"I knew what was going on upstairs. At least I think I did. I was disappointed and heart-broken. I left and spent the night with a friend. I went back to the hotel in the morning, showered, changed and went to work for a late morning shoot at a studio downtown." Iain knew Ira had his back. He was the best money could buy.

"And who is this 'friend,' Iain, that you spent the night with? Can she testify to you being with her?"

"Ira, I can't. I can't tell you who I was with. I know you need to know but it does not matter. What matters is that I had nothing to do with Rebecca's disappearance."

Ira looked at Iain straight in the eyes. The eyes. It always came down to the eyes for Ira. People could lie as much as they wanted but their eyes always betrayed the truth. Ira knew Iain was telling the truth. It wasn't ideal that he did not know all the details but he could work with that.

"What about the money, Iain? Can you at least tell me where that came from?" Ira's tone was always kind and gentle, like a loving father's. Ira looked the part, with soft features and a full head of white hair. Beneath that soft and gentle exterior was a fierce and competitive lawyer who wanted to win at any cost.

"You cannot share this with anyone, Ira."

"Of course, Iain. This is strictly between us, attorney client privilege." Ira smiled his most reassuring smile.

"Matheus Faust, I think. The money was wired to me from a secret offshore bank account. I made a trip to Curacao for work and opened a bank account there." Iain was clearly feeling uneasy. His fingers and hands were shaking.

"Iain, I'm telling you this as a friend and your lawyer. You need to lay off the drugs. At least till this entire thing is over."

Iain closed his eyes and shook his head. Ira had seen many cases where the person involved did himself no favors when the drug habit came to light.

"Why did Matheus pay you so much money?" Ira had a bad feeling about this. "You need to come clean with me, Iain, otherwise I can't help you."

"I didn't have anything to do with Rebecca's disappearance or Dr. Gupta's death." Iain was still nervous and his hands were shaking.

Ira put his hands on Iain's hands. "Look at me, Iain.

I'm here to protect you and I won't let anything happen to you. You need to help me. What was the money for?"

"Like I said, I think it was Matheus. I never met him directly. It was a lawyer. I met him in Los Angeles at a party. He approached me and offered me a proposition, money in exchange for pulling some files periodically from Rebecca's laptop. I needed to copy the files that she backed up on her laptop from work on a pen drive and drop the pen drive at a location he told me about. One time it was inside a waste bin in the bathroom of a Taco Bell. Another time, it was behind some Danielle Steel books on a bookshelf at a Barnes and Nobles. The money would show up in the account a few hours later. It had to be Matheus. He was the only one that this information was useful for."

"And this was all to support your drug habit, I'm presuming?"

"Yes, kind of. I was spending way more than I was making. I made a couple of wire transfers from there to my account in L.A. That is probably how the cops made me." Iain was feeling better letting some this out.

"How many times did you do this?"

"Thrice. I dropped off three pen drives over the course of a few months. The lawyer texted me saying he needed "the latest pics" from me. That was code for the files and I would download the files when she was not around and drop off the pen drive where he asked me to.

"But then something happened. Maybe she got spooked or something. She replaced her laptop and there were several security features. The new laptop needed a password as well as a fingerprint ID. I couldn't access the files any longer and I let Matheus' guy know. That was the end of that. I never heard from him or anyone else ever again." Iain felt a huge weight lifted off his shoulders. He had had conflicting feelings throughout his relationship with Rebecca. So many secrets that he held back from her. Yet, he loved her dearly. Deep inside he knew she did not deserve someone like him, but he still wanted her.

"Well, you will need to declare those assets and pay Uncle Sam taxes and penalties on that money, Iain. But as long as you tell me you had nothing to do with Rebecca's disappearance, and I do believe you, Iain, you have nothing to worry about." Ira was a bit relieved to learn the truth, however partial it may have been.

"Why were you in Cambridge? What took you there?" Ira switched gears to the second case.

"I was there helping a friend who was in distress." Iain was cryptic again. Ira wondered who Iain may have been meeting. In his mind, the industrial espionage was a more serious thing and if anything Iain should've been hiding that instead. Whoever he was meeting, there was clearly something ominous about it. Ira could feel it in his old bones.

"And this is the same friend you were with the night Rebecca disappeared?"

"I can't say Ira. But I did not kill Dr. Gupta. There's nothing to tie me to that."

Ira sighed. "Let's call Timothy in. Let's get you out of here."

• • •

Timothy looked visibly irritated as Iain and Ira made their way out of the precinct. Timothy knew Iain was going to call a lawyer but not that he would call one of the top lawyers in New York City. Ira sandbagged the entire conversation and challenged every assumption that Timothy or Roberta made. Without anything concrete to tie Iain to either of the crimes, they were both soon on their way. Timothy even made a friendly gesture of having them cooperate in a bid to solve both crimes but that just fell on deaf ears.

"What do you think he's hiding?" Roberta asked Timothy.

"He's a drug addict. They're pathological liars. You can never trust them. He's got something to hide. He may have fooled Ira. Ira is a great lawyer but he's mostly a white-collar crime guy. I see hardened criminals and drug addicts every day. They would lie to their own family to gain their trust, steal their money or use their cards to buy drugs. I don't trust him. Get me something on him, Roberta. I want him back in a cell."

Roberta nodded as Timothy crushed the can of Coke in his hand and dunked it into the bin on the other side of the room.

CHAPTER 37

DAY 13, TUESDAY
LINCOLN MYERS BUILDING, NEW YORK CITY

Lincoln Myers was housed in a large fifty-five floor glass tower overlooking Bryant Park in New York. The building was a constant humdrum of activity as traders streamed into the building in the early hours of the day, just as the junior investment bankers were leaving after an all-nighter working on a pitch book or a high-pressure transaction.

Ragnar belonged to the former group. When he was employed there, Ragnar would come to work shortly before 7:00 am and leave at 5:30 pm every day, typically ending the day at a local watering hole on 43rd Street with others from his trading desk before heading home for the evening.

Ragnar had been set up on dates by his co-workers but the dates never ended up anywhere for him. It was always one of two things – either he thought that his date was not intellectually on par with him or his date found him boring and not interesting enough to go on a second date. And then there was the time when he was hiding those losses. He just gave up during that time.

Ragnar had bought a pair of cheap horn rimmed glasses to match Alex Leslie's photo on the stolen card.

He stood just outside the building. He had worn a suit after a long time. He had combed his hair differently to change his look and avoid being recognized. He had even put on a plain navy blue tie, the only one he owned.

When Ragnar had walked into the Charles Tyrwhitt shop close to the Lincoln Myers building and picked the plainest tie he could find, a bald but young sales man told him semi-sarcastically "*Everyone* needs a plain blue tie!" His words echoed in Ragnar's head as he fiddled with the tie a bit.

As a trader, Ragnar typically wore khakis and a buttoned down semi-casual shirt and a sweater vest for the freezing temperature on the trading floor. He never understood why the trading floor was always kept at freezing temperatures.

Ragnar carried an old briefcase in one hand. He looked the part of a banker. He took a deep breath and walked into the building through one of the many revolving glass doors at the entrance. He walked straight towards the turnstiles and held Alex Leslie's identity card in front of the infrared rectangle next to the turnstile. Ragnar fully expected this card to work.

Ragnar held the card and the machine just gave out a small beep declining the card. Ragnar held it there again and the turnstile still would not give. Ragnar knew what that meant. People walked past him and looked irritated at him for holding up one of the three turnstiles. One of the security guards walked up to Ragnar. "Your card's not working?"

"Yeah, I left it in my trousers yesterday and threw them into the washer and then the dryer. Must've screwed up the chip inside."

"What floor do you work on sir?"

"Uh, six."

"Just register with security. They will issue a temporary day pass. You can submit an application for a new one today."

"Okay. Thanks."

Ragnar stood in the line for security. There were three people ahead of him. Ragnar was praying no one would recognize him in the lobby. He felt open and exposed.

"Name?"

"Rag-nex Leslie. Uh, Alex, Alex Leslie."

"What floor do you work on?"

"Uh, six."

The woman behind the security desk looked at her system and then looked at him. Ragnar's heart was racing in his chest.

"Sir."

"Uh, yes?"

"I need you to look straight into the camera."

Ragnar looked at the camera and gave a wide grin. The woman, who probably felt bored out of her mind, printed the pass and handed it to him.

"Next, step forward please."

Ragnar took the pass and walked back to the turnstile. This time the temporary pass did the trick and Ragnar walked into the elevator bank. He typed -1 for the basement and hopped into a designated elevator down to the basement.

The basement of the Lincoln Myers building housed some security desks, the mailroom and a small IT team. Ragnar turned left and walked toward the IT room hoping Eddie was still there.

Ragnar knocked on the door and peered inside. The room was dark and there were several servers with tangled wires coming in and out of them. There were small lights all over the place - green, red, orange and blue showing all the electronic activity within those servers.

"Eddie? Eddie, you there?"

A black office chair with wheels spun out. A short bespectacled boyish man sat on the chair with a wireless keyboard on his lap.

Eddie looked at Ragnar trying to place him. His eyes widened when he recognized him. "Ragnar? That you? What you doing here, bro? Don't they got an arrest warrant or somethin' for you?"

Eddie Juarez was a brilliant but nerdy tech guy who used to work on the trading desk with Ragnar and his team. Eddie had helped Ragnar and his team set up the servers for PatRec. After PatRec was dismantled, Eddie was sent back to the onsite IT maintenance room in the basement where he was more than happy to be, playing online video games between service requests.

Eddie grew up in Queens and still lived there with his parents. He was the third of five children. He was always smiling and helpful like it was his mission in life to help people. His real name was Herberito Juarez but he went by 'Eddie' mostly.

"Eddie, I need your help. Do you still have access to PatRec? Can you log into that system?"

Eddie broke out into a big mischievous grin. "PatRec bro? You mean ShipWreck? What are you goin' do? Trade another hundred million?"

"That's funny, Shipwreck, huh? They might as well have called it that. Eddie, uh, listen. There's a, uh, girl, uh, a girl that's missing. I want to use the pattern algorithms to find where she is. I have some pieces of the puzzle. If PatRec still works and is connected to all the traffic and police systems, I think it may help find this girl." Ragnar pulled out his cell phone and showed Eddie the picture of the van. "She was taken in this van. I just need to find where this van was from or where it went."

"You goin' to get me in trouble bro?" Eddie gave him a smile again. Eddie was always smiling. He could never say no, even if he tried. Ragnar knew Eddie would help.

"Just a quick search and then I'm gone. And no, I don't have an arrest warrant out for me. But I can't be here, you know, after the, uh, the, the thing with the losses. They fired me, Eddie. It wasn't my fault but they still fired me."

"Can't do it bro." Eddie was still smiling back. "Come on, Eddie. You can do this for me. You'll do me a solid. I need to, uh, find her."

"Can't do it from here, bro. I don't have access to PatRec."

Ragnar's heart sank. It was just as he feared. PatRec was probably scrapped. The servers were probably rotting in some junkyard in India or China.

"You know the trading desk can still access it." Eddie was still grinning, even wider now. His leg was shaking at the thought. "You know, if you went upstairs and logged into one of the computers and gave me access, I could access PatRec. But you got to go upstairs for that bro. I don't have access anymore." Eddie was still grinning.

"You're fucking kidding, Eddie. I can't walk back to the trading floor."

"How did you get in, bro?"

"Into the building? Uh, I, uh, acted like someone else."

"Then do that again. Lose that tie and coat. I'll let you borrow a spare shirt and my baseball cap. No one will recognize you with those glasses and the cap. I'll give you a login name and password. The first terminal you see empty, or even an empty office, just walk in there, log in and give me access. 30 seconds tops. Go upstairs at lunch time. Fewer traders then, bro."

"Traders eat their lunch at their desks, Eddie. They hardly ever leave until 5:30 pm."

"Try the exotic equities desk. They were hit hard with all the layoffs. Go that side of the floor. You'll be fine." Eddie was still grinning. Damn Eddie, Ragnar thought, always smiling.

. . .

The elevator doors opened on the sixth floor. Ragnar had a Mets baseball cap on. He continued to look down trying to avoid eye contact with anyone. He entered the doors that led to the trading floor. In an instant, his heart felt a twinge. He missed the excitement and the energy of this place. It was always buzzing with bravado and crazy antics throughout the day. There was never a dull moment.

Ragnar turned right and kept walking toward the exotic equities desks. He walked fast afraid someone may recognize him. As he walked towards the desks, he noticed all the terminals were taken. Maybe the bank moved some other teams here. There were virtually no empty terminals.

Ragnar kept walking trying to find one that maybe available. He turned the last corner and noticed every terminal occupied. He wondered what the odds of something like this would be. He wondered whether it made sense to abandon this altogether and leave.

He was so close and yet. Just then he saw a pregnant lady step out of her office. Ragnar decided this was his chance and started walking towards her office. He walked into her office just as she was leaving. She stopped and looked at him.

"IT security. Did you call earlier? Just need to check your terminal and program some security updates. Can I use your terminal now? Just needs ten minutes."

She glared at him. "I called two days ago. They sent someone now? I need that second screen fixed. Or replaced. You IT guys are the worst."

"Sorry ma'm. I'm on it. I'll fix it for you." Ragnar couldn't help but imagine how she would react when she got back and realized the second screen was still broken. She would be raving mad.

The pregnant lady walked away, likely visiting the bathroom for the umpteenth time of the day, Ragnar thought. He quickly clicked on the working screen and gave Eddie access to her terminal. He dialed Eddie's extension from her office phone. "Eddie, are you in? This is someone's live terminal. I couldn't find an empty one. Will this do?"

"Yes, we good. Come on down, bro." Eddie hung up. Ragnar knew Eddie was smiling and clicking away.

■ ■ ■

Ragnar sat in front of the screen typing away while Eddie looked at him. Ragnar uploaded the photograph of the van. He entered several additional fields of information.

HARDBEII
maroon van New York East Village

. . . .

. . . .

PatRec was designed to access various different databases of information to find trading patterns and buy or sell signals for securities. Rather than use trading information, Ragnar wanted to use the traffic system and the police database.

After the first screen, Ragnar clicked on the NYDOT system, the NYPD database and a few other local city systems.

PatRec went into thinking mode. Eddie was smiling as PatRec seemed to be back in action.

"You want to trade some too, bro?"

"No, Eddie. No trading. This is one-time only. Once I get this, I'm out of here." Ragnar knew Eddie was just excited to see another human being downstairs in the basement. "You think the lady upstairs knows we're in her system accessing PatRec?"

"Well, her system gotta be a bit slower than usual, but no. She won't know. You did good, bro." Eddie was giving him that thousand watt smile again.

"How long do you think this will take?" Ragnar was getting anxious. It was early afternoon already.

"Could be an hour, could be a day. I don't know. PatRec looks like a nervous wreck, bro. If you want to go, why don't you go? I'll be here. I'll email you whatever I find." Eddie was smiling.

"Don't you leave at five to go home, Eddie?"

"Don't worry, I'll stick around till PatRec gives me some answers. I got you covered, bro."

Ragnar was touched by Eddie's offer. "Okay Eddie. I can't stay here all day. I need to leave soon. Please email me anything you find as soon as you find out. This could be a life and death situation."

"I got your back, bro." Eddie smiled back as Ragnar made his way back towards the basement elevator bank.

■ ■ ■

The elevator doors opened at the lobby level. As soon as the doors opened, Ragnar saw Ruby Vohra standing outside the doors. She looked at him and after a couple of moments recognized him.

"Ragnar, what are you... Ragnar, what you are doing... security, this man here..."

Ragnar started sprinting in the other direction towards the turnstiles at the back of the building. The turnstiles opened as he ran towards the main doors. He could hear Ruby's voice behind him telling security which way he went. He did not turn back. He kept running till he got out of the building. He saw a security guard chasing him. Ragnar started running towards Times Square knowing that was his best bet at losing the security guard.

As Ragnar reached the corner of 43rd Street and Broadway, he felt an arm pull him toward the side of the building. The man who stopped him spoke to him quickly. "Ragnar, here take my coat." He handed Ragnar a denim jacket. "Give me your cap. I'll lose the security guy. Walk in that direction. Don't run. Act normal and don't look back. Meet me at 38th and Broadway in fifteen minutes."

Ragnar put on the denim jacket and started walking. He saw this other man put on the cap and run in the opposite direction. The security guard probably just kept chasing the orange baseball cap and ran behind the other man, who looked like he was slowing down. Ragnar kept walking. He paused and turned around to see the other man arguing with the security guard and then both walking towards the Lincoln Myers Building.

It was pretty obvious. The guard was going to take the other man back and Ruby was instantly going to tell the guard that he got the wrong man and they would let him go. Genius, he thought. Ragnar threw away the glasses he was wearing into a bin as he kept walking.

He reached 38th Street and Broadway. Ragnar's head was pounding. He never expected everything that happened today at Lincoln Myers to happen. Then again, he did not know what he was expecting to begin with. He was waiting for this other man to show up when he felt his cell phone vibrate.

Ragnar saw the name, sighed and picked it up. "What the heck, Ragnar? What were you doing in the building today?"

"I don't know what you are talking about Ruby. Why would I be in the building?" Ragnar was almost enjoying this, now that he had slipped away so easily.

"Ragnar, I saw you. You were right there."

"Ruby, I'm in the Hamptons right now sipping a Pina Colada. I've got to go for my afternoon swim in the ocean. Have fun at the mind-numbing job, which by the way sucks. And you sucked at your job even more. Trust me, you sucked, big time! Bye." Ragnar hung up feeling ecstatic.

A few minutes later he saw the man with the Mets baseball cap walking towards him. Ragnar nodded his head and simply asked, "Do you want to grab a coffee? I know this great place in Chelsea away from here where we can sit down and talk."

The other man shook his head.

"You want to, uh, tell me what that was all about? Who are you and why did you help me with that guard?" Ragnar was walking to the curb to hail a cab.

"Ragnar, I'm Gustav Henriksen and I'm looking for Rebecca just like you are."

● ● ●

NEW YORK CITY POLICE DEPARTMENT, 6TH PRECINCT, WEST VILLAGE

Roberta hung up her cell phone and ran towards Timothy's office. She opened his door without knocking. Timothy looked up at her. "What now?"

"James Lin just called. You're not going to believe this. Ragnar and Gustav met outside the Lincoln Myers

Building in midtown. James saw Ragnar running out of that building being chased by a security guard and then Gustav helped him shake off that guy. They're both together now talking in a coffee shop in Chelsea."

CHAPTER 38

DAY 13, TUESDAY
SOMEWHERE IN LONG ISLAND, NEW YORK

The void is scared. The fear is all consuming. The fear feeds the madness and the mental frenzy, makes the void even crazier. The void is pulsating with the madness. There's a strong urge to feed. The void is mad and hungry. The void is all alone. No one can be trusted. No one. No one would protect the void, other than the void itself.

Rebecca was lying face down on her stomach in the cell. She was still hurting from the drugs in her system. She had barely eaten in several days. She lay on her stomach barely conscious trying to make sense of her situation. She could still feel the pain of being burnt in her inner thigh.

Her mind was piecing together the events of the last few days. She tried not to move too much to avoid being drugged again. Pretending that she was still hallucinating was probably a safer alternative. She gave out groans and painful screams every few minutes as a diversion. She knew her captor was behind the door right now peering in.

She recalled her day at the conference. She also remembered her dinner with Iain. A tear formed at the corner of her eye as she thought about meeting Ragnar and spending the night with him. She felt like she had an instant connection with him and now she was here and he had probably moved on. She didn't know if she was ever going to meet him again. The thought of that hurt more right now than the physical pain she was experiencing.

Rebecca heard several latches on the other side of the door. Her captor was opening the door. Rebecca felt a sharp pain in her stomach. It was the fear of anticipation. She did not know what form of torture was in store for her next. She braced herself for the worst. She knew she had to survive this ordeal somehow. She had too much grit and determination in her to give up easily. If the captor wanted her to give up, he was going to have to try harder, a hundred times harder.

The door opened and the cell lit up with daylight. Rebecca was facing the other side, but she flinched with the light. She groaned and lay still on her stomach. The phantom walked up to her and gave her a couple of light kicks to see if she was awake. Rebecca made a light moaning sound as if she was barely conscious.

The phantom knelt down next to her and held her hair and in one quick move pulled her hair back hard. Rebecca felt a jerking pain in her scalp as her head was pulled up backwards. It was then that she realized that she was thirsty and her throat was parched. She gave out a weak groan and looked up at her captor from the corner of her eye. Her captor was wearing a sweatshirt with the hood pulled over and some sort of mask.

The phantom spoke to her in a muffled voice, the mask hiding the voice and identity well. "Are you going to give me what I want Rebecca? Or do you want some more?"

The phantom's voice was muffled but Rebecca's mind was racing trying to place the voice and match it with a face. It was so familiar. She remembered the last call she got when she was at Ragnar's place and then she knew.

"So, it is you, -------."

The phantom froze and then pulled the mask aside.

The phantom let Rebecca see the face behind the mask. "Yeah, it's me."

Rebecca whispered. "Why? Why do you need to do all this?"

"Why? I'll tell you why." The phantom sat down next to her in the cell and started talking to Rebecca. The phantom went back right to the beginning. No detail was too small for this conversation. The phantom went into excruciating detail, every twist, every turn and every justification possible for the phantom's actions. Some of the facts she learned pained her tremendously. She felt a deep sense of betrayal. While knowing the phantom's reasons provided some clarity on the reasons for her captivity, Rebecca now wished she had not asked.

"...and then I killed Dr. Gupta. I injected every vial I could lay my hands on in the lab freezers. I even removed all the old samples from the cryo-freezer and injected him with those. He died a very painful death. Not painful enough though. I wish he suffered more. He deserved much worse."

"What are you waiting for then? Why don't you kill me too? You've already subjected me to a lot of pain." Rebecca countered back. "You're crazy, you know that, right? You can tell yourself whatever you want but your actions make no sense. Nothing can justify what you're doing right now."

"Your time will come when I say it is time. Now you're going to tell me what I need to know." The phantom went closer to Rebecca and whispered something in her ear.

Rebecca heard it and closed her eyes tightly shut.

"If you don't give it to me, I'm going to force it out from you Rebecca. Your choice."

Rebecca looked up and whispered what the phantom wanted to hear. The phantom left Rebecca's hair and caressed her head gently. "Good girl. That's a good girl."

The phantom walked off and closed the door again. Rebecca lay there in the dark running through the identity of the phantom and what that meant for everyone.

CHAPTER 39

DAY 13, TUESDAY
COOKSHOP, CHELSEA, NEW YORK CITY

"I've been in New York since Rebecca disappeared. I saw the story in the *Daily Post* and then I tracked you down. It wasn't very difficult given how many times they called you in to the precinct." Gustav picked up his cappuccino and took a sip.

Ragnar had not been to a place like Cookshop in a long time. "So you've been following me? For how many days?"

"Yes, for the last few days. Look, I know about Rebecca and you. I used to date her. We broke up but I still care about her. I want to find her and I know you're trying to find her as well. I don't know what you were up to in that building but it must've been important for you if you risked going in there." Gustav tried to sound as reassuring as possible. He understood why Ragnar would be suspicious. "You have to trust me. I can help you. We can work together to find her."

Ragnar had been alone for so long, he was glad there was someone who he could speak to, even if he did not completely trust Gustav. Ragnar sighed and decided he was going to use all the help he could get. Ragnar spent the next hour going over everything from the night he first met Rebecca, how he met her, their night at his place, how she disappeared and then how the cops showed up after a few days asking questions.

Ragnar went through how he figured Dr. Gupta was at the hotel the night before he met Rebecca, his trip to Cambridge and then to Evansville. He told Gustav about the van that Rebecca was likely kidnapped in and why he was at the Lincoln Myers Building as well as everything about PatRec.

Gustav shook his head in disbelief. "Wow. You're crazier than I thought. You really love her, don't you?"

Ragnar shook his head in the affirmative.

"I was in your shoes. She has this effect on people. Like I said, I still care about her. A lot. I've been watching all the madness unfolding from the sidelines and I couldn't just sit and watch it idly any longer without doing something about it."

Gustav then told Ragnar about his relationship with Rebecca, their time together in Dr. Gupta's lab and their secret relationship when they were working for the bitter rivals, Atticus Biopharma and Faust Biopharma. He told Ragnar about the leaks, his confrontation with Rebecca and their inevitable breakup as a result of that. He saw Ragnar's expression when he told him about the subsequent leaks.

"If we find out the source of the leaks, we could probably find a lead on who kidnapped Rebecca." Gustav looked at Ragnar seeing if he got the hint.

"No, uh, no, no, no fucking way. I'm not breaking into Atticus Biopharma. Why don't you try a break-in this time?" Ragnar was still shaken from his run-in into Ruby at the Lincoln Myers Building.

"That building is a fortress compared to Lincoln Myers Building. We'll need all the help we can to get in there."

"Why don't you just tell the, uh, police or, uh, the folks at Atticus Biopharma about these leaks? They'd know how to find the person responsible." Ragnar looked incredulously at Gustav.

"Why didn't you take the information about the van to the police? Why haven't you done that?"

"That's different. I'm just trying my bit to find something that the cops obviously missed." Ragnar stood up to leave.

"Ragnar, this is my number. Call me when you need my help. I know you will." Gustav wondered whether Ragnar was just jealous about his previous relationship with Rebecca. If he was, it was understandable, he thought. He finished his coffee, left some cash on the table and left Cookshop.

CHAPTER 40

DAY 14, WEDNESDAY
NEW YORK CITY POLICE DEPARTMENT,
6TH PRECINCT, WEST VILLAGE

Timothy walked up to Roberta. "Pack up. We're going to Chinatown right now."

"Why Chinatown?" Roberta stood up and picked up her cell phone getting ready to leave with Timothy.

"James just called me. We have another body. The Rebecca case." Timothy had turned and was walking out. Roberta walked fast to catch up with him. "Anything from Long Island yet?"

"No, we're running through several leads but nothing yet. Whose body?"

■ ■ ■

Ragnar was pacing his living room as he spoke to Eddie on his cell. He did not have a shirt on. "Eddie, did PatRec find something?"

"Long night, bro. PatRec took forever."

"Hey, thanks, Eddie. I, uh, really owe you one for this." Ragnar was holding his breath in anticipation. "What did it throw up, Eddie? Sounds like you have something."

"Yes, bro. I got something for you. PatRec came through with something. A maroon van was reported missing the day before, on Wednesday, by a business in Long Island. Hard Bend Brothers Saw Mill."

Ragnar could not believe what he was hearing. He pulled a pad and wrote down what he had.

HARD BEII

Ragnar drew a line connecting the two I's.

HARD BEN

He wrote the remaining letters after it.

HARD BEND BROTHERS SAW MILL

"You still there, bro?"

"I am, Eddie. Thanks a lot. This is great." Ragnar sat down on the chair still shaking his head. He could not believe PatRec was able to make the connection with a police report around the dates with the van and the incomplete letters.

"I got more, bro."

"More? What else do you have, Eddie?"

"The van was found next Monday, five days later. It was found a few miles from where it was taken. The cops in Long Island found it. Nothing was missing from the van. I'm guessing they figured it was stolen for some sort of drug delivery or something. I'm emailing the report over to you now."

"That's great, Eddie, can you send me the addresses of where it was stolen and found?"

"Just did. I also ran a quick analysis of likely places the van would've been. There's an old industrial area with several closed factories. It's possible the person you're looking for is being held in one of those."

"Thanks, Eddie. I'm presuming you've emailed your algorithm and results over to me with the report?"

"Just did, bro."

"Eddie, you're the best. You should go home now."

"Can't, bro. But I'll leave at five sharp today. You still got my shirt and Mets cap bro?"

Ragnar remembered how he had to flee the building yesterday and could not return Eddie's shirt and cap. "I do, Eddie. Why don't you come by to the East Village today? I'll buy you a few drinks. I owe you. You got my coat and tie?"

"I do, bro. See you later."

"Thanks Eddie, you're the best." Ragnar hung up, knowing Eddie was tired but probably still smiling. Ragnar clicked on his email and opened up the police report as well as the map output Eddie had emailed him.

The map was an interactive file that had two shaded circles indicating the most likely places the van could've been given the locations where it was stolen from and returned to. Ragnar opened the algorithm that Eddie had run and reviewed the parameters. Eddie had done a good job of running the probabilistic report with the circles on the map. Ragnar made a minor tweak to take into account the fact that the van made its way into Manhattan and back. He switched back to the map where the circles were slightly smaller now.

Even though the circles were small, in reality it covered several square miles of area in Long Island. After eliminating all the open areas, the streets and highways, there were still a lot of places where Rebecca might be.

Ragnar wrote some commands down in the mapping software and pulled up the list of buildings within the two circles. The list was several pages long. Ragnar then added additional parameters to eliminate active businesses. The list was shorter now but still had over forty buildings on it, forty-three to be precise. Better than what Ragnar had earlier but still not great.

Where are you, Rebecca? Where are you being held? I hope you are still alive. I am going to find you.

Ragnar pulled up the list and started searching for details on each name on the list. It was going to be a long night, Ragnar thought to himself.

CHAPTER 41

DAY 14, WEDNESDAY
ELIZABETH STREET, CHINATOWN (CLOSE TO THE MANHATTAN BRIDGE), NEW YORK CITY

Timothy and Roberta made their way up a narrow staircase of a dilapidated building in the heart of Chinatown. There were several onlookers standing around watching the cops make their way up, but did nothing. They all spoke in their native language, almost whispering and stopped talking as the cops passed them.

Timothy and Roberta made their way up to the third floor of the building. James Lin was waiting there for them. "This way." He pointed down the hall and started walking towards an open door at the end of the hallway. Timothy and Roberta followed him there.

The living room was small and sparsely furnished. James led them to the bedroom. Mike Moretti was there with a large camera taking pictures of the victim. There were a few forensic analysts from his team sweeping the room for physical evidence.

Timothy and Roberta were shocked at the scene in front of them. The bedroom was furnished with just a large king-sized bed and a bedside table. Iain was spread eagle naked on the bed. His hands and legs were tied to the corners of the bed. His mouth was tied tightly and so were his eyes. There was a knife handle sticking out of his chest. The killer had stabbed him through the heart and left the knife inside him. There were some signs of a struggle as Iain tried to break loose but he stood no chance after being stabbed so brutally through the heart.

Iain's manhood was exposed and even in his dead state, it was an impressive sight thought Roberta to herself. She understood why Iain was so popular with women.

■ ■ ■

A FEW HOURS EARLIER
ELIZABETH STREET, CHINATOWN (CLOSE TO THE MANHATTAN BRIDGE), NEW YORK CITY

The void covered the face with a mask and walked into the room where Iain lay tied down to the bed. The void motioned the woman in the room to keep quiet and leave. She left without protest knowing without any uncertainty that the void meant business. Bad business.

The void pulled out a long sharp knife and immediately felt excitement rush through the body. A rush of blood to the head felt like heaven.

The void gently climbed on top of Iain. The fool. He was blindfolded and did not even know that his death was sitting on him. He just moaned like a dumb fool, thought the void.

The void lifted the knife high above the head and with one strong motion stabbed him in the chest.

With the knife inside his chest, Iain's heart continued to beat, tearing itself to shreds. There was less immediate blood loss other than knife injuries but the heart was getting damaged beyond repair. Death was almost certain. Iain lost consciousness from the shock within fifteen seconds. He was brain dead in three to five minutes and dead a few minutes after that.

The void's breathing was heavy and labored. The blackness surrounding the void was immediately lifted. Everything around looked bright and hopeful. This was far more satisfying than the last one, the void thought.

The void does not forgive. The void does not forget. The void punishes. The void takes.

Nothing can fill the void.

■ ■ ■

DAY 14, WEDNESDAY
ELIZABETH STREET, CHINATOWN (CLOSE TO THE MANHATTAN BRIDGE), NEW YORK CITY

Mike Moretti stopped taking pictures of Iain and spoke to Timothy and Roberta. "The killer knew exactly what he was doing. He stabbed the heart and left the knife in. With a knife inside, the heart continues beating and tears itself to shreds, damaged beyond repair. Death in such an injury is almost certain. Iain probably lost consciousness from the shock within seconds and died a few minutes after that. Bitch of a way to go, if you'd ask me."

James spoke next. "Someone called it in from a public phone downstairs. This building is a prostitution den and is controlled by the Flying Dragons gang. They're basically the Triad. We're lucky they called the cops and they didn't just dump the body and go back to business as usual. Knowing the gang influence here, I doubt you're going to find anyone who will talk to us."

"So, no witnesses at all. Can't we find the girl he was here for?" Roberta asked knowing what the answer was likely going to be.

"And admit to prostitution? No way anyone here utters a word. Even though the gang is less powerful than it was in the 1980s, it still has a lot of influence in this neighborhood. They run underground gambling rings, drugs, prostitution, human trafficking, you name it and it's going on here, largely unchecked." James had been in this neighborhood several times for all sorts of crimes. I will ask around. I have some sources, but for something like this, Grandma Ang needs to give her blessing."

"Grandma Ang?" Roberta asked. Clearly she knew less about the lay of this neighborhood than some others in New York City.

"Grandma Ang took over activities of the gang in the mid-1990s after her grandson, Jimmy Ang, was arrested and sentenced to thirty years. Jimmy is still behind bars.

There was a brief power struggle after Jimmy went to prison. Grandma Ang ordered the deputy leader who was aspiring to take Jimmy's place eliminated along with members of his family to set an example.

It was a brutal transition and everyone got the message – no one messes with Grandma Ang. Since she assumed power, it's been largely violence-free. No one challenges her authority and everyone recognizes that without her, business would be much harder. Her organization survived the Giuliani years pretty much intact. She has managed to keep the peace and grow the business." James had heard about her ascension to power from old timers at the force.

"Can we speak to Grandma Ang?" Roberta kept pushing.

"Grandma Ang is a ghost. No one has seen her for years in public. She operates secretly, partly for her own protection and partly because she wants everyone to know that she is untouchable. She cannot be found, even if someone tried. Also, she's quite old now. She is hanging on waiting for Jimmy's return to hand over the organization to him."

"James, can you put word out to Grandma Ang. Look, we don't care about her organization or about anything that's going on here or in this building. All we care about is if someone saw the person who did this to Iain." Timothy was wondering if someone could cover Iain's body and give him the dignity of not being paraded naked for the entire forensics team, but he realized that they needed to do their work here.

Okay, I'll try, but don't expect much from this. Like I said, Grandma Ang is a ghost."

"Just let them know that it's either cooperate with the police, help find the killer and we leave the Triad alone or there's a headline in the local papers, 'LA-based Photographer Found Brutally Murdered in Triad-owned Brothel in Chinatown,' with a leaked picture of Iain's body." Timothy was working any angle he could to try and get some information.

"How about 'Chinatown Children Found Playing Soccer with Cop's Head.' My head. You're not seriously asking me to threaten the Triad, threaten Grandma Ang? No one threatens Grandma Ang. She hasn't ruled over the Flying Dragons for two decades by being pushed over, Tim." James was concerned that Timothy may not fully understand the implications of what he was suggesting. And then a thought struck him. "Though I do know someone who can help us, someone who knows Grandma Ang. Your old friend, Raoul Perez."

"Raoul knows Grandma Ang?" Timothy was surprised that he had never heard about this before.

"It's ancient history but Raoul worked on a kidnapping case of a young child. Turns out the child was from the extended Ang family. He found the child just in time. If he had been even a few minutes late, the kidnapper would've killed the child. The Triad and the Ang family owe him. They would listen to him if he reached out." James was glad he did not have to be the one reaching out to Grandma Ang.

"I'll speak to Raoul, try and set up a meeting with her.

How's the crime scene looking here?"

"This room has more DNA than you can find in a football stadium." Mike Moretti was the one to speak this time. "You don't want to touch anything in this room. And not just because of contamination of the evidence."

Despite the grim situation, Timothy gave a hint of a smile at Mike's semi-crude comment. Timothy stepped into the living room and went out into the hallway. Several doors in the hallway were open an inch or so and people we peeping at where Timothy was standing to see what was going on. Timothy ignored them and pulled out his cell phone. He dialed Raoul's number. Raoul picked up his cell phone on the second ring.

"Raoul, it's me, Timothy. I need to update you on a serious development on the Rebecca case and I need your help with that matter."

Raoul was listening patiently to Timothy update him on the developments on the day.

■ ■ ■

NEW YORK CITY POLICE DEPARTMENT, 6TH PRECINCT, WEST VILLAGE

Timothy and Roberta were sitting opposite each other. "Okay, déjà vu. We have another body and another twist in this saga. Let's hear your thoughts on this first, Roberta."

"Well, based on our last conversation with Iain, he was hiding two things from us – one, he spent the night of Rebecca's disappearance with someone he would not tell us about and two, he refused to disclose the source of the three large deposits in his Curacao bank account. Also, it looks like we rattled his cage. He hired a high profile lawyer that probably set off alarm bells for someone who did not want him to talk. Unfortunately for him, the killer did not want to take a chance and silenced him anyway. That's the only thing that explains what happened to him and the timing of his murder."

"I agree with everything you just said. We should speak to Ira, see if he gives us something. I'm sure he's going to be upset with what happened to Iain." Timothy was fidgeting and Roberta could tell that he did not like the direction this case was taking. They were barely making any real headway on the disappearance and the bodies were piling up. "We need to speak to Ira and fast. I have a feeling that whoever is behind this is not done yet."

"I'll reach out to Ira and speak to him."

■ ■ ■

"Ira, this is Timothy and Roberta. How are you doing?" Timothy knew they needed Ira's cooperation to get to the bottom of his complex case.

"How the fuck do you think I'm doing? I just found out that my client was brutally stabbed in his chest, that he was tied up, gagged and blindfolded in a dirty brothel in Chinatown. How do you think it makes me feel?"

"My heart goes out for him, Ira, it truly does. No one deserves to die that way. I'm on your side. We want to get to the bottom of this and find the person who did this." Timothy felt genuine remorse and hearing the pain and angst in Ira's voice made him feel a bit better about Ira's cooperation.

"What do you want from me?" Ira knew what was coming next.

"Look Ira, Iain spoke to you at the precinct. He obviously shared information with you that he did not want to share with us. We need to know what he told you. It could help us find the person who murdered him." Timothy looked at Roberta exchanged a glance. This was it, he thought. Either Ira would go for it or he would stonewall them.

"Timothy, I'm still bound by attorney-client privilege. It survives the death of the client in most jurisdictions. I'm not sure anything I tell you is going to help you, other than muddy Iain's name and I don't want to stab him in the back after his death."

"We understand where you are coming from Ira but we don't have any intention of putting Iain on trial here. This is about us finding his murderer and bringing him to justice. I know if this would've been Iain's call, he would've wanted you to help us. We don't want to see his murderer get away with what he did and we certainly don't want to put anyone else in harm's way. There's a monster on the loose and we need to get him." Timothy was trying his best to get Ira to a place where he could rationalize helping the police by breaching the attorney-client privilege. "Ira, are you still there?"

"Dammit Timothy."

"I hear you Ira and I feel for Iain too, but you've got to help us. We understand the quandary we're putting you in but you know deep down that it's the right thing to do."

There was silence on the line for several moments. Timothy and Roberta looked at each other. "Strictly off-the-record, Timothy. You did not hear this from me. Is that understood?"

"Of course Ira. Totally off-the-record. You have my word on it." Timothy made a small victory gesture with his fist.

"Iain was accessing Rebecca's laptop and selling her research in exchange for cash. He did all his dealings through some lawyer, a middleman basically. He did not meet the ultimate buyer of the information but he strongly suspected it was Matheus Faust, the CEO of Faust Biopharma."

Timothy nodded at Roberta. This made sense given what Gustav had told them about the leaks from Atticus Biopharma. "Ira, there were three payments in Iain's Curacao account. Where did the last two payments go? There were five sets of research papers that were leaked."

"Those were the only three payments he received. He sent three sets of research documents before the folks at Atticus Biopharma caught on. They really increased the security protocols. They issued Rebecca a new laptop that needed fingerprint verification in addition to passwords to access it. He wasn't able to access her laptop any longer after that." At the other end of the line, Ira looked at his notes and wished he had gotten Iain to provide the name of the lawyer who was the middleman between Faust Biopharma and him. "I don't know who it was but you could look into his cell phone records and probably find the lawyer who was the middleman between Faust Biopharma and Iain."

"What about the night Rebecca disappeared? And the day when Dr. Gupta was killed? Iain was in Cambridge that day. What did he tell you about that?" Roberta wanted to make sure she covered everything while they had Ira cooperating.

Ira went over the night of Rebecca's disappearance and what Iain shared with him about being in Cambridge. "So he didn't tell you who he was with at both those times? Doesn't that strike you as odd?" Roberta was surprised that Iain held back something so critical from Ira.

"My clients don't always tell me everything. Sometimes they choose to hold back and I learn things the hard way after the fact, but that comes with the territory. Personally, I don't think Iain had anything to do with Rebecca's disappearance or Dr. Gupta's death. He was probably hiding an affair with some model. That would be my guess." Despite what he said, Ira had a nagging feeling now about not knowing Iain's whereabouts. Maybe there was something important about that after all.

"Ira, you've been tremendously helpful. If there's anything else you remember, please give us a call."

"Do me a favor, Timothy. Nail the motherfucker who did this to him."

"We will, Ira. We will."

. . .

UNDISCLOSED LOCATION, CHINATOWN, NEW YORK CITY

Ning Zhao was around seventeen years old when she landed in the port of Los Angeles. She and eight other girls around the same age were hidden at the back of a container. Half the container was walled off with a makeshift metal separator creating a 'room' at the back. The front of the container was filled with sacks of chemicals to pass off as an import from China.

The container was built as a human smuggling vessel that could easily be placed on or removed from a container ship and shipped to any part of the world. The unfortunate inhabitants of the container had to endure tremendous hardships as part of their journey.

Ning was born in the village of Huangpu in the Guangdong province in China in the outskirts of Guangzhou's city borders. Huangpu is an old port that was in use during the Qing Dynasty. Huangpu, located on the Pearl River, was at the convergence of Eastern and Western cultures in its history.

During a part of the eighteenth century, Huangpu was the only Chinese port open to foreign trade. Huangpu was the center of the thriving opium smuggling during that period despite imperial directives banning the sale of opium. Officials in change of Huangpu condemned the opium trade publicly while they reaped the financial benefits of the illegal opium trade from this imperial port. The opium trade out of the Huangpu eventually led to the Opium Wars that forced other Chinese ports to open up for foreign trade.

Huangpu though no longer held the importance that it held historically. All that remained of the grandeur of its prosperous past were the fancy old brick houses and ancestral temples built in the seventeenth and eighteenth centuries. Fishermen still lived in Huangpu and took their old fishing boats on the Pearl River much like their ancestors did over the last few hundred years Ning's father worked on a fishing boat owned by another fisherman in Huangpu. Life in Huangpu was a hand-to-mouth existence. Lured by promises of a better life in a western country, Ning found herself on a container ship headed to Los Angeles with several other girls. Soon after she landed in Los Angeles, she realized that her father had taken a loan to pay for her journey to America and her family was deeply in debt to the traffickers that helped her make her way to America.

Ning spoke no English when she first landed in America, though she proved to be a quick learner over the next three years. After the first few months in a Chinese-owned brothel in Los Angeles, Ning was sold for a quick profit to a brothel in Chinatown in New York, an operation controlled by the Flying Dragon gang.

As much as her profession pained Ning, she plunged into the flesh trade headlong. Ning was becoming increasingly popular with her clientele in New York for her imagination and her lack of inhibitions in the bedroom. Ning learnt how make her clients' senses tingle and make them experience pleasure for a long time. She was sensual and gentle in the beginning and aggressive and wild as her time with the men progressed. She very gradually notched up the pleasures of having sex. Ning was one of the most expensive 'courtesans' in the Elizabeth Street brothel, likely even the most expensive one in all of Chinatown in New York.

Ning had a steady stream of famous clients in New York City, though she often did not recognize them and when she did, she made it a point not to make it known that she knew them out of discretion and respect for their privacy.

Ning had made quite a few friends with other girls who worked at the brothel and she had almost never had any client trouble during her entire time here in New York City, until now. A client under her care had 'died.' Or put more accurately 'murdered,' and the brothel was swarming with police officers from the NYPD.

Ning was quickly taken away from the brothel shortly after Iain's body was discovered to live in another apartment in Chinatown. Ning feigned ignorance about what happened to Iain when she was first questioned at the brothel. She said she had left Iain tied up and had gone to change into something even more provocative for him and found him bound and murdered when she got back.

In the heat of the moment, no one questioned her story much. Everyone was in a hurry to evacuate the important working women before the police showed up. The men who came to move her to a new apartment were somewhat panicked and kept referring to "Grandma Ang" and her temper in a quivering tone. Clearly, they were all scared of her and she figured she should be too.

Today was the first time Ning had met Iain. Iain had paid for two hours with her and she planned to give him his money's worth. Ning made Iain sit on the bed as she seduced him with a sensual dance. She then proceeded to strip him naked and tie him down to the bed. She sat on top of him and after seducing him by gently running her fingers and nails all over his body, she blindfolded him. Ning then proceeded to pleasure Iain's manhood with her mouth. When he started moaning loudly, she stopped, got on top of him, tied his mouth and slipped back between his legs. It was then that she saw a shadowy figure in the far corner of the room.

Ning's heart started to pound hard in her chest as she recalled what happened next. What she now knew could get her killed. As she sat on her bed in her new temporary apartment, she heard a knock on the door. She walked over to the door and asked who it was, her heart still pounding wildly in her chest.

She heard a male voice speak to her in Mandarin from the other side of the door. "Grandma Ang summons you."

CHAPTER 42

DAY 15, THURSDAY
NEW YORK CITY POLICE DEPARTMENT, 6TH PRECINCT, WEST VILLAGE

Timothy and Roberta sat opposite Matheus Faust who looked more beaten down than when they had last met him. They had read about the failed Glovir trial and the steep decline in the stock price of Faust Biopharma.

"You got anything better than this dull machine coffee?" Matheus had taken a sip from the cup of coffee from the small Keurig coffee machine down the hall and looked disgusted as he put the cup down.

"Maybe I can grab you a Coke or a Diet Coke from the vending machine?" Timothy put down the Dunkin Donuts coffee that he carried in with him today morning. He knew exactly what Matheus' coffee tasted like.

"No, thanks. I don't put that stuff in my body. The caramel coloring that is used in manufacturing these soft drinks produces a carcinogen that can cause cancer. You know what a carcinogen is, don't you?"

"We do. It's anything that can cause cancer in living creatures." Roberta interjected.

"So, no thank you, no soft drinks for me please. I understand the business about Iain but why do you need to talk to me about it?" Matheus looked defeated even before the conversation started.

"We know you paid Iain to steal research from Rebecca's laptop." Timothy wanted to get straight to the point and not beat around the bush any longer.

"You're never going to be able to prove that. My lawyers..."

"Matheus, we strongly suggest that you start cooperating here with us. The bodies are piling up and we're going to do whatever it takes to get to the bottom of this. This is not a corporate espionage case. This is a kidnapping and murder case. Two murders now to be precise. And we're not ruling you out as a suspect, either directly or if you hired someone to do it. So you better start talking and fessing up or you're going to find yourself having a very difficult time in jail over the weekend. We can trace that money back to you. We're going to make sure a warrant gets issued tomorrow and we put you behind bars late tomorrow. You'll be behind bars over the weekend before you're able to make bail. Don't test us. We're not playing games here. We want the truth. Right now." Timothy banged his hand on the table for effect.

Roberta was surprised to see his aggressive move. The deposits in Iain's accounts were not traced to anyone yet but the threat Timothy made sounded credible.

Matheus was calculating his next move in his head. Did he want to take the chance that Timothy was bluffing? What would happen to the stock price of Faust Biopharma if they arrested him for the disappearance of one cancer researcher and the murder of a second one?

Even though the probability of the NYPD having traced the money back to him was remote and infinitesimally small, if that were true, it could be the deathblow for his career at Faust Biopharma and maybe even for Faust Biopharma itself. The Board of Faust Biopharma would certainly not hesitate to oust him from the company that he created. Investors would flee the company. The stock price would collapse dramatically. All his top researchers and managers would head for the exit.

Corporate espionage, on the other hand, was a different matter altogether. It would take forever to prove. It would not really affect the company. We would have an army of lawyers to fight those charges, if the police ever decided to bring charges for that. In addition, it sounded like they did not even really care about those.

"Matheus, what is it going to be?" Roberta asked him sternly.

Matheus snapped out of the trance he was in as he played out all the scenarios in his head.

"I'll talk." Matheus focused back to the people in the room. His survival instincts kicked in and he was the same Matheus who made his way from Brazil to Boston with half a million dollars in cash in a duffel bag.

"As you know, I've always wanted to recruit Rebecca to Faust Biopharma. I've followed her career and wooed her several times. At one point, I was frustrated that I wasn't able to hire her while she was making giant strides with her research at Atticus Biopharma. I tracked down her boyfriend, Iain. Iain cheated on Rebecca quite often and I had hired a private detective to dig up dirt on him.

"With the proof of his indiscretions in hand, I had a lawyer I hired reach out to Iain and blackmail him. I did not want to deal with Iain directly for obvious reasons. We were able to get Iain to provide us with information on Rebecca's whereabouts and everything she shared with him about her work. During those conversations, he told the lawyer about how Rebecca backed up her research on her travel laptop. Through the lawyer, I then offered Iain money for downloading those documents and passing them along to the lawyer who in turn passed those to me."

All of what Matheus told them made sense given what Gustav and Ira had told them.

Matheus continued his side of the story. "Iain provided three distinct downloads from Rebecca's laptop to the lawyer. I sanitized the documents and passed along the research that Iain provided to my team at Faust Biopharma, all to Gustav, to replicate the research and findings in our labs. Gustav probably knew whose research he was getting but he never said anything. He went along without asking any questions."

"Did you say three downloads?" Roberta asked. "That's the crazy thing that I don't understand. After the first three sets of documents we got, Iain stopped sending any documents. He told the lawyer that they had clamped down and tightened security at Atticus Bio- pharma. At first we thought he was bluffing so we threatened to send the pictures of him with the other women to Rebecca, but he did not flinch. And then the damnedest happened."

"Let me guess, more documents started showing up miraculously." Timothy tried to catch the expression on Matheus' face.

"That's right. The lawyer started getting pen drives mailed to his office. At first we thought we were being fished with bait. We had the pen drive thoroughly analyzed for tracking software or anything that might give away our location. But it was apparent that someone with far greater access than Iain, likely someone at Atticus Biopharma, was downloading documents and sending them to us."

"Matheus, you need to come clean about this. Who else was helping you at Atticus Biopharma? Why would someone just start sending you the information you needed for free, especially after all the trouble you went through in baiting and blackmailing Iain? What else are you hiding? No games, Matheus."

"You can speak to the lawyer and he'll tell you the same thing I just told you. I can give you his name and number. Bring him in. I'm telling you the truth." Matheus looked straight into Timothy's eyes, which Timothy read as Matheus telling the truth.

"You know I've always wondered about Gustav. He is probably as ambitious as I am. He did not flinch for a second when he had to join Faust Biopharma and breakup with Rebecca. He never questioned any of the research I gave him or how I got it." Matheus picked up the coffee cup in front of him, took a sip and remembered again how horrible the coffee was and immediately put the cup down, making a mental note not to forget that again.

Timothy and Roberta looked at each other taking in what Matheus just said. "Can we get a copy of the pictures or whatever it was that you used to blackmail Iain?" Roberta asked Matheus after exchanging glances with Timothy.

"Of course. They're not with me. I'll track them down and have them sent to you."

■ ■ ■

"Spit it out Roberta." Timothy wanted to know what she thought.

"Gustav could be our guy. A lot of it seems to make sense when you put him into the equation. Rebecca was his former flame. She breaks up with him. He wants Rebecca and at the same time he wants her research, even though he won't ever admit it to anyone. She's been kidnapped and is being held somewhere but she's not dead. On the other hand, Dr. Gupta was killed, probably due to some old vendetta from their days in his lab. And then you have Iain, who was engaged to Rebecca at one point of time. After they broke up, Iain was trying to get back together with her. Maybe he was just plain jealous."

"By that logic, Ragnar should be next, don't you think?" Timothy was playing out the possibility of Gustav being the guilty one.

"He very well could be. There is another possibility as well though." Roberta looked visibly excited about analyzing the situation from another angle.

"What's that?" Timothy knew what was coming. "That the kidnapping and the murders are related in some way but not the handiwork of the same person. Someone may have kidnapped Rebecca and put in motion some chain of events that led to the two murders, but by someone else, maybe someone totally unrelated to the kidnapper. What do you think?"

"I've been grappling with that question in my head as well. That could put Ragnar back on the list of suspects. And Gustav along with him." Timothy could feel he was missing something. "We have to find Rebecca. Maybe then we'll make some sense of this case."

Where are you, Rebecca? Who has you right now?

CHAPTER 43

DAY 15, THURSDAY
EAST VILLAGE, NEW YORK CITY

Ragnar was topless and wearing a pair of black sweatpants. He had installed a pull-up bar in his tiny apartment. He was doing pull-ups in his apartment. Getting some exercise in always helped him. The soreness in his body after some serious exercising relaxed his mind and put him at ease. Ragnar's mind was racing over the events of the last few days and he needed the exercise to calm his mind. He had spent the whole day going through the list of buildings that Eddie had sent him and he was no closer to getting to a shorter list of possible places where Rebecca may be held.

When Ragnar had a job, he had a membership at the Equinox close to his office building, which was something he could not afford in his current situation. When he had the membership, Ragnar did not make it out to the gym more often than once or twice a week. He missed his old gym now. Turning a small apartment in the East Village into a gym required a lot of creativity.

Ragnar heard his cell phone ring. Ragnar received very few phone calls these days. He did not have any close friends. He did not keep in touch with his colleagues from work, especially after what happened at Lincoln Myers. It was also true that no one there wanted to be associated with him any longer. Recruiters barely ever returned his phone calls. The only calls were the occasional rejection calls he got after an interview, but he hadn't been for an interview in some time now.

As Ragnar thought about his last interview, he realized that he had stopped his job search altogether since he met Rebecca two weeks ago. Her disappearance had all but consumed him. He wondered who would be calling him today. Ragnar stopped what he was doing, walked over to his desk and picked up the phone.

"Ragnar, uh, Ragnar Johnson here."

"Ragnar, it's me Liz Nelson."

"Who?"

"Liz Nelson, Joshua Nelson's grandmother. You came by my house in Evanston a few days ago."

"Uh, yes, uh…Mrs. Nelson, of course." Ragnar was still catching his breath.

"You told me to call you about anyone who knew about Joshua's treatment. I think there may be someone you could speak to."

"Is it Dr. Gupta? I spoke to him recently, though, he, uh, sounded like he, uh, was…"

Liz Nelson cut off Ragnar mid-sentence. "It's a woman actually. When my daughter, Marge and her husband David committed suicide, we held a funeral at a local church here in Evanston. Most of the people who showed up at the funeral were folks who knew our family here locally. I was struck with a mountain of grief at the funeral. Several people from town spoke at their funeral. They praised my daughter and son-in-law and how they gave everything they had in trying to find a cure for Joshua. This woman, who knew them, spoke briefly at the funeral. She said something about knowing Marge and David from when they were treating Joshua and praised their strength and endurance during that difficult time."

Ragnar's head was spinning. "Do you know what she looked like?"

"I do. She was a middle-aged blonde woman. Her name was N. Mulligan. She spoke to me after the funeral and left flowers for them with a thoughtful note. I kept the note and remembered today morning about her at the funeral. I found the note when I looked for it among a few other things that I saved from the funeral."

"Did you mean, uh, Nancy Mulligan?"

"That's the one Ragnar. She was a doctor of some sorts."

"Was there anyone else with her at the funeral?" Ragnar wondered if Rebecca or Dr. Gupta were at the funeral. Maybe they went there and Nancy accompanied them.

"I can't say. I was a wreck at the funeral. You should track her down. She could help your son."

Ragnar just remembered the lies he told her about his own sick son and felt a wave of guilt wash over him. "Mrs. Nelson, thank you so much. You've been immensely helpful."

"Anything I can do to help your little one, Ragnar. May God bless you."

Ragnar hung up his cell phone.

Ragnar darted towards his computer and started typing furiously. It did not take long for him to track down Nancy's address in New York City. She lived in a nice co-op apartment in the Upper East Side in the city.

What was Nancy Mulligan doing at the funeral for Marge and David Nelson? She was not involved in the Joshua Nelson trial. Or was she? That trial happened before Rebecca joined Atticus Biopharma. Why did she go there to attend the funeral? She would not know Joshua Nelson, other than through Rebecca, or Dr. Gupta.

■ ■ ■

FIFTH AVENUE, UPPER EAST SIDE, NEW YORK CITY

Nancy was lying on her stomach on the floor of her apartment as she regained consciousness very briefly. She could not feel most of her body due to the numbness and the trauma. She was lying in a pool of blood and her clothes were drenched in it. She had been shot several times and she knew she had only a few moments before she passed out again, this time for good. In her dying moments, she dipped her left finger in her blood and scribbled a few letters and numbers next to her body. She had a faint smile on her face and felt a sense of achievement at her final action before she slipped unconscious again.

Nancy breathed a few ragged breaths before her body finally gave up and life slipped out of her.

...

STATEN ISLAND, NEW YORK CITY

Timothy's cell phone rang just as he was entering his house.

"Timothy Burns."

"Timothy, this is Raoul."

"Hey Raoul, what's going on?"

"We're meeting Grandma Ang tonight. Meet me at the Chinatown bus stand on Allen Street in an hour."

"It's going to take me longer than an hour to get there. And I want Roberta to be there as well." Timothy turned around stepping outside and shutting the door behind him as he jogged towards his car to make the journey back into Manhattan.

"Okay. Please be there as soon as you can. This is your one and only chance to speak to Grandma Ang."

"Buy me some time. I'm on my way." Timothy started his car and stepped on the gas.

Timothy hung up his cell phone. Just as he was about to dial Roberta, he saw an incoming call from her.

"Roberta, we're meeting Grandma Ang tonight. I just got a call from Raoul. Meet us at the Chinatown bus stand, the one on Allen Street." Timothy glanced at his watch as he spoke.

"Timothy, I just got a call. Nancy Mulligan has been shot dead in her apartment. A neighbor reported some gunshot sounds and called 911. Minutes before the police arrived there, Ragnar was downstairs in the lobby. He wanted to meet Nancy. The building doorman was calling her just as the cops arrived. They still have Ragnar there. Moretti and the rest of the forensics team are on their way. I'm headed over there as well."

"You mean, Nancy from Atticus Biopharma?" Timothy felt like someone had punched him really hard in the stomach when he heard the news. He couldn't believe there was one more body so soon after they found Iain's body.

"Yes, the same one. I'll take care of the crime scene. We'll have to divide and conquer tonight. Will you be alright without me?"

"Yeah, that makes sense. I'll tackle Grandma Ang. I'll be over as soon as possible. You cover the crime scene there."

"Please be careful, Timothy."

"I will."

■ ■ ■

FIFTH AVENUE, UPPER EAST SIDE, NEW YORK CITY

Ragnar was sitting in the lobby of Nancy's apartment building. Her building was a co-op on Fifth Avenue, opposite Central Park and the Metropolitan Museum of Art. The building, which was constructed in the 1920s as a hotel was converted into a residential co-op in the mid-2000s. Nancy purchased a large four thousand square feet apartment in the building when it was converted to a co-op.

The NYPD walked into the lobby of the building just as the doorman was calling Nancy's apartment to ask her if he could send Ragnar upstairs, but her house phone was ringing with no answer. When the NYPD asked about her apartment, he told them about Ragnar who was also waiting to go upstairs. They asked him to wait and a junior detective was sitting in the lobby with him watching over him.

Ragnar immediately knew something was seriously wrong. Ragnar tried to strike up a conversation with the detective who was watching him. "So what brought your team and you over here?"

"Gunshots. Neighbor reported hearing gunshots from Nancy's apartment and called 911. What were you doing trying to meet her at this hour?"

"I, uh, I, wanted to speak to her, err, about a funeral she attended a few years ago. She spoke at that funeral.

It was the funeral of a couple that died together. Their son died of cancer a few years before them and I, uh, think Nancy, uh, I think she knew him." Ragnar knew how crazy he sounded right now.

The detective just nodded at Ragnar. He had seen people like him before, semi-delusional and out of their mind. They commit gruesome crimes when they are in a state of trance and don't remember their crimes. Even in a normal state, they sound incoherent. Nothing Ragnar just said made any sense to the detective. He was pretty certain that Ragnar would be hauled off soon to the precinct.

Ragnar looked at his watch and wondered how long a night this one was going to be.

■ ■ ■

FIFTH AVENUE, UPPER EAST SIDE, NEW YORK CITY

Mike Moretti put his camera away after taking pictures of Nancy's body and the crime scene. There appeared to be no signs of a struggle. The murderer knew Nancy and given that the body was so far away from the entrance and closer to a sitting area in the living room, it was likely that Nancy and her murderer were having a conversation before she was shot.

Mike pulled out his recorder again as he stepped closer to the body to take a look. "There are five gunshot wounds in the victim's back. The victim has been shot once in the right upper back, once in the mid right back, twice in the lower back and the fifth bullet hit her in the right lateral chest wall. The bullets likely perforated several vital organs including her lungs and heart. The victim fell to the floor after what appears to be five shots in quick succession when she was standing. The victim used her right hand to scribble some words using her blood before she died. It looks like O L T 9 0. Blood from her injuries seemed to have merged into the first letter. She was probably shot with a Colt Series 90 gun." Mike switched off his recorder.

There were no signs of a struggle or a forced break-in. Some of the forensic team was reviewing security tapes from the building's security system in parallel.

Roberta walked in just then. Mike looked at her with a look of resignation. "What a mess. We have another body and we're no closer to solving these crimes. Hopefully, we can nail the bastard today. My team is going through the security cams as we speak."

"What is an OLT90? She probably meant COLT 90, I'm guessing."

"That's my guess as well. I would bet the person who did this had a registered Colt 90 gun." Mike was wiping the sweat off his forehead as he saw his tech analyst walk up. "What is it? Did you find anything?"

"We'll have to take this down to the precinct and run through all the faces again. The apartment has a back door with access to a service staircase and a service elevator. The cameras there caught a figure in a sweatshirt and a hood covering most of the face. The perp looked away from the cameras intentionally hiding his face. The back door handle and the bell button have been wiped clean for fingerprints. The perp came into the apartment from the back door, murdered her and slipped out again from there. We'll have to interview the folks downstairs, but I suspect the perp knew the building well and used a service exit to leave the building."

Mike looked visibly frustrated and angry as he dropped his hands in an animated fashion. Roberta's jaw dropped but she tried to compose herself. "Let's get everything we can from the security cams and forensics. We need to nail this bastard. Get Ragnar to the precinct."

CHAPTER 44

DAY 15, THURSDAY
NEW YORK CITY POLICE DEPARTMENT,
6TH PRECINCT, WEST VILLAGE

"How many times, huh? How many times are we, uh, going to go over this, this, this game?" Ragnar was frustrated as Roberta refused to believe his story of why he was in the lobby of Nancy's building.

"So you're telling me it's a coincidence that you were there at exactly the same time she was murdered? How many coincidences are we to believe, Ragnar? You were there just before Dr. Gupta was killed. What have you been involved in? Someone is following you or there's something else about your night with Rebecca that you're not telling us."

"I know this sounds crazy, but I don't think Nancy had anything to do with Joshua Nelson's experimental treatment. Why would she fly to Evanston half the way across the country to attend the funeral of his parents? There's something about that boy's death that I think is connected. Rebecca and Dr. Gupta were part of that trial when Joshua died. Nancy claimed to have been involved in the trial and she even attended the funeral. Iain I can't explain but it may have been something he knew about that trial from Rebecca."

"Do you own a Colt 90 gun, Ragnar?"

"What?"

Rebecca pushed a picture of the letters scribbled by Nancy for him to look at. "Do you own a Colt 90 gun? These were Nancy's last words before she died."

Ragnar looked at the picture of the letters in Nancy's blood and his mind started racing immediately. A small but indistinguishable smile appeared on his face. It looked like he was trying to solve a three-dimensional puzzle in his head.

"Do you own a Colt 90, Ragnar?" Roberta sounded sterner when he did not reply.

"No, I don't own a, uh, Colt 90. Never did. In fact, I've never, uh, ever, uh, touched a gun in my life. I mean a real, uh, gun. Any chance I can get a copy of that picture?"

"Not a chance in hell, Ragnar. Are you crazy? You have some sort of murder fetish now? I'm going to let you go but don't leave town. We may want to speak to you again. Don't, and I repeat, don't go anywhere near anyone else connected to Rebecca. For their sake really."

"I get it. I'm the grim reaper, La Santa Muerte and Lord Yama, uh, all-in-one now."

"What?"

"Uh, death, personified."

"Don't act smart with me Ragnar. Go home. Get some rest. We'll call you again. This case is far from over." Roberta stood up and walked out of the room.

■ ■ ■

NEW YORK CITY POLICE DEPARTMENT, 6TH PRECINCT, WEST VILLAGE

Ragnar stepped out of the precinct. It was dark and silent outside other than the cars zipping along on 10th Street. He pulled out his cell phone and dialed a number, one he knew would be glad to hear from him. The call went straight to voicemail. "Gustav, it's me, uh, Ragnar. I need your help. Please call me when you get this message."

■ ■ ■

NEW YORK CITY POLICE DEPARTMENT, 6TH PRECINCT, WEST VILLAGE

It was late but Roberta was hoping to make some more progress on the case before she called it a night. "Julia, hi. This is Roberta calling from the NYPD." She paused for a moment. "I'm sorry for your loss."

Julia sounded clearly distraught at the other end of the line.

"I have a few questions for you and I'm hoping you could answer those."

"Of course, Roberta. Do you want me to come down to the precinct?"

"No, that won't be necessary. What did Nancy have to do with the treatment and death of Joshua Nelson?"

"Everything. Nancy was instrumental in having Joshua Nelson get accepted by Dr. Gupta in his lab for his treatment. She oversaw the experimental treatment protocol for Joshua. If the treatment had been a success, we would've licensed the technology for further development in our labs at Atticus Biopharma. So Nancy was intimately involved in all the key scientific decisions of his treatment." Julia paused for a few seconds. "And so was I, though Nancy spent more time visiting the lab than I did."

"Could you please send us a list of everyone at Atticus Biopharma that was involved in that treatment? We need all the details we can lay our hands on."

"Do you think Nancy's death has something to do with Joshua's treatment?" Julia sounded extremely surprised.

"We don't want to rule out anything at this point.

We're exploring every angle in this case right now."

"Okay. I'll have Christy from my team download all the files and have them sent to you as soon as possible."

"One other thing, Julia. Do you own a Colt 90 gun?"

Julia took a deep breath. "Yes, I do." She knew what coming next.

"We will need to get your gun for a forensic examination. Unless you want us to get a warrant, in which case we'll get one, but would you voluntarily allow us to get your gun for some tests?" Roberta knew she made a veiled threat, but she was running out of patience. It had been a long day and it was still not over.

"Roberta, I have three hand guns including a Colt 90. You can come by tonight and pick them up."

"I'll be there in half an hour. Thanks for understanding, Julia." Roberta hung up in a hurry.

Julia dropped her cell phone on the coffee table and walked up to a cabinet in the living room. She pulled aside a panel in one of the shelves of the living room cabinet to reveal a small pistol safe. Julia pressed her fingers on the biometric fingerprint recognition pad. She heard a clicking sound as the safe unlocked. She pulled open the door of the safe and pulled out the Colt 90 along with the two other pistols. It had been a while since Julia had used the Colt 90.

She walked back to the coffee table and dialed a number. "Christy, its Julia. I need you to download all the files related to the Joshua Nelson treatment, cut it on a disk and bring it by my apartment tonight. As soon as possible please."

Julia then dialed Raoul's cell phone but his phone was switched off. It was highly unusual of Raoul not to answer Julia's calls. She left a voicemail for him.

She placed the three pistols on the coffee table in front of her and waited for Christy and Roberta to show up.

■ ■ ■

ALLEN STREET, CHINATOWN, NEW YORK

Timothy pulled his car into the parking lot, jumped out of the car and sprinted towards where Raoul was waiting for him.

Timothy spotted Raoul standing at a corner and he slowed down as he walked over to him. "So where are we meeting Grandma Ang?"

"Wait." That was all Raoul said and pulled out a cigarette and lit it up.

"Since when did you start smoking?"

Just then a white van pulled up next to where Raoul and Timothy were waiting. Raoul threw the cigarette down and Timothy realized that that was the signal for Raoul and Timothy being ready to go meet Grandma Ang. Two tough Chinese strongmen stepped out of the van. Both of them wore black wife beaters and were heavily tattooed on their arms. They slid open the side door of the van and made a gesture to Raoul.

Raoul recognized several of the tattoos on each of their arms. The dragons across their arms symbolized allegiance to the Flying Dragons gang. The spider webs on the elbows depicted the time spent in prison, typically a lengthy term. One of the two strongmen had a tattoo of five dots between his thumb and forefinger. This also represented time done in prison with the four dots outside representing the four walls of the prison and the fifth dot inside representing the prisoner. Both strongmen had a similar tattoo on their forearm that not many law enforcement officers had seen before or knew about. They both had the Xingfu symbol – 幸 福 – along with a dragon circling the symbol. Raoul knew from his previous life that the symbol stood for the words 'blessed.' Both the men were 'blessed' by Grandma Ang as being loyal, fully trustworthy and ready to die for her. They were part of the elite guard protecting her.

"Get in, Timothy. We're going to meet her soon."

Timothy stepped into the van and Raoul followed him in. The van had two sets of seats facing each other. Raoul and Timothy sat on the seats facing the front of the van. The two strongmen hopped inside and sat opposite them.

"Cell phones." The strongman uttered just a couple of words to them. Raoul and Timothy pulled out their phones and handed it to him. The strongman put their phones into a small cloth bag and handed it to a third gang member who was now standing outside the van. He looked like a younger, more recent recruit with fewer tattoos and none that indicated a stint in prison. He did not have the 'blessed' tattoo either. The third gang member then pushed the van door shut.

One of the strongmen sitting opposite them pulled out a couple of blindfolds and plastic zip ties.

"Is this really necessary?" Timothy looked annoyed at being treated like a criminal by these two gang members.

Raoul signaled to Timothy indicating that they would be fine. "Trust me, we'll be fine. Just do like they say, otherwise we're not meeting Grandma Ang tonight."

Timothy sighed and reluctantly held his hands forward. The strongman zip tied Timothy's hands together and then leaned forward and tied the blindfold on him. He then proceeded to do the same with Raoul.

He uttered something in his native language and the van started moving. Timothy wondered whether this was really worth all the trouble they were going through to meet Grandma Ang. Raoul and Timothy were driven around for almost half an hour before the van came to a complete stop. Timothy wondered whether the van was just driving around in circles and they were still in Chinatown.

Both of them were led out of the van still tied up and blindfolded. Timothy found it ironic that Iain was found dead in the same state, blindfolded and tied up. At least Timothy had his clothes on and if he died, it would be with his modesty intact and not a swarming team of forensics and detectives hovering over a fully naked body. He felt a tinge of guilt at the thought.

The strongman pulled the blindfolds off. Their hands were still zip tied. Both of them were standing in a rundown empty barn with a couple of ceiling light bulbs. Timothy noticed a figure at the far end of the barn pushing a wheelchair and two more strongmen accompanying them moving towards them. A strikingly beautiful Chinese lady accompanied them. The entourage came to a halt a few feet away from where Raoul and Timothy were standing.

Raoul had seen this show before. Grandma Ang was really old and needed a wheelchair to get around. The person pushing her wheelchair was her nurse. The two strongmen were the elite of the 'blessed' elite. They stayed close to Grandma Ang and protected her day and night. If required, they would willingly lay down their lives to protect her. The beautiful woman accompanying Grandma Ang was her translator. Grandma Ang knew little English and she never bothered to learn it either.

"Good evening, gentlemen. To what to do we owe the pleasure of your company tonight?"

"Grandma Ang, we are extremely grateful that you accepted our invitation to meet with you and make a humble request. My friend here, Timothy, is working on a case of a missing woman and several murders, one of which took place in a place of business. Timothy has the utmost respect for your place of business and has no intention of disrupting it. He just needs to talk to one of your employees to get a description of the killer who brought disgrace to your place of business." Raoul tried to be as diplomatic as possible in Grandma Ang's presence. He knew there was already a risk of his message being misinterpreted or lost in translation.

The translator conveyed the message and got a response from Grandma Ang.

"What does your friend offer for our help?"

"Grandma Ang, we would be happy to consider any requests you make that could be within my friend's power to provide. If you kindly recall, when I helped find and return the young Xiao Jun from your family, who was kidnapped and was going to be killed by the sadistic serial killer who took him, you had told me that I could ask you for your help if I ever needed it. We need your help with finding this person that my friend is looking for."

After a brief exchange, the translator looked at them again. "My grandson Jimmy is serving a long sentence. He still has over sixteen years left. We want Jimmy's sentence to be cut to five years. He has already served a long time. He deserves to be free if you want us to help you."

Timothy looked at Raoul. He knew this was going to be near impossible. Raoul had been in Timothy's shoes as a cop and knew what Timothy was thinking.

"Grandma Ang, what you ask is honorable, but frankly outside of what my friend can do. He will try, he certainly will, but we strongly ask you to reconsider. We're asking for your help in exchange for the life of Xiao Jun that we saved."

After a brief exchange the translator retorted in an angry tone. "How about we spare your lives in exchange for Xiao Jun's life? We won't chop your heads off right here. Does that sound like reconsideration enough?"

"Grandma Ang, as much as I respect you, you don't

want to off a cop and an ex-cop. You're a survivor. You know that's not good for business. A dead body in your shop is not good for business either. Add to that the fact that it will be unsolved will only cause business to suffer."

"Find out how you can help Jimmy get out sooner and we'll have this exchange again. For now, go back to your lives thankful that you are still alive."

. . .

ALLEN STREET, CHINATOWN, NEW YORK

The van dropped off Raoul and Timothy at another deserted location in the heart of Chinatown and sped off. It had gotten really late at night.

"What was all that about?" Timothy switched on his cell phone, which the strongmen had returned just before they left.

"You're going to find a way to reduce Jimmy's remaining sentence, even if it's by a few years, if you want any help from them."

"How is that going to help? Jimmy does not get out for another fifteen to sixteen years. I could try and get a deal for three or five years less, but I don't see how that would help. Grandma Ang is not going to last another ten years."

Raoul gave him a smile. "You didn't see what I saw. Grandma Ang is old and almost senile now. I recognized the translator with her. She was Cynthia Ang, Jimmy's daughter. She's grown up since I last saw her. She is now the head of the Flying Dragons gang. She is using Grandma Ang as a front to hide in plain sight. Everyone thinks Grandma Ang is still running the operation, but it is Cynthia."

"Let me see what I can do. Wow! So a twenty-something-year-old dangerous gang leader threatened to chop both our heads off."

"She's hot blooded. Be glad she didn't follow through with the threat. Grandma Ang would've kept her word but Cynthia owes me nothing." Raoul switched on his cell phone and saw several voicemails from Julia. This could not be good, he thought.

CHAPTER 45

DAY 16, FRIDAY
EAST VILLAGE, NEW YORK CITY

Ragnar woke up with the persistent ringing of his cell phone. He looked at the time, cursed himself and reached for his cell phone.

"Ragnar, here."

"Ragnar, this is Gustav. I got your message. I also heard about Nancy. What do you need my help for?"

"Not on the phone. Meet me at the same coffee shop, where we first met, in an hour. I'll tell you everything then." Ragnar hoped Gustav remembered Cookshop in Chelsea and the cross street. "Do you remember the address?"

"I do. I'll see you there in an hour." Gustav hung up.

. . .

COOKSHOP, CHELSEA, NEW YORK CITY

Cookshop was even more crowded than usual. New Yorkers had started their weekend early with several folks having brunch at the place. Ragnar was sitting at a small corner table for two when Gustav walked over.

"I'm glad to hear from you, Ragnar. Tell me how I can help? What did you find?" Gustav sounded more curious than usual. Ragnar wanted his help but at the same time did not trust him completely.

"I need your help tracking down a very old clinical trial, uh, one from the 1990s. Specifically, I need help tracking down someone who participated in that clinical trial."

"What? I don't understand."

"I'll get straight to the point. When Nancy was found murdered, uh, she scribbled a few letters using her blood just before she died. She wrote the letters, err, O – L – T 90. Would that mean anything to you?"

"A Colt 90 gun maybe?"

"Nancy was a scientist, not a, uh, gun enthusiast. She was shot and killed by someone she knew, so probably happened, uh, fast, really fast. She was a researcher her entire life. I'm pretty certain 90 stands for the year, uh, 1990 and O L T are initials or more likely the name of someone who ran or participated in that 1990 trial." Ragnar motioned the server to let her know that they were ready to order. "I'll have a cappuccino, with brown sugar, please. Gustav?"

"Double espresso, please." Gustav waited for a few moments for the server to leave and then turned to Ragnar. "That's sounds quite far-fetched to me. What would a trial from 1990 have to do with Rebecca? She would've been a teenager then."

"I think something went wrong in that trial, uh, seriously wrong. Just like Joshua Nelson's trial. Nancy was involved in both those trials. I'm willing to bet Dr. Gupta was also involved in that 1990 trial. Whoever did this to both of them probably has Rebecca." Gustav turned white in the face. It actually made sense to him.

"Why didn't Nancy just write the name of the killer before she died? Wouldn't that be easier than this cryptic clue she left?"

"I think she, uh, was trying to tell the whole story with her last words, not just a name or a murder weapon. The shortest possible narration for a long story. O L T 90. She was saying, '*my killer, something O L T, was involved in a clinical trial in 1990 that I worked on and he killed me because of what happened in that trial.*' Doesn't that sound more plausible than '*my killer used a Colt 90 to kill me or my killer wore some god-damned perfume before he killed me*'?"

The server walked over with the coffee and both of them stopped the conversation immediately. They gave her a smile and nod. She gave Ragnar a big smile just as she was leaving. Gustav noticed that and gave Ragnar a strange look.

"Nothing happened. I used to come here, uh, a lot. Flirting, but nothing happened." Ragnar was blushing a bit as he picked up his coffee.

"Are you sure? You banged Rebecca the very night you met her."

"That was different. Don't change the subject. I need to get access to details of that trial."

"And how do you think I could help with that?" Gustav looked confused. His espresso was particularly good. He made a mental note to visit this place again, if just for the espresso.

"I need access to the, uh, old records at Atticus Biopharma. Specifically, I need to, uh, break into Atticus Biopharma's building in Boston and access Nancy's old clinical trial records."

Gustav almost spat out his coffee when he heard what Ragnar was asking. "Are you crazy? Break into Atticus Biopharma? Just like that? I don't even work for Atticus Biopharma. I work for their archenemy, Faust Biopharma. You think I could just waltz into the Atticus Biopharma building, with you, and tap some computers and pull those records? On what is basically a hunch…"

"Basically, yeah." Ragnar sipped his cappuccino. It had been a while since he had one at Cookshop. The cappuccino was exactly as he remembered it to be.

Gustav stared at Ragnar for several moments, trying to make up his mind about whether Ragnar was clinically insane or a stuttering genius. Ragnar kept sipping his coffee, knowing Gustav would see things his way and agree with his reasoning, as crazy as it may be.

Gustav sighed. "Okay, I'll help you but only if I go in there with you. I know someone who might help." Gustav looked at the ceiling and couldn't believe he was actually going to do this. "I'm over. My career is going to be over after this."

"Even if it is, we'll, uh, find Rebecca."

Gustav picked up his small espresso cup and held it up as a toast. "To Rebecca."

Ragnar picked up his cup and toasted Gustav. "To Rebecca."

. . .

NEW YORK CITY POLICE DEPARTMENT, 6TH PRECINCT, WEST VILLAGE

Timothy slammed the phone down on his desk and then just stared at it. He had one hand on his waist. He was trying to think of his next move.

Roberta walked into his office and noticed he looked upset. "Everything okay?"

"I just got off the phone with the District Attorney. Jimmy Ang has a rap sheet the size of the Empire State Building, including several beatings in prison. He continues to have contact with several lieutenants of the gang from behind bars. And this is despite him being in solitary confinement for twenty-three hours a day. The District Attorney has explicitly refused to reduce his sentence by even a day, let alone a few years."

"We knew this was going to be a long shot, Timothy. We'll catch the bastard soon."

"We probably have an eyewitness to the murder here and we can't even speak to her." Timothy picked up the phone again to call Raoul and give him the news.

...

OUTSIDE COOKSHOP, CHELSEA, NEW YORK CITY

Ragnar saw Gustav walking away in the other direction. He told Ragnar that he would connect with his contact at Atticus Biopharma and get in touch with Ragnar. Without wasting any time, Ragnar pulled out his cell phone and called his favorite IT technician, Eddie Juarez at Lincoln Myers.

"Eddie?"

"Ragnarrrrrr, bro! What's up? You comin' to break in again, bro?"

Ragnar chuckled. "No, Eddie. I need your help. I'm going to be, uh, in Boston in a couple of days. I'm, uh, believe it or not, uh, breaking into another building there. I need to access some very old information. I need you to come with me to access the server. I can't trust anyone else with it. I'm begging you, Eddie. Please do this for me."

Eddie gave an innocent laugh. "I'll do it, bro. I'm not doing any John McClane stuff though. And you gotta promise me somethin', bro."

"What is it, Eddie?"

"You gotta come for my cousin Gabriella's birthday party. It's on a weekend in Queens."

"Is it safe? Are there going to be any street gangs there?" Ragnar was pulling Eddie's leg with a long-running joke about Queens being dangerous and unsafe relative to Manhattan.

"Bro, yeah, many street gangs. You've gotta see my prison tats, bro. We'll make you swear allegiance to our nerd gang."

"You got it, Eddie. I'm down for the birthday party if I'm not, uh, behind bars on that day."

"Later, bro. Just text me so I can give my supervisor some notice."

"You got it, Eddie."

Ragnar hung up on Eddie and put his phone back into his pocket. Ragnar was headed to Penn Station to catch a train to Long Island. After a lot of thought, Ragnar decided that he would probably scout out all the possible buildings that Rebecca could be in. He figured his time was best spent trying to find her directly. Maybe he would get lucky and find her before he needed to break into Atticus Biopharma. Maybe, just maybe.

■ ■ ■

JULIA'S APARTMENT, 15 CENTRAL PARK WEST, NEW YORK CITY

Raoul was sitting opposite Julia in her apartment. Christy was also there sitting with a laptop that was logged into the Atticus Biopharma server.

Raoul spoke first. "Christy and I went through Nancy's internet browsing history on her work computer from here. The thing that stood out was that she was going through private investigator websites shortly after Rebecca disappeared. I'm willing to bet she hired one. If I can get access to her bank and phone records, I could track down the specific one she hired and get the scoop on why she needed a PI."

"Are there many names on the list?" Julia looked visibly upset now.

Raoul spoke as he pointed to the screen in front of Christy. "She went through a few websites which had long lists but then she looked up eight or nine names in detail. She probably called each of them. Unless I know which one it was, it may be difficult to call them and have the one she used confess to having been hired by her."

Julia rubbed her face. None of this made any sense. Word of Nancy's death had gotten out and Atticus Biopharma put out a statement about her untimely death. Atticus Biopharma stock had fallen again but Julia appeared unfazed by that. Her legacy was crumbling before her eyes. Her working partner, Nancy, was murdered. Her research collaborator, Dr. Gupta, was murdered in a gruesome manner. Her most promising researcher, Rebecca, was kidnapped and missing for almost two weeks now.

"I'm next, aren't I, Raoul?"

"If it's a vendetta, I would agree with you Julia. I think both you and Christy are at risk. Both of you need to hire more security for your protection. Nancy knew her murderer. How fucked up is that?"

Christy looked visibly shaken at the suggestion of her being at risk. "You don't say, I could be at risk here?"

"Christy, I would not underestimate what's going on in the killer's head. You need to be really careful. You worked closely with Rebecca."

Julia shook her head in agreement in Christy's direction. "Christy, you need to be careful. I've lost Rebecca. I've lost Steve and now Nancy. I don't want to lose you." Julia then looked at Raoul to give him the update. "That cop, Roberta, came over last night. I had to hand over my pistols and a disk with data on a sick child we tried treating unsuccessfully. I'm wondering what that would have anything to do with Nancy's death. But then again, Dr. Gupta and Rebecca were both involved in the treatment of that boy. And so was I." She turned to Christy. "So were you Christy. Weren't you there when Joshua was treated?"

Christy had a semi-guilty look on her face. Raoul sensed that she was still not over the collective guilt of Joshua's death. She spoke in a subdued tone. "Yeah, I was there. I worked with Rebecca on the T cell treatment that we administered to him. We have all the data from her treatment, right up to his...uh..."

"Can I get a copy of that disk as well?" Raoul's sixth sense told him this was something that was crucial to this case.

"Of course. I'll have Christy get another copy for you today. Keep me posted on what you find out about the private investigator that Nancy hired." Julia walked over to the balcony still lost in her thoughts about her place in history. They were so close and it felt like everything she worked for turned out to be a sandcastle after all and it was collapsing right before her very eyes.

∎ ∎ ∎

OUTSIDE COOKSHOP, CHELSEA, NEW YORK CITY

Gustav pulled out his cell phone and went through his contacts. He wasn't sure if he even had Christy's number on his phone. It was so long ago. Rebecca, Christy and Gustav had worked together in Dr. Gupta's lab. Christy had worked as a junior cancer researcher with them. The three of them had been through a lot together working in Dr. Gupta's lab. Despite Rebecca and Christy joining Atticus Biopharma and Gustav joining archrival Faust Biopharma, they shared a deep tie that could not be broken despite the different directions life took them.

Gustav has not spoken to Christy since they had all parted ways from Dr. Gupta's lab. Working with Rebecca had given Christy the opportunity to become a part of the small inner circle at Atticus Biopharma. Gustav hoped Christy would help him for old times' sake, for Rebecca's sake.

As he scrolled his cell phone, Gustav found Christy's phone number. He dialed her number and waited for the call to go to voicemail.

"Gustav? Is that you?" Christy sounded extremely surprised. Gustav could sense warmth in her voice and he instantly knew he had made the right move reaching out to her.

"Christy, hey. Yeah, it's me. Long time, no speak." Gustav, Rebecca and Christy had spent many nights in Dr. Gupta's lab, surviving on pizza and fries, working on biological puzzles that would change the world one day.

"It's been a while, Gustav. How are you doing?"

"I'm doing fine, Christy. To tell you the truth, I'm really worried about Rebecca." Gustav was surprised they could have a civil conversation after so long. Their bond had not weathered with time.

"Me too, Gustav. I'm worried like hell about her. I don't know what to think after what happened to Dr. Gupta, Iain and Nancy. I don't know, something tells me she may not even be alive."

"Christy, I have a lead. I need your help finding her."

"Of course, I'll help. What lead do you have, Gustav?" Gustav explained everything about Ragnar, the clue that Nancy left next to her body and Ragnar's interpretation of that clue. Christy listened patiently.

"We need access to the central server at Atticus Biopharma in Boston to get details on that clinical trial from 1990. We need your help getting into the building and a terminal to access the records." Gustav wondered whether Christy would play along. He was asking an awful lot of her.

Christy thought about what Gustav was asking and then finally replied. "Okay, I think it can be done. I need a little time to set this up. The tricky part will be accessing the server. I have access to several levels, but there are areas that I don't have access to. Have you spoken to the police and told them what you just told me?"

"No. They are never going to believe Ragnar. He has one too many strikes against him on this case. Also, I don't think Julia would go for this. What do you think?"

"I don't think so either. She is fiercely protective of everything she's built at Atticus Biopharma. She is not going to tarnish the company with any innuendo of any wrongdoing or anything that went wrong in 1990. That would make everyone question the very foundation of the company. Give me some time and I'll do something."

"That'll be swell Christy. Thanks a lot for your help."

"I'll be in touch Gustav. Please take care and stay safe."

"You too, Christy." As soon as Gustav hung up, he felt he was now officially as crazy as Ragnar was. He thought Ragnar was crazy to even suggest something like this and now, here he was, carrying out the crazy plan that Ragnar was suggesting.

■ ■ ■

SOMEWHERE IN LONG ISLAND, NEW YORK STATE

The first location on Ragnar's list of forty-three buildings, that he had created using the interactive map that Eddie had sent him and that he had whittled down to a manageable number using a mapping software, was an old school building in Long Island. The school building was a large 125-year old brick building with three stories, complete with spires, gargoyles and a pitched slate roof. It looked like the kind of place where Harry Potter and his friends may have studied magic a half of century ago when the school was a thriving military school serving as one of the top prep schools in the country.

The walls of the building inside were etched with names of students from a bygone era. The school closed in the early 1990s and was the subject of several ongoing cases with the town proposing to demolish the building altogether pitched against preservationists who wanted to preserve the building by designating it as a landmark.

Scouting through this large building was going to take several hours. Ragnar pulled his backpack and pulled out a torch and headed towards the entrance. Ragnar knew that if he was caught, he would be charged with trespassing. The building itself could be crumbing due to dilapidated ceiling, stairs and other structures.

In addition to these risks, he had to be careful in case he was in the building where Rebecca was being held. Her kidnapper was equally dangerous, having used biological agents, a knife and a gun to kill. What else could the kidnapper have up his sleeve, he thought? Maybe a bear trap for trespassers? Nothing would surprise him anymore. He had to be extremely careful. He wondered what else he would put on his list and he was surprised that there could be many more – sharp objects, broken glass, falling concrete, holes in the ground, wild animals, snakes, asbestos, territorial homeless people and graffiti artists.

The main entrance of the building was locked with a heavy iron chain. Ragnar walked to the closest window, knocked out the glass with the back of his torch, opened the window and climbed into the building.

Ragnar was carrying several essentials in his backpack including water, a pocket knife, a second torch, extra batteries as well as some cash, just in case he had to buy his way out of trouble with the homeless.

The main lobby of the building looked grand and must've been a grand entrance in its heyday. Ragnar could hear from birds flapping in the enclosed space. There were several holes in the ceiling through which sunlight pored through into the structure. The building smelt like death inside though. Ragnar was sure the building would've been a haven for the homeless at some point. Maybe they were still there, hiding somewhere in the dark in some crevasse or corner.

Ragnar swallowed hard and he figured this was going to take all the courage he could muster. He was going to do a full sweep of this building. And forty-two other buildings like this. He hoped to hit pay dirt before building forty-three. Hopefully, Murphy's Law did not work against him in this case, whereby Rebecca is in the very last building he looks into.

On the list of craziest things he had ever done, this was definitely all the way up there. With that thought in mind, Ragnar proceeded to start his reconnaissance of the building.

CHAPTER 46

DAY 17, SATURDAY
EAST VILLAGE, NEW YORK CITY

For the second day in a row, Ragnar woke up to the ringing of his cell phone. His body hurt in numerous places all over. Ragnar had spent the previous day scouting three buildings in Long Island in his search for Rebecca. After the school, which turned up nothing other than several dead birds, rats and dangerous stairwells, he moved on to an abandoned cake factory and then an old warehouse. There were no signs of Rebecca in any of those buildings.

He did run into a small group of aggressive homeless people in the warehouse. They wanted nothing to do with him poking around there. He had to pay them some money, fifty dollars to be precise, to let him scout the last location properly, though he was pretty certain that the kidnapper would never hold Rebecca in a building that was inhabited by the homeless.

Ragnar looked at his bedside clock and then answered his phone. It was Gustav. "Ragnar, pack your stuff and head to Boston. We're going to work in the Atticus Biopharma building today."

Ragnar immediately jumped up in bed. "How?"

"An old colleague of mine, Christy, works at Atticus Biopharma. She used to work very closely with us in

Dr. Gupta's lab. She joined Atticus Biopharma and was close to Rebecca. She's agreed to help us find the information you need."

Gustav paused for a moment to make sure Ragnar was listening and then he continued explaining the plan. "She had a delegation visiting from the University of Washington in Seattle in a couple of days. They canceled last minute due to some conflicts. You and I are going to pretend we're from the University of Washington and we're going to be led into the building. She's instructing security that we will be there early, as we wanted to get a headstart on the work and meetings at Atticus Biopharma. I'll meet you in Boston and tell you your new name."

"How many people are they expecting? I need one of my IT buddies, uh, to also come today. His name is Eddie. He is great about IT." Ragnar remembered that he had not told Gustav about Eddie when he last met him.

"Dammit Ragnar. Why does he need to be there? You and I will be there. Christy, who's helping us, will be there as well. We don't need anyone else." Gustav sounded irritated at the last minute addition, adding to the complications involved in planning a break-in at such short notice.

"Eddie needs to be there, Gustav. He is a real asset. I can't be confident we'll have looked at the right places on the server unless he's there."

Gustav thought about this development for a few moments and then spoke. "Let me check with Christy and call you back. Don't ever do this again to me, Ragnar. Tell me everything upfront. There's no need to hold back." Gustav hung up the phone.

Ragnar did not trust anyone anymore. There was no way he was going to trust Gustav.

Gustav called back in a few minutes. "We're in luck. There were several people in that team from University of Washington. Eddie can come as well. Please meet me in Boston as soon as possible."

"I'm on my way Gustav."

. . .

ATTICUS BIOPHARMA HEADQUARTERS, CAMBRIDGE, MASSACHUSETTS

The Atticus Biopharma Headquarters is located on a site close to the Charles River. The thirteen-floor glass building was designed by a famous architectural firm based in Los Angeles that had designed several famous glass towers in the Cambridge area, though the Atticus Biopharma Headquarters was certainly their crowning achievement. The building was designed as a vertical city of sorts with individual offices and conference rooms, several public areas and gardens within the building. The building had an open staircase that started in the lobby and proceeded through all the floors. A majority of the building was illuminated naturally through a combination of a skylights, top-lit central atrium and re- directional blinds.

The building had a security desk and turnstiles in the lobby. Christy had briefed Gustav, Ragnar and Eddie on their story. They were researchers from the University of Washington that were in town to jointly review some lab results by comparing it against a similar set of trial results at Atticus Biopharma. Christy had briefed them on what they needed to say in case someone else in the building asked any questions. Christy had added their real names to the roster of attendees yesterday. There was no way they were going to be able to create fake IDs within a short period of time, but their real IDs with Christy's backstory might just work.

Ragnar's body still ached from his exploration in Long Island yesterday. He still had forty buildings left on his list. Ragnar was glad he was in Cambridge today. The thought of venturing out into Long Island made him feel sick.

Gustav was wearing thick black-framed eyeglasses, likely as a partial disguise. Ragnar thought he looked ridiculous but he kept his opinion to himself. Christy escorted the three men to the security desk. A couple of them were carrying sodas in their hand and making casual conversation, acting as if they just had a meal together and were headed back to the building for work.

The employees at Atticus Biopharma were known to be hard workers and it wasn't unusual for people to come in on weekends to work. The security desk quickly verified the IDs against Christy's request in the system and let the group pass through the turnstiles.

"Well, that was easy." Gustav smiled as he looked at Christy.

"Wait till they catch us snooping in the database. They're going to go into lockdown in an instant and I'll be held back for letting this rag tag bunch into the building."

"Who are you calling rag tag? Hopefully not me, right? Maybe Ragnar and Eddie here could pass for rag tag."

"We need to hurry." Ragnar looked visibly nervous and was not amused at Gustav's jokes.

The foursome made their way to an office on the seventh floor. Christy switched on the terminal, logged into the system and stood up. "All yours Eddie. Be quick and don't do anything crazy to get me into trouble. If you find you don't have access to something, don't try to brute force your way into it please. The firewalls and security is state-of-the-art."

"I got it, bro." Eddie smiled and sat down on Christy's chair in front on the terminal and started typing wildly. "State-of-the-art bro. This is awesome. This is even more advanced than what we have at Lincoln Myers." Eddie continued typing.

"Eddie, did you find the trial yet?" Ragnar kept looking over his shoulder at the door of Christy's office.

He feared they would be found any moment and building security would barge into the office.

After over twenty minutes of typing into a Unix window, Eddie turned around. "Can't do it, bro. She does not have access."

"Dammit." Ragnar whispered under his breath.

"We could use a terminal that has master access, even if Christy logs in from there. That could work, bro. I could make that work."

"Master access? Who has master access?" Gustav feared he knew the answer.

"Says Julia Fitzpatrick on the system." Eddie looked at Christy innocently and asked her. "Do you know where her office is?"

Christy was dumbfounded. "No *FUCKING* way. There's no *FUCKING* way we're logging in using Julia's terminal." Christy's emphasis on 'FUCKING' said it all to Gustav and Ragnar, but Eddie didn't seem to get the message.

"Why not? It should be easy. If the office is not locked, we can slip in, download the files and slip out. I can erase all records of the login from your terminal here." Eddie kept looking at everyone's faces from his chair.

"For starters, there is fingerprint biometric recognition required to log into her computer. What if there is something that triggers an alert as soon as you log in as me?" Christy couldn't believe this was even an option.

"Fingerprint is not an issue. If she has even a single print left in her office, I know how to pick it up using scotch tape and create a usable fingerprint using a special glue I have. I'm carrying it all today, bro."

Ragnar just burst out laughing. He had taken Eddie to be a genius hacker, and here he was part IT nerd, part cat burglar capable of fooling biometric sensors.

Gustav looked equally confounded by this conversation. "Where did you find this guy?"

"In the basement where I used to work."

Gustav looked at Christy. "Christy, we have to take a chance. We're not going to find Rebecca if we don't."

"I'm royally screwed if we're caught, you know that right?" Christy wanted to call it a day. She had tried and given it a good shot.

"I'll get Matheus to hire you at Faust Biopharma, no questions asked. You have my word." Gustav knew Matheus would snap her up in a second.

Ragnar started to doubt Gustav intentions when he mentioned Matheus. He wondered if Gustav was here really to help Rebecca or for more nefarious reasons, including help bringing down Atticus Biopharma in case someone there was involved in the crimes. Ragnar decided to focus on the task at hand. They had come too far to turn back.

"We need to do this for Rebecca. We all owe her. We need to find her. Julia will understand." Ragnar made his most touching appeal to Christy.

"Time is running out Christy. Are we doing this or not?" Gustav was getting impatient.

"Okay, okay. Let's go to Julia's office. She never locks her office. Eddie, are you sure you can lift a fingerprint and bypass the biometric security?"

Eddie did not reply. He just gave her his widest smile and nodded his head.

"Julia's office is on the thirteenth floor. We'll be on the security footage. As long as we don't trigger the systems logging in, we should be fine. Come with me."

The three men followed Christy to the thirteenth floor. The thirteenth floor of the Atticus Biopharma building was where all the executive offices were. The walls were decorated with expensive paintings. There were several statues among the artwork as well. This was clearly the money floor, Ragnar thought. He recognized a Lichtenstein, a Pollock, a Warhol and a Kahlo painting. There were several others that he could not identify but figured they were expensive paintings as well. Julia certainly had good taste in art, he thought.

The four figures made their way to Julia's office. Christy quickly ushered them all inside and closed the door behind them. Julia's office was tastefully decorated. There was a seating area within the office complete with a sofa, a coffee table and some cushy leather chairs. Julia's desk at the other end of the office had three computer screens and a separate Bloomberg terminal.

Ragnar noticed a small biometric scanner on Julia's desk. "Is that the fingerprint biometric device?" Christy nodded in reply. "Okay Eddie, get to work."

"I got this, bro." Eddie was smiling. He removed a small toolkit from the bag he was carrying. He started inspecting various surfaces in the office for fingerprints using a brush and a magnifying glass. Eddie finally got to a bright yellow stainless steel Klean Kanteen water bottle on Julia's desk. He inspected the bottle with his magnifying glass. "This will work, bro. I got it." Eddie was smiling again.

Eddie removed a wide scotch tape from his bag and carefully pulled some prints from the side of the bottle. Next, he used a wide steel ring and wrapped the scotch tape around it carefully so that Julia's fingerprint was in the hollow part of the ring. Eddie removed a glue bottle from his bag and poured some glue into the hollow of the ring.

"We need to wait for a few minutes for the glue to dry and pick up the finger print." Eddie looked at the others and smiled. Ragnar was glad he got Eddie today. Gustav wondered whether this was going to really work. He had never seen anything like this. Christy looked visibly nervous but surprising well composed given the circumstances.

After a few minutes, Eddie pulled out the dried glue 'fingerprint' from the steel ring. "I'm ready." He walked over to the desk, used the fingerprint to activate the terminal and logged in as Christy. The system immediately provided him with access. "See, easy peasy, bro." Gustav wondered how many times Eddie had done something like this before.

Eddie started typing furiously and kept at it for several minutes. His smile disappeared and he looked serious. Ragnar had almost never seen Eddie without a smile. He knew what this meant. Eddie kept typing away and then all of a sudden he stopped.

"It's not there. There's no trial in 1990 with an O – L – T, T – L – O or any such combination. There weren't that many trials in the system. I ran the queries for a few years before 1990 and after as well. Nothing there. Sorry bro. I know this sucks." Eddie looked up at Ragnar.

Ragnar was shell-shocked. How could he have been so wrong, he wondered. Gustav was disappointed as well. He had held up hope that Ragnar was somehow right and they would find a clue that could lead to Rebecca.

"We need to leave. Now." Christy signaled that it was time to leave. They had been lucky so far and she did not want to take a chance.

The four of them quickly made their way out of Julia's office and went straight down to the lobby and left the building.

"I'm sorry for the trouble, Christy." Gustav removed his glasses that he had used for the partial disguise.

"No, it's fine. We had to try. Please let me know what you find as you continue to look for Rebecca. I would really like to know and I could help wherever possible. Promise me, Gustav." Christy took Gustav's hand in hers.

"I promise, Christy. We'll keep looking. I'll let you know if we find something or need your help again."

Ragnar was surprisingly silent. Gustav figured he was probably the most disappointed of the four of them since it was his idea to look for a 1990 trial at Atticus Biopharma.

Christy gave Gustav a goodbye hug and they parted ways.

When Ragnar and Eddie were alone by themselves, after Gustav and Christy left, Eddie turned to Ragnar and gave him his trademark smile. "I got you, bro."

"Holy shit, did you actually find something, Eddie?" Ragnar perked up. He was probably right in his hunch after all, he thought.

"You told me not to trust anyone, bro."

"Eddie, you're a genius. What did you find? Did you find the trial? Did you mail it to yourself?"

"No, bro. I did not find the trial."

"I'm confused. So what did you find?"

"Someone deleted the file of that trial yesterday morning. I was able to find out that the file did exist but was deleted. Yesterday morning. No one accesses those old files. It's probably not a coincidence that someone deleted it just when you were looking for it."

"How does that help though, Eddie? We still don't have that file."

"I got that too, bro. See before the records were computerized, all trial records were manually maintained on paper. A trial in 1990 would've had paper records. The records were computerized but the paper records still exist.

And I know where. All the trials from 1988, 1989, 1990 and 1991 are still available. They're in storage in a highly secure warehouse outside Cambridge. Paper records from 1992 onwards are in storage in the basement of the building we just left. All the trials had electronic tags of the original paper records."

"So, we need to go to this warehouse and get the paper records of that trial, correct?"

Eddie had a full-blown smile on his face. "You going to break into a third building this time? You're crazy, bro."

"Can you find out who deleted those files?"

"Can't, bro. I tried that already. Someone used a dormant administrator login to delete those files."

"So it's someone who works there that did it, correct?"

"Could be. Or someone who knows someone who stole a password. You never know. I logged into Julia's terminal using her fingerprint today. What does that tell you, bro? It could be anyone with some sort of access. Any sort of access. Maybe, someone who has a secret backdoor into their system."

Ragnar immediately thought of Matheus and his vendetta against Atticus Biopharma. He could not be sure. There was no way to know for sure. Other than get the file from storage.

"What do you know about that warehouse building, Eddie?"

"Everything, bro. It's a tough one, but not impossible. I have a cousin, who has a friend, whose girlfriend is an expert at these types of break-ins."

"Your cousin's friend's, uh, girlfriend? Are you kidding, Eddie?"

"She is going to be at my cousin Gabriella's birthday party too, bro. You can trust her. I can take care of bypassing the electronic security but she's the best cat burglar there is. She will help you get into the building." Eddie was smiling again. He just wanted Ragnar to say yes.

Ragnar could not believe he was even contemplating doing something like this. But then Eddie turned out to be everything he promised. He had managed to access data bypassing some complex security procedures in the Atticus Biopharma building. Surely Eddie and his cousin's friend's girlfriend had some more tricks up their sleeve. Ragnar figured this was worth a shot.

"Okay, Eddie. I trust you. Uh, let's do this."

"I got to track her down and speak to her first, bro." Eddie was still smiling.

■ ■ ■

JULIA'S APARTMENT, 15 CENTRAL PARK WEST, NEW YORK CITY

Julia's cell phone rang but the caller ID showed up as 'Unknown' on her cell phone. Julia answered the phone anyways.

"Julia?"

"Julia speaking."

"Julia, this is Matheus."

"What do you want, Matheus?"

"I'm sorry to hear about Nancy. I'm sorry for your loss."

Julia knew there was more. She had known Matheus for a long time and he was the most opportunistic person she had ever met. "Thank you, Matheus. Was that all you called about?"

"Julia, you know me well. In fact, you know me too well. You are I are two sides of the same coin. I have a compelling proposal that may interest you." Matheus had rehearsed his pitch numerous times before he called Julia.

"I'm listening."

"We should combine Atticus Biopharma and Faust Biopharma. Merge the two companies together. We would create a behemoth and you and I can run the combined company together. You need a seasoned leader after Nancy's loss. I could be that person. You could be the Chairman of the combined company and focus on your vision of curing cancer. I'll take care of the day-to-day headache of running the combined company as the CEO." Matheus knew this was not going to be an easy sell.

"You mean you want to take over my company, Matheus?"

"Julia, your company lost Rebecca and Nancy. Everyone perceives weakness in Atticus Biopharma. Your stock price has taken a heavy beating. There will be an exodus of talented employees from your company. You've built a great company and you've had a great run. Cash in your chips before the tide turns completely against you."

"If I knew any better, I would be asking you where you're holding Rebecca. And why you had Nancy killed." Julia decided she no longer needed to play around and just be direct with Matheus.

"I had nothing to do with either of those, Julia. That's a baseless accusation."

"Next you're going to tell me you had nothing to do with Iain stealing our research from Rebecca's laptop."

"Julia, just think about it, please. We've been so successful despite each other. Imagine how strong the combined company will be with both of us working together."

"Fuck off, Matheus. Go fuck yourself." Julia hung up on Matheus and threw her cell phone across the room.

CHAPTER 47

DAY 18, SUNDAY
NEWTON, MASSACHUSETTS

It was late evening and the sun had finally set. Ragnar, Eddie and Adrianna, Eddie's cousin's friend's girlfriend, were sitting in a van close to the document storage facility in Newton that housed the old documents from Atticus Biopharma.

Adrianna, who stood all of five feet in height and weighed probably a hundred pounds, was an extremely promising gymnast in high school until an accident on the pommel horse. She tore her anterior cruciate ligament, or ACL, in her knee, which ended what could've been an Olympic level gymnast. Adrianna's father passed away a few months later. In a bid to support her mother and siblings, after her knee had healed completely, Adrianna used her gymnastic skills as a cat burglar, something that she found out she was very good at, after all.

With her small frame and agility, Adrianna was able to scale the side of buildings and squeeze into narrow vents to get in and out of buildings. To her credit, she had never been caught, not just because of her ability to break into buildings, apartments and mansions, but also because of her style. She never stole large amounts of money or valuables and always cashed her loot quickly with only one person whom she trusted.

Adrianna had grown up in the same neighborhood as Eddie and knew him through her boyfriend. When Eddie called and explained the situation, she decided it was a worthy cause and agreed to help.

"Okay, I've re-routed the security camera to my laptop and I will disable the alarms once both of you start getting into the building. I'll wait outside for you in the van." Eddie was the resident IT hacker cum getaway driver today. "Adrianna will get into the building through the small window on the side and open one of the side doors for you to get in, Ragnar. All the best."

"You bet." Ragnar pulled down the black ski mask and followed Adrianna as she stepped off the van and made a sprint for the side of the warehouse building.

Within minutes, Adrianna had scaled the wall on the building making her way to the small circular window. She broke the glass using her elbow and in a swift gymnast-like move disappeared into the building. Ragnar heard a click on the door he was standing next to and it opened up to reveal Adrianna.

"Come on. We need to be quick."

Adrianna and Ragnar turned on their torches and quickly made their way to the temperature-controlled room that housed the documents. Eddie had unlocked all the doors electronically from outside by hard wiring into the system.

Adrianna and Ragnar opened the door gently to make sure no alarms went off. Ragnar was finding it hard to breathe in the mask. That combined with the darkness and the fact that he was illegally inside a building stoked his anxiety level. His breathing elevated and he started hyperventilating.

Adrianna turned around, held Ragnar's shoulders and quickly made him sit down. She removed his mask. "Breathe. Calmly. Breathe. Long deep breaths."

Ragnar opened his mouth and took in several deep breaths. "I'm alright."

"Are you sure?"

"Yeah, let's go."

Ragnar passed a long line of shelves that were stacked with boxes. The files were arranged by year. Ragnar made his way to the shelf with all the 1990 boxes. There were only four of them. Ragnar pulled the boxes to the floor, held the torch light in his mouth and quickly shuffled through the documents in each of the boxes. Each box housed all the documents of a human clinical trial and included lists of the patients taking part in the trials, their address and other personal details, trial protocol, data readouts and a summary paper describing the trial results. In the third box, Ragnar found a list of patients which included Isabella Holt. Isabella was thirty-two years old and suffered from breast cancer. She had been admitted into the trial for an experimental drug to treat her cancer. Isabella had died during the course of the trial. The therapy did not work for her. Her cancer continued to progress and she had died as a result.

"Gotcha." Ragnar muttered and put all the documents from that box into his backpack. He made a thumbs-up sign to Adrianna.

Within the next five minutes, Ragnar, Adrianna and Eddie were in the van on their back to a motel in Worcester.

. . .

MOTEL CLOSE TO I-95 SOUTH, WORCESTER, MASSACHUSETTS

Ragnar was up till late with Eddie and Adrianna reading through the documents. The trial in which Isabella Holt died was run by three investigators, Dr. Steven Gupta, Julia Fitzpatrick and Nancy Mulligan. No surprises there, Ragnar thought.

Isabella Holt was one of twenty-three cancer patients recruited into the trial. Based on what little Ragnar could decipher, Isabella was the sickest of the patients admitted with the most advanced cancer among the cohort. It would've hardly been surprising then that she died during the trial.

How is Isabella Holt connected to Nancy's death? And to the deaths of Dr. Gupta and Iain? What about Rebecca? She was probably a young girl then. What does she have to do with this trial? Who is Isabella Holt?

Ragnar explained everything that he read about Isabella Holt to Eddie and Adrianna. "I can Google through whatever I can but need PatRec to make sense of the connections here, Eddie. What do you think? You open for another break-in?"

Eddie was smiling his usual 100-watt smile. "You underestimate me, bro!"

This time Ragnar spotted clear mischief in his smile. "Eddie, what did you do?"

"I installed the software on the computer I asked you to access the last time you were there at Lincoln Myers. I've created a backdoor into her desktop computer. I can remotely access in my office computer from here, then access the backdoor into that other computer and access PatRec." Eddie quickly pulled out his laptop and started it up.

"Jesus, Eddie. You're a genius. Fire it up, Eddie.

Let's do this."

"The results are not going to be done tonight though, bro. They should be done by tomorrow." Eddie typed furiously, pulled up a query window and handed his laptop to Ragnar. Ragnar entered several pieces of information into the PatRec window.

Primary Searches:

Isabella Holt

Secondary Searches:
Nancy Mulligan
Dr. Steven Gupta
Julia Fitzpatrick
Atticus Biopharma
Rebecca Chase
Joshua Nelson
Margaret Nelson
David Nelson

Ragnar selected several public and private databases to query this information. He handed the laptop back to Eddie. He was glad he did not have to break into another building for this.

CHAPTER 48

DAY 19, MONDAY
NEW YORK CITY

Raoul was on a call with Isaiah Walker, a private investigator based in Harlem. Raoul had spent the last twenty-four hours tracking him. With Julia's help, he was able to retrieve Nancy's credit card information using the passwords he found on her laptop. Nancy had made some minor store purchases and ordered Ubers to drop her and pick her up a couple of times from Isaiah's office in Harlem.

With some help from his friends in the NYPD, Raoul also managed to get some information that he could use as leverage.

"Isaiah, I know Nancy hired you for something. Like I told you, I need to know what it was that you were looking for and what you found."

"I already called Nancy and told her what I found. I can't share any of that with you."

"Isaiah, when did you speak to Nancy? Nancy is dead, murdered last week on Thursday."

"What? She's dead? How? I, I, I think I spoke to her on Thursday last week, gave her a call and told her what I had found."

"Isaiah, whatever it is that you told her got her killed. I need to know what you told her and I need a copy of your report and findings as well."

"I can't. I have a business to run. My reputation is everything. If people see me as someone they cannot trust..."

"Isaiah, I know about your sister. I know that she's struggling from addiction, that she's living with you and that you are trying to help her get straight. I have a photograph of her picking up some coke yesterday evening. I can go to the cops with this and this will be her third offense. What do you say?"

Isaiah was silent for a minute. "Did you say Nancy is dead?"

"She is." Raoul had known that Isaiah had paid for his sister's legal defense and bailed her out several times. He knew this would work.

"I want you to trade the picture for the report. How do I know that's the only copy?"

"I don't want to get your sister or you into trouble. I don't care about that, unless you make me care about it. All I need is the report. I promise you I'll give you the picture. Now tell me what you told Nancy."

"No, we're trading the report and the information for the picture. I'm not telling you anything till I see and get the picture. Meet me today evening in Central Park. Deal?"

"Deal."

Raoul wrote down the address and time that Isaiah suggested for that evening.

I've got you. I've got you, you crazy murderer. You're not getting away with this. Not this time.

Raoul picked up the cell phone to give Julia an update.

■ ■ ■

UNDISCLOSED LOCATION, CHINATOWN, NEW YORK CITY

Ning was pacing around in her small apartment. She was taken to meet Grandma Ang last week. Ning had told Grandma Ang and her young caretaker everything about what she had seen when Iain was murdered.

Ning recalled everything that had happened and relayed it in detail to Grandma Ang. Ning had met Iain for the first time the day he was murdered. Ning was asked to describe everything in graphic detail including the foreplay with Iain and how she stripped him naked, tied him up to the bed and blindfolded him. Ning was then pleasuring Iain's manhood with her mouth when she saw a figure standing in the far corner of the room. The figure was wearing a sweatshirt with a hood covering the head completely. The figure was also wearing a skull face mask so only the eyes were really visible to Ning.

The figure was holding a large knife in one hand and held up the index finger of the other hand gesturing Ning to keep quiet and threatening her with the knife using hand gestures. The figure then pointed to door gesturing Ning to leave the room immediately.

Iain, who was tied to the bed and blindfolded, was completely oblivious to the sinister presence in the room. Ning quickly stood up from between Iain's legs and walked out to the room, leaving Iain alone with the figure. But what the figure did not realize was that Ning went into a room next door, which was sometimes used by the pimps to keep an eye on the prostitutes. There was a hole in the wall that was somewhat hidden by what looked like a painting on the other side of the wall, in the room in which Iain was currently in. Ning stood next to the peephole and peered in. The figure made its way and sat on Iain's chest. Iain was probably a bit confused with the weight of the person sitting on him but assumed it was Ning and continued to moan, unaware of the danger he was in. His mouth was tied tightly. The figure raised the knife his above the head and plunged it into his chest.

Iain's whole body jerked up in a sharp reaction to the stabbing and then gently lowered until it was limp.

The figure got off Iain's chest. And then it had happened. The figure pulled aside the mask to wipe Iain's blood that had squirted out of his chest on the killer's face. In that moment, Ning saw the face and it was seared into her memory. She vowed never to forget that face until she died.

Ning was here in another apartment where she was moved after the murder. There was a bodyguard placed outside the door to make sure she did not leave. The windows in the apartment all had iron bars. The apartment was effectively a temporary prison, she thought.

Today was different though. Ning had finally decided that she had had enough of this modern day slavery. She was going to break free today. Ning had pulled out the wooden leg of the sofa in the bedroom. She held it in her hand and inspected the thickness. Used properly, the leg could be used as a deadly club.

Ning hid the club in the bathroom and went to the main door of the apartment. She knocked on the door until the bodyguard opened it from outside. They spoke to each other in their native Mandarin.

"What is it Ning? Are you hungry?"

"There's a half-dead rat in the shower. It's still moving, I think. I'm really scared. Can you please kill it and throw it away?"

The bodyguard sighed and came inside. He walked towards the bathroom and Ning followed behind him. The shower curtain was drawn.

"It's behind the curtain. It's really big."

As the bodyguard turned around and reached for the shower curtain, Ning picked up the club, held it with both hands, aimed for his head and swung it extremely hard.

She heard a cracking sound and the bodyguard just collapsed where he was standing. She hoped the man was still alive. She dropped the club and darted for the door.

Within minutes, Ning was downstairs and in a very busy street in Chinatown. She walked really quickly making her way out of the crowd. She saw an NYPD patrol car at the corner. She quickly made her way to the car and spoke to the cop in the car.

"Please help. I need help. I saw Chinatown murder. I witness murder. Please help me. Take me to station. They follow. Please let me in."

"Who is following you?"

"Flying Dragon gang. Please, I need to hide."

The cop looked at her and decided that he could trust her. No one uttered the name of the gang in broad daylight in Chinatown to a cop. There would be serious consequences.

"Hop in the back, lady." He let her into the patrol car and quickly drove off.

• • •

JULIA'S APARTMENT, 15 CENTRAL PARK WEST, NEW YORK CITY

Julia's cell phone was ringing and the caller ID showed up as 'Unknown' again. Julia imagined this was Matheus calling to urge her again about merging their companies.

"Julia here."

A deeply disguised and muffled voice spoke to her at the other end. The person at the other end of the line was using some sort of software to disguise their original voice. "Julia, I have Rebecca."

Julia held her breath and tried to be calm. "I could choose to believe you but I need to speak to her first to make sure she's alive and alright."

After a pause of fifteen seconds, Julia heard a weak sounding voice at the other end of the line, which she instantly recognized. "Julia, it's me."

"Rebecca dear, are you alright?"

"You could say that."

With that the kidnapper was back on the call with Julia. "Do you believe me now, Julia?"

"What do you want?"

"I want you to bring three million dollars in cash. I'll give you an address. Be there today evening at six sharp. Don't bring anyone. Don't call anyone. Don't speak to anyone. If I suspect anything at all, Rebecca dies a horrible, horrible death. And then I will find you and kill you too."

"So this was all about a few million dollars? You killed all these people, took Rebecca, all for a few million?"

The kidnapper ignored Julia's question. "Write down the address…"

Julia scribbled the address down and the kidnapper hung up the phone. The money would be no problem. Julia had a safe in the apartment with over five million dollars of cash. This did not sound right. Julia knew this was about her. Today would probably be her last day on earth. She was ready for it. She had lived a fruitful life and would leave behind a lasting legacy. If she could secure Rebecca's safe release, her legacy would be secure, Rebecca would make sure of it.

Julia went to her bedroom and opened the door of her walk-in closet. She put on the light and walked into the closet. Julia walked to a section where several designer dresses hung from the closet rod. She reached one of her hands behind the dresses and pressed a button. She heard a clicking sound. She pulled the section with the dresses to reveal a large hidden vintage safe behind the shelf.

Julia started turning the knob of the combination lock to her safe and had the safe open in minutes. There were several stacks of cash, bars of gold, jewelry boxes as well as some pouches of loose diamonds inside. Julia grabbed a duffel bag from one of the shelves in the closet and started throwing the bundles of hundred dollar bills in cash into the bag.

CHAPTER 49

DAY 19, MONDAY
EAST VILLAGE, NEW YORK CITY

Ragnar was pacing around his apartment waiting for his phone to ring. He had called Eddie several times during the day to check in on the results from PatRec to see if it was able to identify the connection between Isabella Holt and her clinical trial in 1990, the kidnapping and murders that were taking place now.

Ragnar's cell phone started ringing. Ragnar saw the caller ID. It was Gustav. Ragnar decided he would ignore the call for now. The cell phone stopped ringing but Gustav did not leave a voicemail. Ragnar was not sure who he could trust. Gustav was helpful in breaking into Atticus Biopharma but Ragnar still could not get himself to trust him.

Ragnar pulled his top off and started doing pull-ups on his pull-up bar out of frustration. He kept doing pull-ups without stopping. His arms started to hurt sharply but Ragnar continued to push himself, doing more reps than he typically did. On his last rep, he let out a scream and let the bar go and let himself fall to his feet. The wait was killing Ragnar.

Ragnar decided a cup of coffee was in order. He poured himself some water and added a couple of spoons of instant coffee and let it heat in the microwave for a full sixty seconds. He pulled the mug out, opened the refrigerator and added several cubes of ice into his coffee. Ragnar started sipping his 'cold coffee.'

• • •

CENTRAL PARK, NEW YORK CITY

Raoul was sitting on a bench in Central Park where Isaiah had asked him to meet. He held a paper folder with the pictures of Isaiah's sister. Raoul saw Isaiah walking up to him. He recognized him from his picture on the website.

"Raoul?"

"Yes. Isaiah?"

"Yes. I have what you want. Did you get the pictures I asked you for?"

"I have them here." Raoul handed the folder over to Isaiah. "Can I get the investigation that you did for Nancy?"

Isaiah took the folder from Raoul and looked at all the pictures. The pictures were clearly incriminating and would not bode well for his sister, a recovering addict. He sat down next to Raoul. "How do I know you don't have another copy of these pictures?"

"You don't. As long as you hand over everything you found out for Nancy, you have nothing to worry about. You have my word Isaiah."

Isaiah took a deep breath. "So you said Nancy died because of this?"

"I believe so."

"It's all here in the folder. Let me tell you what I found..."

. . .

NEW YORK CITY POLICE DEPARTMENT, 6TH PRECINCT, WEST VILLAGE

Timothy and Roberta were sitting opposite Ning. Ning had run them through how she got to Los Angeles from China and then to Chinatown in New York City. She described her working conditions in the brothel where the NYPD had found Iain's body. Her English was surprisingly good for someone who never spoke a word of English for a majority of their life.

Timothy and Roberta felt like they finally had a break in the case. There was no need to negotiate with Grandma Ang or Cynthia Ang for that matter. Here, in front of them, living and breathing, was an eyewitness in the case who had witnessed a murder and could identify the murderer.

Just then a detective poked his head into the room and made a gesture for Roberta. Roberta stood up and walked to him.

"What is it?"

"Messenger parcel for you. I dropped it on your desk. It was sent by Matheus Faust."

Roberta remembered that Matheus had agreed to share the pictures of Iain with other women that he had used to blackmail him. "Okay, I'll go through those once I'm done here."

She walked back and sat down at the table. "Ning, now please tell us about the day Iain was murdered. Please tell us everything. We need to know everything you know."

Ning told them about her encounter with Iain in the room. She told them how the killer ushered her out. She told them about how she spied on the murder and witnessed the murder and even got a glimpse of the killer's face.

"What did he look like?" Timothy jumped in.

Ning described the killer's face. Timothy and Roberta looked at each other. They were confused and couldn't exactly match the description to anyone obvious who was a suspect in the investigation. They wondered whether Ning was mistaken.

"Are you sure, Ning? It was a small peep hole we're presuming, the killer would've been moving and the whole wiping of the face couldn't have taken more than a few seconds."

"I sure. I see clearly. I remember."

"Let's get a police artist to make a sketch." Timothy stood up to leave. Roberta followed him out of the room.

"Make sure there's a detective watching her twenty-four hours. She is in danger from the Flying Dragons gang." Roberta nodded and walked to her desk to retrieve Matheus' parcel.

Roberta sat down at her desk and picked up the parcel addressed to her. She took an envelope opener and tore open the parcel. The contents of the parcel included a folder with several large photographs. There were color pictures of Iain kissing women, holding hands and often heading into seedy hotels. There were some pictures of Iain in compromising positions taken through a window opposite one of his hotel rooms. Roberta saw one picture that had a person who looked exactly like the one Ning had just described.

Roberta turned the picture over. All the pictures had names of the people in the pictures scribbled at the back with a pencil. This picture was no exception. Roberta read the name at the back and felt like she was hit by a speeding train.

She picked up the picture and ran towards the room that Ning was sitting in.

■ ■ ■

EAST VILLAGE, NEW YORK CITY

Ragnar's cell phone rang loud and he jumped and picked it up. "Eddie, is it done?"

"Yeah, bro. I'm sending you the results now. You're not going to be believe it."

"Eddie, what is it?"

"Read it, bro."

. . .

CENTRAL PARK, NEW YORK CITY

Isaiah started relaying his side of the story to Raoul. "Nancy contacted me and asked me to run background checks on two names. One of them turned out to be nothing. But the other one had an interesting and secretive background. This goes back to 1990 when Nancy and her colleagues were working on a clinical trial together. They recruited a thirty-two year old woman, Isabella Holt, a divorcee who had breast cancer into a clinical trial for a new drug. Isabella was dying and the clinical trial was her only hope. She was put on a regimen of pretty strong drugs. It looked like the cancer was receding but her body could not tolerate the drug itself and her organs failed. She died during the trial.

"Isabella had a child who was only nine years old then. The child lived with the grandparents after Isabella died. Several years later, her child joined Harvard Medical School to study medicine. During her last year of medical school, her child started using her mother's maiden last name...

■ ■ ■

EAST VILLAGE, NEW YORK CITY

Ragnar was reading the results from PatRec in his email and talking to himself as he was piecing together all the facts.

"...and as a result, Isabella's daughter went from Christy Holt to Christy Cassidy which became effective shortly before she graduated, so it went largely unnoticed among her peers. She emerged with a different persona and after graduation Christy Cassidy joined the lab of Dr. Steven Gupta in Cambridge, one of the researchers on the 1990 clinical trial during which her mother died. Christy likely blamed Dr. Gupta, Nancy and Julia for her mother's death..."

■ ■ ■

NEW YORK CITY POLICE DEPARTMENT, 6TH PRECINCT, WEST VILLAGE

Roberta pushed open the door to the room where Ning was sitting and placed the photograph in front of her. "Is this her? Is this the killer, the one in this picture kissing Iain?"

Ning went white in the face and looked up. "Yes. She killed Iain. She stabbed him."

Roberta turned the picture over again to re-read the name.

Christy Cassidy, Atticus Biopharma

. . .

EAST VILLAGE, NEW YORK CITY

Ragnar rapidly dialed Eddie's number. "Eddie, what the fuck? It's Christy! She's the one, Eddie."

"I know, bro. I would've never guessed. She's something, huh?"

"Eddie, we need to find where Christy is, where she is holding Rebecca right now." Ragnar was pacing nervously around his apartment as he spoke.

"I got you, bro."

Ragnar was confused but could picture the grin on Eddie's face. As always, he had something up his sleeve. "What do you have, Eddie?"

"I dropped a program and created a backdoor to Christy's computer when we were at Atticus Biopharma. I did that for Julia's computer as well, just in case we ever needed to access them again."

"Eddie, you're a genius. Can you access her computer and see if you can find anything that points to where she may be holding Rebecca? See what you can find."

"On it, bro. Speak to you soon."

"Eddie, one more thing. I'm going to start heading to Long Island right now. Call me on my cell if you find anything as soon as you do."

"Okay, bro. I'll call you."

. . .

CENTRAL PARK, NEW YORK CITY

Raoul dialed Julia's number as she ran towards the street. Julia's cell kept ringing eventually transferring Raoul to her voicemail. "Julia, this is Raoul here. Listen, I found out who's behind all of this. It's Christy, Christy Cassidy. You need to be careful. I will explain everything when we meet but it is really important that you make no contact with Christy. Do not, I repeat, do not let her anywhere close to you. She is extremely dangerous. Please call me back as soon as you hear this message."

Raoul ran out of Central Park and across Fifth Avenue despite the oncoming traffic that made its way down Fifth Avenue as he ran towards his parked car.

. . .

LONG ISLAND

Julia checked the address on her GPS and slowly drove her car through the rusted metal gates into the compound of an abandoned factory building. The factory was a large red brick building. Several of the windows were broken and the elements had wreaked havoc with the structure. The building was adorned with colorful graffiti of all sorts. There was a green skull monster with red eyes, several cartoonish figures as well as letters that did not mean much to Julia.

Julia glanced at her cell phone and noticed that Raoul had called and left a voicemail for her. Just as Julia picked up her cell phone to check her voicemail, her cell phone rang with an incoming call from an 'Unknown' number. She knew this was the kidnapper again.

A deep baritone and muffled voice spoke to her from the other end of the line. "Julia, get out of the car along with the money. There is a van parked several yards away to your left. Walk to the van and open the back door. Drop the money at the back. Don't do anything stupid. I can see your every move from here."

Julia looked around but did not see anyone close by. But then again there were many places the kidnapper could be hiding and keeping an eye on her. She figured the kidnapper was hiding somewhere in the factory building and watching her every move. "Where is Rebecca, you sick freak?" Julia was visibly upset and wanted this whole charade to be over soon.

"Not so fast, Julia. I'll take you to her but you need to follow my instructions first."

Julia was seething but knew she had to do whatever it took to get Rebecca back. She started walking towards the van. "Okay, you'll get your money now. What then?"

"There's a blindfold and a pair of handcuffs in the back as well. Get into the back of the van with the money, cuff your hands and put on the blindfold. No funny business, Julia. I promise you'll be with Rebecca soon. I'll take you to her."

"This doesn't sound like a fair exchange. What if I just turnaround and walk away? I don't see how you're going to keep your word after you have the money and I don't have Rebecca."

"Do that, but know this. You're going to get bits and pieces of her mailed to you every day for the next few months to come. And I promise you she will be alive for that entire time, as I pull pieces of her apart to send it to you. How does that sound, Julia?"

"You sick fuck."

"Get into the van and I'll take you to her. You can see her with your own eyes and I'll bring you both back here. You can take her back with you after that. I just need to know that no one followed you here when we leave in that van. If someone is following us, that'll be it. I'll shoot you and then I'll kill Rebecca as well. Do you understand why I need you to come with me?"

"If anything happens to me or Rebecca, you're going to pay dearly, you understand that?"

"Don't worry about me, Julia. Drop your cell phone outside the van when you get in the back. Don't want your cell phone being tracked to where I'm taking you."

Julia knew the kidnapper was bluffing to entrap her and make her a part of whatever sick fantasies that they had. She pegged her chances of making out of this trap alive at fifty-fifty at best. Still, she figured this was her best chance to securing Rebecca's release.

Julia stopped when she got to the back of the van. She ended the call and threw her cell phone gently to the ground so that the kidnapper could see her clearly. She opened the doors at the back of the van and held it wide open. She then gently placed the bag in the van, turned around and got in.

She saw the blindfold and the handcuffs at the back. She picked up the blindfold, placed it on her eyes and tied the back tightly behind her head. The blindfold was a thick black cloth that was fairly wide and covered her eyes quite well. She used her hands to grope for and reach the handcuffs. She picked them up as soon as she felt the cold metal. She fumbled for a second and then slipped them on her wrists one by one and snapped them shut.

Julia felt extremely vulnerable but tried to relax her breathing and took deep breaths as she waited anxiously for the kidnapper's next move. She heard footsteps approaching her. A pair of hands reached for her and checked her blindfold to make sure it was firmly over her eyes. The kidnapper then reached for her handcuffs. In one quick move, the kidnapper unlocked one hand, pulled her hands and cuffed her hands behind her back. The kidnapper then gave Julia one push to throw her into the back of the van.

■ ■ ■

LONG ISLAND

Christy pushed Julia into the van. She planned to reveal herself after she took Julia to the warehouse where she was holding Rebecca.

Christy pulled out the bag of money and shut the door. She picked up Julia's cell phone, switched it off and dropped it on the ground. She then proceeded to pull out a hammer from the backpack she was carrying. She slammed the hammer into the cell phone several times until Julia's phone broke into several pieces.

Satisfied that Julia's phone was destroyed for good, Christy walked to the front of the van, tossed the bag across the seat and got into the driver's side and slammed the door shut. She adjusted her cap under the hood and looked at the rear view mirrors. She started the van and drove out of the parking lot, while constantly checking her rear view mirrors.

After driving around on the side streets for several minutes, Christy was content that no one was following them. She turned the van and started driving in the direction of the warehouse where she was holding Rebecca.

She finally got what she had wanted for a very long time. Julia and Rebecca were hers to do as she pleased.

The void was ecstatic. Her heart pounded wildly and blood rushed into her head as she thought about what she had in store next. The void's fantasies were vivid – she was going to torture Julia as Rebecca watched. The void was getting turned on thinking about it. She would operate on Julia where it would hurt her most. She would heap the ultimate insult on her. First she would amputate both her breasts without anesthesia. Her heart pounded even faster as she thought of what she would do after that...

. . .

FIFTH AVENUE, NEW YORK

Raoul jumped into his car and hit the gas pedal. His car jerked forward as a result of the sudden acceleration. He started driving in the direction of NYPD's 6th precinct.

"Timothy, Raoul here. I know who's behind everything. It's Christy Cassidy. She kidnapped Rebecca. She also murdered Dr. Gupta."

"We know. We just found out as well. We have an eyewitness who saw her murder Iain in Chinatown. We're putting out an APB on her and start a manhunt to bring her in. How did you find out?"

Raoul quickly explained that he tracked down Isaiah who dug into her background and found out about her past and how her mother's death was tied to Julia, Nancy and Dr. Gupta.

Timothy was stunned. "That is absolutely unbelievable. Why don't you bring everything you have to the precinct? We need to find Julia and make sure she's safe."

"That's what I'm calling you about. Julia is not answering her cell phone and I can't seem to get hold of her. I'm worried something bad is about to happen to her. We need to find her as soon as possible."

"I'll get a couple of detectives to track her down. We need to move fast here, Raoul. I don't think we have much time."

"I don't think we do either. I'll meet you at the precinct soon. We need to find Julia and then we need to find Christy. Julia is in grave danger. She is the third person who was involved in the trial in which Christy's mother died. She has to be Christy's next target." Raoul drove through the New York traffic like a NASCAR driver.

Raoul pulled out a rotating red light from next to his seat and put it on the roof of his car. The light had a magnet at the base that affixed itself firmly on the roof. He kept the red light for emergencies like these and had used it only once before. It was, after all, illegal for him to use the red light since he was no longer on the force, but at this moment, all he could think about was tracking Julia and getting her to safety.

Raoul's phone rang. This time it was Timothy calling him back. "Raoul, I just spoke to Julia's housekeeper. She left the house an hour ago. She was alone. She took her car and drove herself to wherever she was going. The housekeeper said Julia was carrying a large black duffel bag."

"Dammit. She's meeting Christy. Can you track her cell phone?"

"We pinged her cell but it looks like it is switched off completely. Or maybe it's damaged. We're going to track down every lead."

"We need to find Julia and Christy fast. I don't think we have much time."

"I know. I need to run. I'll let you know if I hear anything." Timothy hung up the call. Raoul felt a sinking feeling in his stomach. Before Raoul started working on Rebecca's disappearance, his primary job was to protect Julia. And he was failing now. Failing miserably, to say the least, he thought. If only he had gotten this information to Julia a bit earlier, things would've been different. If she died at Christy's hands, Julia's death was going to be on him.

Raoul hit the gas even harder making his way to the precinct.

CHAPTER 50

DAY 19, MONDAY
LONG ISLAND

Ragnar was driving an expensive Lexus making his way through the traffic to the area where Rebecca was most likely being held, based on what his algorithm had told him previously. Ragnar had emailed the list of forty buildings to Eddie before he left his apartment.

His first stop was his neighbor, Mr. Gao. Mr. Gao had previously helped Ragnar when he acted as a translator between Ragnar and the Chinese delivery man who had seen the van across his building in which Rebecca was kidnapped minutes later. Ragnar asked Mr. Gao if he could borrow his car because Ragnar did not own one. He told Mr. Gao it was a matter of life and death and that he was close to finding his friend who was kidnapped.

It turns out, Mr. Gao, who lived a frugal life in the rundown apartment building was actually quite rich. He was retired and wanted a simple life but was indeed relatively well off. Mr. Gao happily gave Ragnar the keys to his new Lexus. "You find her, Ragnar. Whatever it takes."

Ragnar's cell phone rang and it startled him. He had turned the ringer up all the way to the loudest setting on his phone. "Eddie, what did you find?"

"We have a hit, bro. I think I know where Rebecca is being held."

"Shoot Eddie. What did you find?"

Of all the people Ragnar understood how multiple individual pieces of information did not mean much by themselves. But once you start pulling them together, patterns start to emerge. If you are able to discern the patterns, the information starts to make sense. Add additional data and information to those patterns and you start getting even more concrete information from what were disparate pieces of information to begin with.

Eddie was cross-referring everything he could find on Christy against Ragnar's list of forty potential buildings on the list of places where Rebecca may be. And he had finally hit pay dirt, it seemed.

"I was able to access Christy's computer and went through some credit card statements that she had saved. Her credit card statements were pretty clean except for one minor expense that stood out. Christy got an Uber to pick her up from a location in Long Island around four weeks ago. The location the Uber driver picked her up from was 10 minutes from one of the buildings on your list. She probably went there to scout the location and maybe left her car behind. Or maybe a cab dropped her off there. She was careful to some extent. She probably walked away from the location before she ordered the Uber, but I have the list now, so I was able to locate the building nearest to the pick-up location from your list." Eddie was grinning as he spoke to Ragnar.

"How did you find the pick-up location from her credit card statement?" Credit card statements would show the expense for the Uber but would never include the pick-up or the drop-off details. Ragnar wondered how Eddie pieced that together.

"She charged that Uber expense to Atticus Biopharma. Her expense statements and receipts were also saved on her computer. Can you believe that? She inadvertently charged that Uber ride and saved the receipt as a result. She really messed up and we got her bro."

"But what if it's not that building? What if it is another one further away? How can you be sure?"

"Bro!"

"Spit it out, Eddie. What else you got?"

"I looked up the building close to her pick-up location. It's an old warehouse. The owner had put up one of the smaller buildings on the property for rent. He pulled the ad for the rent one day before Christy's Uber ride."

"You're the best, Eddie. You're crazy, but you're good. Give me the address of that warehouse. After we hang up, you should call 911 and ask them to connect you to Detective Timothy Burns. Tell them it's about the Rebecca Chase case. Once they put you through to him, just let him know that we found the building where Rebecca might be held and give him the address as well."

Eddie gave Ragnar the address and he quickly punched that into the GPS of Mr. Gao's car. Ragnar recognized the address. It was among the next four or five buildings that he planned to scout.

"Remember, this is not in the main warehouse. There is a separate shed behind the main warehouse building where she will be. You be careful, bro. I'll ring the cops now. Stay safe."

"I will, Eddie. I will." Ragnar hung up the call and looked at the GPS. Ragnar was barely twenty minutes away from the location now.

...

WAREHOUSE BUILDING 8, LONG ISLAND INDUSTRIAL PARK, LONG ISLAND

The kidnapper had led Julia into a building while she was still blindfolded. Julia did little to protest or resist. Julia knew it would be only a matter of time before they would track this location down. She had made sure of that.

The kidnapper tied her to a metal chair that was bolted into the ground. Both her feet were zip tied to the legs of the chair. The kidnapper undid her handcuffs and zip tied both her hands to each of the arms of the metal chair. Julia, still blindfolded, could hear ragged breathing coming from the other corner of the room and she knew Rebecca was there, breathing and alive.

"You have what you want. You have the money and you have me. Now remove my blindfold and let me see

Rebecca. Let her go now." Julia spoke calmly to the kidnapper.

She felt a hand tug at her blindfold. There was a single naked bulb in an otherwise dark damp room. The bulb was bright and Julia squinted as her eyes adjusted to the light after being blindfolded for so long. As her eyes adjusted to the light, she finally saw the kidnapper's face and a wave of confusion swept through her head. She could not believe what she was seeing.

"Christy? You? What in the… why did… was it… I don't understand. So you took Rebecca? And killed everyone?"

Christy pulled back the hood and removed her cap. She ran her hand through her hair as if to set her hair and make sure it looked fine, somewhat out of habit.

Julia looked across the room. Rebecca was at the other end of the room opposite her. She was tied facing Julia on a similar metal chair that was also bolted to the concrete ground. Rebecca looked physically gaunt and weak but her eyes were alert as she looked at Christy and then Julia. Rebecca was wearing an oversized white t-shirt and her mouth was gagged shut.

Julia noticed a desk in the bare room with a steel tray. Julia recognized the surgical instruments in the tray including a scalpel, forceps, clamps, scissors, spreader and dissecting knives among others. Noticeably absent was any anesthetic equipment.

"Okay, so I'm going to get started on you first, Julia. I hope you ate light before you came here, because what you're going to see is not for the faint-hearted. I am going to perform a double mastectomy on you. I am going to give you just a local anesthetic shot in and around your breasts. Then I'm going to make a surgical incision right here on your right breast and extend the incision around those fake bags you have in your chest. Then I'm going to do the same with your left breast."

Cold shivers ran down Julia's spine as Christy spoke about butchering her breasts in an even tone, as if she were talking about something as banal as cooking pasta or shopping for pantyhose. Rebecca let out a muffled scream.

"Don't worry, Rebecca. You will have a front row view of the entire operation." Christy turned to Julia again. "Once I'm done with your breasts, I'm going to slowly cut you open and pull your stomach and intestines out as you watch. I'm going to keep you alive throughout all of this. How does that sound?" Christy was grinning looking for a reaction and she got more than she hoped for. Julia was quivering with fear, her legs shaking uncontrollably as her mind imagined the horrors that her body was about to experience.

"Shall we get started now?" Christy started walking towards Julia with a marker in her hand. Tears were streaming from Rebecca's eyes.

■ ■ ■

NEW YORK CITY POLICE DEPARTMENT, 6TH PRECINCT, WEST VILLAGE

Timothy had just finished briefing a room full of detectives about the latest developments on the Rebecca Chase disappearance and the murders that followed. He briefed everyone on the prime suspect, Christy Cassidy, and the importance of finding Christy as well as Julia Fitzpatrick, who was likely in custody of Christy by now. It would only be a matter of time before Christy struck again.

As soon as the meeting was over, he saw Raoul running down the hallway towards him. "Anything yet?"

"We've put out an APB and mobilized everyone to track down Christy and Julia."

"I have another way to track Julia." Raoul was still catching his breath but felt like he did not have a moment to lose in the race to track down Julia. "You see, I've been working on her security detail for several years. The car that Julia took today is one that I outfitted with a GPS device that is sync'd to the security programs at Atticus Biopharma. I have access to where that car went. All Julia had to do was use the GPS system and the location would get logged into the Atticus Biopharma security system. That way we can always trace the car or her, if we needed to. Julia knew that and probably used the GPS system, knowing fully well that it would lead us to wherever she went. I called Atticus Biopharma security on my way here and got the address. Her car is still there."

Timothy led Raoul to a workstation where a tech analyst was seated. "Punch this address in, will you?"

At the same time, Roberta came running towards Timothy. "There's a call on your line that got patched through from the 911 system. It's some techie named Eddie who worked with Ragnar. He says he knows where Rebecca is being held."

"Put him through to this desk."

Timothy spoke to Eddie who relayed the address and the background in brief to Timothy. He urged them to meet Ragnar at that address. Timothy assured him that they would follow-up right away and then hung up.

"It's Ragnar again! Ragnar and a friend of his, some techie named Eddie, seem to have tracked down Christy's whereabouts. Unbelievable!" Timothy had a look of sheer disbelief on his face. "Type in this address as well, will you?" Timothy provided the analyst with the address that Eddie gave him.

Raoul looked at the map on the screen. "That's it. This is a few minutes from the address Julia drove to. Christy probably took her to this nearby location. We should go now."

"Roberta, alert everyone in the field. Have them rush to this address right away. I'm leaving now with Raoul. Follow us and meet us there."

"You got it, boss." Roberta sprinted in the other direction to get the word out.

...

WAREHOUSE BUILDING 8, LONG ISLAND INDUSTRIAL PARK, LONG ISLAND

"Once I'm done with you Julia, it's going to be Rebecca's turn." Christy turned towards Rebecca. "Rebecca, do you remember the charity event you hosted at the headquarters, the one that raised money for child victims of landmines?" Rebecca was gagged and could not reply. She had a confused and terrified look on her face. "Well, you are going to experience what it feels like to be one of them. I'm going to amputate your left leg, just above your knee. And then I'm going to remove your right arm, just below the elbow."

Rebecca was now livid and uttering obscenities at Christy from under her gag. Even though the words were muffled, Christy could make out that Rebecca was cursing her. But she did not seem to care much. "I specially picked out a bone saw just for you, Rebecca." Christy was grinning as she pointed at the gleaming saw on the table with all the other surgical instruments.

Julia's legs were still shaking uncontrollably but she felt a surge of determination run through her. "Why are you doing all this? Don't you want to tell us? You can mutilate me and then kill me, but for all I know, you're just some crazy nut job who lost it and killed me. That's going to be my last thought. Don't you want to tell me why I deserve this, why I deserve to die this cruel, horrible death?"

Christy's eyes widened as put down the syringe she was holding in her hand. "Of course. The why of all of this. Of course…"

. . .

Sometimes I wondered how my life would've turned out if I never knew. Wondered how it would have panned out if grandma had never told me about my mother.

I was raised by my grandma. My father died when I was just two years old. I was just nine years old when my mother died from an illness, the ultimate and ruthless killer – cancer.

I have no memories of my father but I took the death of my mother really hard. I still remember the soft touch of her skin, the smell of her perfume on her neck and her angelic voice. Her death was a devastating blow and I took it really hard. At first, I started acting out in school, talking back to my teacher, getting into fights and once was even caught trying to set a classroom on fire. My world felt empty without my parents, an emptiness that only grew as the years passed. Inside me grew a deep and dark void that nothing could fill.

I lived my teenage years recklessly, getting into trouble at every turn, though I never cared much for the consequences. It was the thrill that I chased. I was angry at the world but didn't know who to direct it at so I directed it at the world.

I had no real friends. All the other girls avoided me. But the boys, they were a different story altogether. They could not avoid an angry rebellious girl. They were attracted to me like moths to a fire. And I reveled in the short-lived attention of it all. I slept with them. Every last one of them. Fucked them just to fill the emptiness inside me, even if it was just for a few fleeting moments. And then the rage would come back and the feeling of being vulnerable and abused.

I was in high school when my grandma was on her deathbed. She was worried about me her entire life and now she was going to leave me forever. She cried as she was breathing her last breaths. She told me that my mother had died fighting for her life. She did not go down without a fight. She found her way into a clinical trial for an experimental cancer drug and placed her life in the hands of the doctors running the trial.

I understood very little about clinical trials then. After my grandma died, I found my mother's medical records and a bunch of documents about her enrollment in the trial. For several years, I did not think much about it. For a few years after grandma's death, I channeled my rage and anger into my studies and got into medical school.

I don't know why I did that. Maybe it was my destiny. Maybe deep down inside I felt I could make a difference. That I could maybe save a life to redeem my troubled soul.

It was during that time that I chanced upon my mother's medical records again.

I finally understood what my mother was going through. She was suffering from breast cancer that could've been fought with conventional chemotherapy. She had a real chance of beating her cancer. But instead, she was recommended for a clinical trial for an experimental cancer drug, one that was being developed by Dr. James Fitzpatrick, Dr. Nancy Mulligan and Dr. Steven Gupta. They somehow convinced my mother to join the trial. In those days, they were facing difficulties in finding patients to enroll in their trial. They had somehow convinced my mother to become their sacrificial lamb.

My mother's cancer progressed and gathered much more momentum. The experimental drug was clearly not working. At the same time, she was now beyond the point of benefiting from conventional chemotherapy. The cancer had spread throughout her body. Instead of switching her to chemotherapy to give at least one last shot, they increased the dosage of the experimental drug. The cancer in her body responded by attacking her even more aggressively. She died a few weeks later. The trial was later discontinued and the drug was abandoned altogether.

■ ■ ■

Julia had never really spoken to Christy about her family or asked her about her background. She was always around but it never dawned on Julia earlier that she knew very little about where Christy was from or that she did not have a family and that their lives were intertwined like this.

"I remember that trial. It was the only one that I've worked on where we had to abandon it midway during the trial. It weighed on my soul, heavily, if you must know. I did not sleep for weeks after that. I walked around like a ghost, nearly having lost my purpose in life."

Christy walked up to Julia with a scissor. She pulled a corner of Julia's black turtle neck sweater and started cutting it. "Don't worry Julia. I've practiced this operation in my head a million times. It's going to go beautifully. I know you're going to love my handiwork."

．．．

At first, I didn't know what to make of this information. I tracked down Dr. Gupta in Cambridge and soon realized that he was eager to recruit promising medical students into his research lab. I was still naïve then, and thought I could learn more about my mother. Maybe even help others in her predicament. I changed my name shortly before I graduated. I wanted to be a different person, a better person, a less empty person.

I joined Dr. Gupta's lab as a research assistant. That was where I met Rebecca for the first time. I worked with

Dr. Gupta, Rebecca and Gustav on next generation cancer therapies – the CAR-T cells – modifying the human body's immune cells to fight cancer.

While the whole premise looked promising, arming the body's defenses to fight cancer, this was an approach that was never done before. The actual modification of the body's immune cells at the cellular level was immensely challenging and needed years and years of breakthrough.

But that did not stop you from testing a nascent therapy on the young Joshua Nelson. Joshua Nelson was just a five-year-old child. He was suffering from a rare childhood cancer.

■ ■ ■

"Joshua was just a five-year old child, Julia. Dr. Gupta, Nancy and you agreed to test the CAR-T cell therapy on him." She turned around and pointed her finger at Rebecca. "And you, Rebecca, you eagerly supplied the CAR-T cells developed based on your research to treat Joshua. The cells you made were defective, just not potent to cure his cancer. Instead of attacking his cancer cells, the CAR-T cells attacked Joshua's normal cells, his healthy organs. He died a cruel death."

Christy finished cutting the sweater off Julia's body. Julia was sitting there exposed and feeling vulnerable. She was hoping the talking would buy them time. Maybe Raoul had tracked down her car and he was on his way here. She hoped he would find them both in time. She winced as she hoped they would find at least Rebecca in time.

Julia spoke up trying to offer some explanation. "Joshua was on his last legs, Christy. His parents had tried every therapy and he had not responded to any. His death was certain. The CAR-T cell therapy was a Hail Mary that did not work, but at least we tried. We gave him the best shot he had at beating his cancer."

There was a marked change in Christy's voice. Her anger was rising and she could feel her inner demons take control over her. She tossed the scissors at the wall in a blind rage and screamed, "You killed my mother in your clinical trial, you crazy bitch. And she killed little Joshua. You both slaughter people in the name of science, running your crazy experiments, regardless of the cost."

Julia tried to rationalize with someone she knew did not want to listen to reason. "But Christy…"

"My mother died a cruel death, thanks to you, Julia. And Joshua died a torturous and early death in a cold laboratory in Cambridge, all thanks to you and your crazy experimental treatment, Rebecca. You both are just so blind because of your own ambitions that you don't care who lives and who dies. Joshua's death is on you, just like my mother's death is on you, Julia."

"Is that when you unraveled?"

■ ■ ■

I was completely devastated when Joshua Nelson died on that operating table in the Cambridge laboratory. All I could think of was how my mother must have died, just like Joshua Nelson, a guinea pig, for a vain, old, greedy fool and others like her who were blinded by ambition. It was then that I decided that all of them would pay. They would all have to answer for their sins. They would all die painful deaths at my hands. All of them.

Julia Fitzpatrick
Nancy Mulligan
Steven Gupta
Rebecca Chase

■ ■ ■

"Why didn't you just kill Dr. Gupta and Rebecca at the lab four years ago? Why did you have to do all this?"

Christy smirked at Julia. "The end game, Julia. You were the end game. I needed to get to you and you were the most difficult of the lot to get to. You were the reclusive billionaire who hardly made any public appearances. Even when you did, you were surrounded by your security. I knew I had to get close to you, become part of your inner circle and lure you out."

"Is that why you kidnapped Rebecca?"

"Rebecca turned out to be the key to my plans after all. Shortly after Joshua Nelson's death, you recruited

Rebecca to Atticus Biopharma and I convinced you to recruit me as well. When I saw how close Nancy and you were with Rebecca, I knew I had to use her as bait to lure both of you out."

■ ■ ■

I laid out my plans to kidnap Rebecca and made it look like a murder to throw everyone off. One by one, I planned to contact Julia, Nancy and Dr. Gupta, getting them to come to rescue Rebecca. She was the ultimate bait.

I found an empty warehouse building to hold Rebecca. I made sure the warehouse was far away from anything but close enough to New York City to be able to pull this off.

On the night when Rebecca met Ragnar, I followed her to the bar and then to East Village outside Ragnar's building. I called Rebecca in the early hours of Friday morning to tell her that I was in trouble, that I was drunk and that I got mugged and beaten up. I asked her to come pick me up. As soon as she emerged from the building, I gagged her with a napkin soaked in chloroform and brought her to this warehouse.

I left her blood-soaked dress for the police to find and throw them off the trail. They would be searching for a body in the Hudson as opposed to tracking her down.

■ ■ ■

"But you killed Dr. Gupta in his lab. Why?"

"Everything was going according to plan until Ragnar showed up on the scene. He started asking too many questions. Raoul was following him and reporting back to you…"

Julia interrupted, "And I was sharing the progress of his investigation with you all along. So that's how you knew…"

"Yeah, you got that right. That's how I always knew and was always a step ahead."

■ ■ ■

Raoul was following Ragnar to Cambridge where he was planning to meet Dr. Gupta. I figured I could frame Ragnar for his death. I made my way to Cambridge and followed Ragnar to Dr. Gupta's lab. After he left, I returned that evening, put on my mask and hood and made my way into the lab from a back access door. I had used the back access door on several occasions when I had worked there to sneak in and out of the lab unnoticed. There was only one security camera and I knew the blind spots.

I got into the lab and sneaked up on Dr. Gupta from behind. I struck him at the back of his head with a laughing Buddha statue from his office. He hit the ground and was nearly unconscious from the blow to his head. I then injected him with every vial of experimental biologics that was stored in the freezer. I even injected a deadly biologic into his eyes. His internal organs probably melted from the agents that I injected into him.

. . .

Julia had tears in her eyes as she heard first-hand what Christy had done to Dr. Gupta. "He trusted you. He hired you in his lab. How could you do that to him? He was only trying to help his patients, patients who otherwise had no other options."

"You always have a choice. My mother could've lived longer had she not participated in that trial. Joshua could have lived a few more months. He would not have died a cruel and painful death. He could've been at home with his loved ones instead of a sterile lab in Cambridge." Christy picked up a syringe and started walking towards Julia.

"What did Iain have to do with all of this? Why did you kill him?"

A large smile emerged on Christy's face. She stopped and turned to look at Rebecca. "You're going to love this, Rebecca."

. . .

I hated Rebecca. Really hated her. When she got engaged to Iain, I couldn't bear to see her happy. I knew Iain's kind. They loved their wives and girlfriends but could never be completely faithful to them. A conquest always excited them.

I seduced Iain and started sleeping with him. He was carrying on an affair with me. I satisfied his deepest darkest sexual desires. He was a rabid animal in bed and I fueled his wild side. I let him bring other women into our bed. First, I would fuck them and then he would fuck both of us. He would even photograph me having sex with the other women. It turned him on. He was an animal and I recognized that the moment I laid my eyes on him.

One night, when we were really drunk, Iain confided in me. He told me that he had betrayed Rebecca in the worst way possible. He was downloading copies of her research from her laptop and sending it along to Matheus. Matheus was blackmailing him and paying him a lot of money to do it. A boatload of it.

I encouraged Iain to continue doing it. I was surprised I did not think of this myself, feeding Julia's biggest enemy with research from Atticus Biopharma. When Rebecca came to know about the leak and Atticus Biopharma clamped down hard on cyber security, Iain was no longer able to send anything to Matheus. I then took it upon myself to continue where Iain left off. I started downloading the research and passing it along clandestinely to Matheus. Anything I could do to bring down Julia.

■ ■ ■

"But why kill him? How did he hurt you?"

"Iain was an idiot. The police were closing in on him. They were pressing him really hard and it was just a matter of time before he spilled the beans on my relationship with him. If the police came to know that I knew about the leaks and never reported it, they would've been on my tail. I could not let that happen. I followed him to Chinatown and took care of him."

"You mean you killed him? Brutally stabbed him in the heart? How could you, Christy?" Julia was praying for more time, but she knew she was running out of time.

Rebecca was weeping and moaning loudly now. This was the first she had heard about Iain. She tried screaming under her gag.

Christy walked up to Julia and knelt down on her knees. She took the syringe and quickly injected the contents into the side of Julia's chest. She got a second syringe and injected the contents on the other side of Julia's chest. "This should numb the pain locally, enough to keep you from passing out during the operation."

Christy stood up and walked out of the room. In a couple of minutes, she pushed and brought in a long floor mirror with wheels attached at the bottom. She turned the mirror a bit so that Julia could see herself in there clearly. She realized that Christy wanted her to see the horrors first hand in the mirror.

"What happened with Nancy? Why just shoot her?"

"Nancy, huh?"

■ ■ ■

I got a call from Nancy saying she wanted to see me and that she wanted to discuss something urgently. I sensed something was off from her voice. I knew she was on to me, that she found out something about my past. I could not take a chance.

I went to Nancy's apartment building. I used the back entrance of her building and went to her apartment using the stairs. I used a mask and hood to hide my face just in case there were any security cameras. I don't understand why she wasn't more careful and why she decided to confront me rather than just pass along the information to the police. When I met her, she asked me if the name Isabella Holt meant anything to me. I feigned ignorance at her question. Just then her cell phone rang and she turned to pick it up. I did not waste a moment. I pulled out my gun and shot her from behind at point blank range and made my way out of there.

■ ■ ■

"Did you say Isabella Holt? She was your mother? You're… you're… you're Isabella's daughter?" Julia was stammering in disbelief. Julia just stared at her with a blank stare. The sheer disbelief of the sequence of events and coincidences overtook her.

"Yes. I'm her daughter, Christy Holt. I took my mother's maiden last name, Cassidy, in high school before I joined Dr. Gupta's lab. I'm glad you remember my mother. This is going to be totally worth it." Christy felt a sense of elation to hear her mother's name from Julia. She was a bit surprised that Julia knew her previous name before she changed it.

Julia started laughing. And laughing loudly at the irony. "You don't understand, Christy. Your mother's trial is not what you think it was. There's no way you could've known what she meant to me. Your mother was…"

Christy was now confused and even more enraged. "Know what? You killed her. That's all that matters."

"You obviously don't understand. Oh Christy, what have you done?"

"What do you mean?"

Julia looked at Rebecca and took a deep breath. Life had come to a full circle but not in the way she had expected it. All three people in the room were intimately connected by events from over two decades ago and did not even know it.

"Your mother meant more to me than you could ever imagine. She was a huge contributor to science and our program."

Christy was convinced Julia was creating a ploy to save herself, telling her blatant lies to avoid her inevitable fate. "My mother was a simple woman. She was no scientist. You need to stop lying, Julia."

"I can show you. Why don't you come with me? We can access the records at Atticus Biopharma. You don't realize the importance of…"

"Shuutttttttt upppppppppp." Christy could not believe the gall Julia had. She was going to pay dearly, Christy thought. Christy put on a pair of surgical gloves, picked up a scalpel and walked towards Julia. She unhooked her bra from behind and let it fall to the floor. She knelt down on her right side and pointed at the mirror, as if informing Julia that she should now watch her operation in the mirror.

Christy had an evil grin on her face. Rebecca looked at the horrific scene in front of her and started screaming under her gag. She was horrified at what she was about to witness.

Christy took the scalpel and in one quick move pierced it into the side of Julia's right breast. A stream of blood started to drizzle from the incision. Julia gave out a chilling scream that pierced the entire room. Christy looked up at Julia to make eye contact, her hand steady, as she spoke in a calm voice. "This is it. I'm going to slide through around your breast. Brace yourself."

Christy held the breast with one hand as her other hand deftly used the scalpel to make an even deeper cut. Blood starting flowing out of Julia's breast. Julia couldn't decide whether it was the horror of what was happening here in this room or the pain that was worse. Rebecca's eyes were bulging as she let out a loud muffled scream. Tears were streaming down her face. The Christy she knew was virtually unrecognizable, replaced by a monster capable of horrors beyond imagination.

Christy continued to smile as the scalpel made its way down along the side of the breast. Julia was screaming in pain.

Christy paused and looked up at Julia. "Keep screaming, Julia. There is no one around here who can save you now. I'm half way through the incision around your breast. Just a few more minutes and I'll cut through all the tissue inside and remove all the skin along with the breast implant. You'll love my work."

Rebecca was now virtually hysterical in her chair. The abhorrent and ghastly revenge taking place in this room was beyond belief. Seeing Julia undergo this ordeal at the hands of someone she trusted made it even worse.

"Keep your eyes open, Julia. Don't give up on me yet. I'm just getting started here." Christy smiled at Julia and looked down to continue her handiwork. The smell of blood, fear and death sickened Rebecca to her stomach, but she continued her muffled shrieking. Christy let out a loud laugh and steadied her hand, the one that held the scalpel, for what was going to come next.

Just then, a loud cracking sound replaced all the screaming in the room. Christy went limp and in the next moment before she could turn around to see what had happened, a dull pain took over. The scalpel fell from her hand and she collapsed on the floor and fainted.

Julia looked up at the figure standing in front of them. Ragnar stood there with an iron pipe in his hand. He had struck Christy on her head and she had collapsed a moment later.

Ragnar quickly untied Julia's hands and legs, picked up the torn pieces of her sweater and pressed the wound on the side of Julia's breast. Julia put her hands on the wound, pressing it hard and pointed to Rebecca. "I'll be fine. Get her."

Ragnar stood up, paced to Rebecca and undid the gag on her mouth. He started to untie her when she spoke up in a hoarse voice. "Ragnar? What are you doing here? How did you even find us? You... you... we just... barely knew..."

"Shhhhh. Soon. You're both safe now. The cops are on their way with paramedics."

"Is she dead?" Rebecca was holding her wrists and rubbing them where her hands were tied. She could still feel a burning sensation where she had been tied.

Julia was holding the sweater next to her side to stop the bleeding. She was sitting next to Christy and weeping.

Ragnar looked at Rebecca. "No. Help me tie her up."

CHAPTER 51

DAY 23, FRIDAY
ATTICUS BIOPHARMA HEADQUARTERS, CAMBRIDGE, MASSACHUSETTS

Rebecca held Ragnar's hand as she led him through her laboratory. "I still can't believe everything you did to get to me."

"I, uh, I… I love you."

Rebecca planted a kiss on his cheek. She then held his hand again and led him through the lab.

It was late in the day on Friday and most people had left early for the weekend. A dull white light lit up the lab.

Rebecca had spent a day in the hospital being treated for the injuries she had endured in captivity. Ragnar had been with her the entire time. They had spent the next few days holed up in a hotel room in New York City getting re- acquainted with each other. The chemistry between them was undeniable. It was still there and the bond was even stronger now.

Julia's injuries were much more severe. She went through several surgeries to fix the damage to her breast. However, her injuries were expected to heal well. Ragnar had found the warehouse just in time to intervene and save both Julia and Rebecca from the hands of a deranged killer. Julia was thankful that she was alive but even happier that Rebecca was alive and had made it out of her ordeal.

Christy was taken into custody by the police. She was charged with kidnapping and torturing Rebecca and Julia and for the murders of Dr. Gupta, Iain and Nancy.

"What is it that you could not just tell me? What did you want to show me?" Ragnar was perplexed at Rebecca's mysterious behavior but agreed to come with her to the lab.

"You see, I've been working on a universal vaccine, ATCS-1010, to cure cancer. ATCS-1010 works when your body has the ability to detect a cancer, identify the mutation that caused the cancer in the first place and then alert all other immune cells to develop a defense against the cancer."

"Okay." Ragnar was trying to follow Rebecca's train of thought.

"Cancers develop because they have developed mechanisms that evade the body's defenses to begin with. When someone has cancer, his or her immune cells basically don't detect the cancer. The cancer cells multiply unchecked and spread through the body. But what if there was a mutation or a set of mutated immune cells that had developed the ability to detect the cancer, any cancer, and mount a response against it. What if such cells existed?"

"Then those cells could alert the rest of the immune system about the cancer and develop a defense against it."

"That's right, Ragnar. Those cells will activate the immune system and attack the cancer cells. They could beat the cancer, any cancer. If we were able to find such cells in someone's body, we could engineer them to be injected into anyone who had cancer. Or even people who don't have cancer as a preventative vaccine. That would be a universal vaccine for cancer. We could eradicate cancer forever."

Rebecca reached a chamber that had several security features. She placed her hand on a screen that scanned her hand. She then looked into a retinal scanner that scanned her eye as a security measure. She typed a password into a keypad.

Ragnar heard some bolting sounds that indicated that the chamber unlocked itself. A small door slid open and Ragnar noticed a vial inside.

"Julia was treating a cancer patient years back whose body developed this mutation. The patient had died during treatment but when Julia was performing the autopsy and doing a biopsy, she realized that the patient had developed his mutation. Cancers in one part of the patient's body had disappeared largely due to the mutation. Unfortunately, it had developed when the patient was in the latter stages of the cancer and her other organs had failed by then.

"The mutation was a freak of nature but something that could be harnessed to develop the universal cancer vaccine. We've been using the blood of this patient all along to work on the development of the universal vaccine. There are several technical and biological challenges of converting these mutated cells into something that could be used universally but we're making good progress."

"Wow. That sounds really exciting. Almost like science fiction. Is that a common mutation?" Ragnar looked into her eyes and could still feel his heart beating like the first time he set eyes on her.

"Not really. We still don't understand what genes were affected to cause the mutation but we know it works effectively. This is the Holy Grail of our cancer research at Atticus Biopharma. This will one day save the lives of millions of people suffering from cancer. It will give them a new lease of life. Maybe even extend the life span of humanity."

Rebecca removed the vial and handed it to Ragnar. Ragnar hesitated to take the vial but Rebecca insisted that he take it.

"Hold it. Be careful though. Julia was the only one who ever had access to this chamber and the vial. She gave me access to this yesterday but I thought you must see it too."

"How is Julia feeling now?"

"She's recovering from her surgeries but feeling better. She is on a regimen of painkillers and will be confined to her bed for a few weeks. She's still in shock over the fact that Christy is Isabella Holt's daughter." Rebecca held out the vial for him. "Here, hold this now."

"Why did that upset Julia so much?"

"Hold this, Ragnar." Rebecca was now opening his hand to place the vial in there.

"Are you sure? I don't know how I feel about this. What if I, uh, if I drop it or something?"

"I know you won't. Hold it. After everything you've done for us, you need to see this." Rebecca handed the vial to Ragnar. The vial felt cold in his hands. He still wasn't sure why Rebecca wanted him to hold it. Maybe she wanted him to see her life's work, he figured.

Ragnar took the vial in his hand and looked down at it. There was a small typed label on the side. He turned the vial to read the label. The liquid in the vial was a light shade of orange. Ragnar actually felt like he was holding the Holy Grail in his hands. He looked up and handed the vial back to Rebecca.

Rebecca placed the vial back into its place and pressed a few buttons to close the chamber. Ragnar's eyes were still fixed on the tiny label on the vial. The chamber doors closed slowly.

Rebecca took Ragnar's arm and started walking him out towards the entrance. She smiled widely as she led Ragnar out. "Are you in the mood for some tapas? There's a great Basque place that I know that serves the best wine in Boston. Are you up for it?"

"Sure, let's do Basque." Ragnar smiled back, happy that he was with this wonderful woman whom he was crazy about since he first saw her at that bar. He could still remember her sitting there in her black dress as her diamond bracelet shone in the dim light of the bar. Rebecca was wearing that bracelet right now.

Ragnar's thoughts immediately returned to the text he had read on the vial moments earlier. The irony was not lost on him. He felt a sense of sadness as he pushed those thoughts out of his mind and focused back on Rebecca. He pushed the words on that vial into a far corner inside his mind, stored out of sight, but never to be forgotten.

ISABELLA HOLT 1990

Dear Reader,

Thank you for taking the time to read 'The Girl At The Bar.'

I would love to hear your feedback on the book. Please take a minute to review it on Amazon and Goodreads. I read all the reviews.

Also, I am very excited to share the first chapter of my next book, which will be based on events in the aftermath of World War II. It is a historical psychological thriller. For a free copy of the first chapter, please feel free to send me an email. Hope you enjoy it!

Best wishes,

Nicholas Nash

Email: thegirlatthebar@gmail.com
Facebook: @AuthorNicholasNash
Instagram: @NicholasNashAuthor

www.ingramcontent.com/pod-product-compliance
Lightning Source LLC
Chambersburg PA
CBHW030651120726
47905CB00001B/155